Cakes and Ale

William Somerset Maugham was born in 1874 and lived in Paris
until he was ten. He was educated at King's School, Canterbury,
and at Heidelberg University. He spent some time at St Thomas's
Hospital with the idea of practising medicine, but the success of
his first novel, *Liza of Lambeth*, published in 1897, won him over
to letters. *Of Human Bondage*, the first of his masterpieces, came
out in 1915, and with the publication in 1919 of *The Moon and
Sixpence* his reputation as a novelist was established. His position
as a successful playwright was being consolidated at the same
time. His first play, *A Man of Honour*, was followed by a series
of successes just before and after World War I, and his career
in the theatre did not end until 1933 with *Sheppey*.

His fame as a short-story writer began with *The Trembling of a
Leaf*, sub-titled *Little Stories of the South Sea Islands*, in 1921,
after which he published more than ten collections. His other
works include travel books such as *On a Chinese Screen* and
Don Fernando, essays, criticism, and the autobiographical
The Summing Up and *A Writer's Notebook*.

In 1927 Somerset Maugham settled in the South of France and
lived there until his death in 1965.

D0726109

W. Somerset Maugham

Cakes and Ale

or The Skeleton in the Cupboard

Pan Books in association with
William Heinemann

First published 1930 by William Heinemann Ltd,
This edition published 1976 by Pan Books Ltd,
Cavaye Place, London SW10 9PG
in association with William Heinemann Ltd
19 18 17 16 15 14 13 12 11 10

All rights reserved
ISBN 0 330 24729 8
Printed and bound in Great Britain by
Anchor Brendon Ltd, Tiptree, Essex

Author's preface

It was as a short story, and not a very long one either, that I first thought of this novel. Here is the note I made when it occurred to me: 'I am asked to write my reminiscences of a famous novelist, a friend of my boyhood, living at W. with a common wife, very unfaithful to him. There he writes his great books. Later he marries his secretary, who guards him and makes him into a figure. My wonder whether even in old age he is not slightly restive at being made into a monument.' I was writing at the time a series of short stories for the *Cosmopolitan*. My contract stipulated that they were to be between twelve hundred and fifteen hundred words, so that with the illustration they should not occupy more than a page of the magazine, but I allowed myself some latitude and then the illustration spread across the opposite page and gave me a little more space. I thought this story would do for this purpose, and put it aside for future use. But I had long had in mind the character of Rosie. I had wanted for years to write about her, but the opportunity never presented itself; I could contrive no setting in which she found a place to suit her, and I began to think I never should. I did not very much care. A character in a writer's head, unwritten, remains a possession; his thoughts recur to it constantly, and while his imagination gradually enriches it he enjoys the singular pleasure of feeling that there, in his mind, someone is living a varied and tremulous life, obedient to his fancy and yet in a queer wilful way independent of him. But when once that character is set down on paper it belongs to the writer no more. He forgets it. It is curious how completely a person who may have occupied your reveries for many years can thus cease to be. It suddenly struck me that the little story I had jotted down offered me just the framework for this character that I had been looking for. I would make her the wife of my distinguished novelist. I saw that my story could never be got into a couple of thousand words, so I made up my mind to wait a little and use my material for one

5

of the much longer tales, fourteen or fifteen thousand words, with which, following upon *Rain*, I had been not unsuccessful. But the more I thought of it the less inclined I was to waste my Rosie on a story even of this length. Old recollections returned to me. I found I had not said all I wanted to say about the W. of the note, which in *Of Human Bondage* I had called Blackstable. After so many years I did not see why I should not get closer to the facts. The Uncle William, Rector of Blackstable, and his wife Isabella, became Uncle Henry, vicar, and his wife, Sophie. The Philip Carey of the earlier book became the I of *Cakes and Ale*.

When the book appeared I was attacked in various quarters because I was supposed in the character of Edward Driffield to have drawn a portrait of Thomas Hardy. This was not my intention. He was no more in my mind than George Meredith or Anatole France. As my note suggests, I had been struck by the notion that the veneration to which an author full of years and honour is exposed must be irksome to the little alert soul within him that is alive still to the adventures of his fancy. Many odd and disconcerting ideas must cross his mind, I thought, while he maintains the dignified exterior that his admirers demand of him. I read *Tess of the D'Urbervilles* when I was eighteen with such enthusiasm that I determined to marry a milkmaid, but I had never been so much taken with Hardy's other books as were most of my contemporaries, and I did not think his English very good. I was never so much interested in him as I was at one time in George Meredith, and later in Anatole France. I knew little of Hardy's life. I know now only enough to be certain that the points in common between his and that of Edward Driffield are negligible. They consist only in both having been born in humble circumstances and both having had two wives. I met Thomas Hardy but once. This was at a dinner-party at Lady St Helier's, better known in the social history of the day as Lady Jeune, who liked to ask to her house (in a much more exclusive world than the world of today) everyone that in some way or another had caught the public eye. I was then a popular and fashionable playwright. It was one of those great dinner-parties that people gave before the war, with a vast number of courses, thick and clear soup, fish, a couple of entrées, sorbet (to give you a chance to get your second wind), joint, game, sweet, ice, and savoury; and there were twenty-four people all of whom by rank, political eminence, or artistic achievement, were distinguished. When the ladies retired to the drawing-room I found myself sitting next to Thomas Hardy. I remember a little man with an earthy face. In his evening clothes, with his boiled shirt and high collar, he had still a strange look of the soil. He was amiable and mild. It struck me at the time that there was in him a curious mixture of shyness and self-assurance. I do not remember what we talked about, but I know that we talked for three-quarters of an hour. At the end of it he paid me a great compliment: he asked me (not having heard my name) what was my profession.

I am told that two or three writers thought themselves aimed at in the character of Alroy Kear. They were under a misapprehension. This character was a composite portrait: I took the appearance from one writer, the obsession with good society from another, the heartiness from a third, the pride in athletic prowess from a fourth, and a great deal from myself. For I have a grim capacity for seeing my own absurdity and I find in myself much to excite my ridicule. I am inclined to think that this is why I see people (if I am to believe what I am frequently told and frequently read of myself) in a less flattering light than many authors who have not this unfortunate idiosyncrasy. For all the characters that we create are but copies of ourselves. It may be of course also that they really are nobler, more disinterested, virtuous, and spiritual than I. It is very natural that being godlike they should create men in their own image. When I wanted to draw the portrait of a writer who used every means of advertisement possible to assist the diffusion of his works I had no need to fix my attention on any particular person. The practice is too common for that. Nor can one help feeling sympathy for it. Every year hundreds of books, many of considerable merit, pass unnoticed. Each one has taken the author months to write, he may have had it in his mind for years; he has put into it something of himself

7

which is lost for ever, it is heart-rending to think how great are the chances that it will be disregarded in the press of matter that weighs down the critics' tables and burdens the booksellers' shelves. It is not unnatural that he should use what means he can to attract the attention of the public. Experience has taught him what to do. He must make himself a public figure. He must keep in the public eye. He must give interviews and get his photograph in the papers. He must write letters to *The Times*, address meetings, and occupy himself with social questions; he must make after-dinner speeches; he must recommend books in the publishers' advertisements; and he must be seen without fail at the proper places at the proper times. He must never allow himself to be forgotten. It is hard and anxious work, for a mistake may cost him dear; it would be brutal to look with anything but kindliness at an author who takes so much trouble to persuade the world at large to read books that he honestly considers so well worth reading.

But there is one form of advertisement that I deplore. This is the cocktail party that is given to launch a book. You secure the presence of a photographer. You invite the gossip writers and as many eminent people as you know. The gossip writers give you a paragraph in their columns and the illustrated papers publish the photographs, but the eminent people expect to get a signed copy of the book for nothing. This ignoble practice is not rendered less objectionable when it is presumed (sometimes no doubt with justice) to be given at the expense of the publisher. It did not flourish at the time I wrote *Cakes and Ale*. It would have given me the material for a lively chapter.

chapter one

I have noticed that when someone asks for you on the telephone and, finding you out, leaves a message begging you to call him up the moment you come in, as it's important, the matter is more often important to him than to you. When it comes to making you a present or doing you a favour most people are able to hold their impatience within reasonable bounds. So when I got back to my lodgings with just enough time to have a drink, a cigarette, and to read my paper before dressing for dinner, and was told by Miss Fellows, my landlady, that Mr Alroy Kear wished me to ring him up at once, I felt that I could safely ignore his request.

'Is that the writer?' she asked me.

'It is.'

She gave the telephone a friendly glance.

'Shall I get him?'

'No, thank you.'

'What shall I say if he rings again?'

'Ask him to leave a message.'

'Very good, sir.'

She pursed her lips. She took the empty siphon, swept the room with a look to see that it was tidy, and went out. Miss Fellows was a great novel reader. I was sure that she had read all Roy's books. Her disapproval of my casualness suggested that she had read them with admiration. When I got home again, I found a note in her bold, legible writing on the sideboard:

Mr Kear rang up twice. Can you lunch with him tomorrow? If not what day will suit you?

I raised my eyebrows. I had not seen Roy for three months and then only for a few minutes at a party; he had been very friendly, he always was, and when we separated he had expressed his hearty regret that we met so seldom.

'London's awful,' he said. 'One never has time to see any of the people one wants to. Let's lunch together one day next week, shall we?'

'I'd like to,' I replied.

'I'll look at my book when I get home and ring you up.'

'All right.'

I had not known Roy for twenty years without learning that he always kept in the upper left-hand pocket of his waistcoat the little book in which he put down his engagements; I was therefore not surprised when I heard from him no further. It was impossible for me now to persuade myself that this urgent desire of his to dispense hospitality was disinterested. As I smoked a pipe before going to bed I turned over in my mind the possible reasons for which Roy might want me to lunch with him. It might be that an admirer of his had pestered him to introduce me to her or that an American editor, in London for a few days, had desired Roy to put me in touch with him; but I could not do my old friend the injustice of supposing him so barren of devices as not to be able to cope with such a situation. Besides, he told me to choose my own day, so it could hardly be that he wished me to meet anyone else.

Than Roy no one could show a more genuine cordiality to a fellow novelist whose name was on everybody's lips, but no one could more genially turn a cold shoulder on him when idleness, failure, or someone else's success had cast a shade on his notoriety. The writer has his ups and downs, and I was but too conscious that at the moment I was not in the public eye. It was obvious that I might have found excuses without affront to refuse Roy's invitation, though he was a determined fellow and if he was resolved for purposes of his own to see me, I well knew that nothing short of a downright 'go to hell' would check his persistence; but I was beset by curiosity. I had also a considerable affection for Roy.

I had watched with admiration his rise in the world of letters. His career might well have served as a model for any young man entering upon the pursuit of literature. I could think of no one among my contemporaries who had achieved so considerable a position on so little talent. This, like the wise man's daily dose of Bemax, might have gone into a heaped-up tablespoon. He was perfectly aware of it, and it must have seemed to him sometimes little short of a miracle that he had been able with it to compose already some thirty books. I cannot but think that he saw the white light of revelation when first he read that Thomas Carlyle in an after-dinner speech had stated that genius was an infinite capacity for taking pains. He pondered the saying. If that was all, he must have told himself, he could be a genius like the rest; and when the excited reviewer of a lady's paper, writing a notice of one of his works, used the word (and of late the critics have been doing it with agreeable frequency) he must have sighed with the satisfaction of one who after long hours of toil has completed a cross-word puzzle. No one who for years had observed his indefatigable industry could deny that at all events he deserved to be a genius.

Roy started with certain advantages. He was the only son of a civil servant who after being Colonial Secretary for many years in Hong Kong ended his career as Governor of Jamaica. When you looked up Alroy Kear in the serried pages of *Who's Who* you saw '*o.s.* of Sir Raymond Kear, KCMG, KCVO, *q.v.*, and of Emily, *y.d.* of the late Major-General Percy Camperdown, Indian Army.' He was educated at Winchester and at New College, Oxford. He was president of the Union and but for an unfortunate attack of measles might very well have got his rowing blue. His academic career was respectable rather than showy, and he left the university without a debt in the world. Roy was even then of a thrifty habit, without any inclination to unprofitable expense, and he was a good son. He knew that it had been a sacrifice to his parents to give him so costly an education. His father, having retired, lived in an unpretentious, but not mean, house near Stroud, in Gloucestershire, but at intervals went to London to attend official dinners connected with the colonies he had administered, and on these occasions was in the habit of visiting the Athenaeum, of which he was a member. It was through an old crony at this club that he was able to get his boy, when he came down from Oxford, appointed tutor to the delicate and only son of a very noble lord. This gave Roy a chance to become acquainted at

11

an early age with the great world. He made good use of his opportunities. You will never find in his works any of the solecisms that disfigure the productions of those who have studied the upper circles of society only in the pages of the illustrated papers. He knew exactly how dukes spoke to one another, and the proper way they should be addressed respectively by a member of Parliament, an attorney, a bookmaker, and a valet. There is something captivating in the jauntiness with which in his early novels he handles viceroys, ambassadors, prime ministers, royalties, and great ladies. He is friendly without being patronizing and familiar without being impertinent. He does not let you forget their rank, but shares with you his comfortable feeling that they are of the same flesh as you and I. I always think it a pity that, fashion having decided that the doings of the aristocracy are no longer a proper subject for serious fiction, Roy, always keenly sensitive to the tendency of the age, should in his later novels have confined himself to the spiritual conflicts of solicitors, chartered accountants, and produce brokers. He does not move in these circles with his old assurance.

I knew him first soon after he resigned his tutorship to devote himself exclusively to literature, and he was then a fine, upstanding young man, six feet high in his stockinged feet and of an athletic build, with broad shoulders and a confident carriage. He was not handsome, but in a manly way agreeable to look at, with wide, blue, frank eyes and curly hair of a lightish brown; his nose was rather short and broad, his chin square. He looked honest, clean, and healthy. He was something of an athlete. No one who has read in his early books the descriptions of a run with the hounds, so vivid and so accurate, can doubt that he wrote from personal experience; and until quite lately he was willing now and then to desert his desk for a day's hunting. He published his first novel at the period when men of letters, to show their virility, drank beer and played cricket, and for some years there was seldom a literary eleven in which his name did not figure. This particular school, I hardly know why, has lost its bravery, their books are neglected, and, cricketers though they have remained, they find difficulty in placing their articles. Roy ceased playing cricket a good many years ago, and he has developed a fine taste for claret.

Roy was very modest about his first novel. It was short, neatly written, and, as is everything he has produced since, in perfect taste. He sent it with a pleasant letter to all the leading writers of the day, and in this he told each one how greatly he admired his works, how much he had learned from his study of them, and how ardently he aspired to follow, albeit at a humble distance, the trail his correspondent had blazed. He laid his book at the feet of a great artist as the tribute of a young man entering upon the profession of letters to one whom he would always look up to as his master. Deprecatingly, fully conscious of his audacity in asking so busy a man to waste his time on a neophyte's puny effort, he begged for criticism and guidance. Few of the replies were perfunctory. The authors he wrote to, flattered by his praise, answered at length. They commended his book; many of them asked him to luncheon. They could not fail to be charmed by his frankness and warmed by his enthusiasm. He asked for their advice with a humility that was touching, and promised to act upon it with a sincerity that was impressive. Here, they felt, was someone worth taking a little trouble over.

His novel had a considerable success. It made him many friends in literary circles and in a very short while you could not go to a tea-party in Bloomsbury, Campden Hill, or Westminster without finding him handing round bread and butter or disembarrassing an elderly lady of an empty cup. He was so young, so bluff, so gay, he laughed so merrily at other people's jokes that no one could help liking him. He joined dining clubs where in the basement of an hotel in Victoria Street or Holborn men of letters, young barristers, and ladies in Liberty silks and strings of beads, ate a three-and-sixpenny dinner and discussed art and literature. It was soon discovered that he had a pretty gift for after-dinner speaking. He was so pleasant that his fellow writers, his rivals and contemporaries, forgave him even the fact that he was a gentleman. He was generous in his praise of their fledgeling works, and when they sent him manuscripts to criticize could never find a thing amiss. They thought him not only a good sort, but a sound judge.

He wrote a second novel. He took great pains with it and he profited by the advice his elders in the craft had given him. It was only just that more than one should at his request write a review for a paper with whose editor Roy had got into touch and only natural that the review should be flattering. His second novel was successful, but not so successful as to arouse the umbrageous susceptibilities of his competitors. In fact it confirmed them in their suspicions that he would never set the Thames on fire. He was a jolly good fellow; no side, or anything like that: they were quite content to give a leg up to a man who would never climb so high as to be an obstacle to themselves. I know some who smile bitterly now when they reflect on the mistake they made.

But when they say that he is swollen-headed they err. Roy has never lost the modesty which in his youth was his most engaging trait.

'I know I'm not a great novelist,' he will tell you. 'When I compare myself with the giants I simply don't exist. I used to think that one day I should write a really great novel, but I've long ceased even to hope for that. All I want people to say is that I do my best. I do work. I never let anything slipshod get past me. I think I can tell a good story and I can create characters that ring true. And after all, the proof of the pudding is in the eating: *The Eye of the Needle* sold thirty-five thousand in England and eighty thousand in America, and for the serial rights of my next book I've got the biggest terms I've ever had yet.'

And what, after all, can it be other than modesty that makes him even now write to the reviewers of his books, thanking them for their praise, and ask them to luncheon? Nay, more: when someone has written a stinging criticism and Roy, especially since his reputation became so great, has had to put up with some very virulent abuse, he does not, like most of us, shrug his shoulders, fling a mental insult at the ruffian who does not like our work, and then forget about it; he writes a long letter to his critic, telling him that he is very sorry he thought his book bad, but his review was so interesting in itself, and if he might venture to say so, showed so much critical sense and so much feeling for words, that he felt bound to write to him. No one is more anxious to improve himself than he, and he hopes he is still capable of learning. He does not want to be a bore, but if the critic has nothing to do on Wednesday or Friday will he come and lunch at the Savoy and tell him why exactly he thought his book so bad? No one can order a lunch better than Roy, and generally by the time the critic has eaten half a dozen oysters and a cut from a saddle of baby lamb, he has eaten his words too. It is only poetic justice that when Roy's next novel comes out the critic should see in the new work a very great advance.

One of the difficulties that a man has to cope with as he goes through life is what to do about the persons with whom he has once been intimate and whose interest for him has in due course subsided. If both parties remain in a modest station the break comes about naturally, and no ill feeling subsists, but if one of them achieves eminence the position is awkward. He makes a multitude of new friends, but the old ones are inexorable; he has a thousand claims on his time, but they feel that they have the first right to it. Unless he is at their beck and call they sigh and with a shrug of the shoulders say:

'Ah, well, I suppose you're like everyone else. I must expect to be dropped now that you're a success.'

That, of course, is what he would like to do if he had the courage. For the most part he hasn't. He weakly accepts an invitation to supper on Sunday evening. The cold roast beef is frozen and comes from Australia and was over-cooked at middle day; and the burgundy – ah, why will they call it burgundy? Have they never been to Beaune and stayed at the Hôtel de la Poste? Of course it is grand to talk of the good old days when you shared a crust of bread in a garret together, but it is a little disconcerting when you reflect how near to a garret is the room you are sitting in. You don't feel at ease when your friend tells you that his books don't sell and that he can't place his short stories; the managers won't even read his plays, and

15

when he compares them with some of the stuff that's put on (here he fixes you with an accusing eye) it really does seem a bit hard. You are embarrassed and you look away. You exaggerate the failures you have had in order that he may realize that life has its hardships for you too. You refer to your work in the most disparaging way you can and are a trifle taken aback to find that your host's opinion of it is the same as yours. You speak of the fickleness of the public so that he may comfort himself by thinking that your popularity cannot last. He is a friendly but severe critic.

'I haven't read your last book,' he says, 'but I read the one before. I've forgotten its name.'

You tell him.

'I was rather disappointed in it. I didn't think it was quite so good as some of the things you've done. Of course you know which my favourite is.'

And you, having suffered from other hands than his, answer at once with the name of the first book you ever wrote: you were twenty then, and it was crude and ingenuous, and on every page was written your inexperience.

'You'll never do anything so good as that,' he says heartily, and you feel that your whole career has been a long decadence from that one happy hit. 'I always think you've never quite fulfilled the promise you showed then.'

The gas-fire roasts your feet, but your hands are icy. You look at your wrist-watch surreptitiously and wonder whether your old friend would think it offensive if you took your leave as early as ten. You have told your car to wait round the corner so that it should not stand outside the door and by its magnificence affront his poverty, but at the door he says:

'You'll find a bus at the bottom of the street. I'll just walk down with you.'

Panic seizes you and you confess that you have a car. He finds it very odd that the chauffeur should wait round the corner. You answer that this is one of his idiosyncrasies. When you reach it your friend looks at it with tolerant superiority. You nervously ask him to dinner with you one day. You promise to write to him and you drive away wondering whether when he comes he will think you are swanking if you ask him to Claridge's or mean if you suggest Soho.

Roy Kear suffered from none of these tribulations. It sounds a little brutal to say that when he had got all he could get from people he dropped them; but it would take so long to put the matter more delicately, and would need so subtle an adjustment of hints, half-tones, and allusions, playful or tender, that such being at bottom the fact, I think it as well to leave it at that. Most of us when we do a caddish thing harbour resentment against the person we have done it to, but Roy's heart, always in the right place, never permitted him such pettiness. He could use a man very shabbily without afterward bearing him the slightest ill-will.

'Poor old Smith,' he would say. 'He is a dear; I'm so fond of him. Pity he's growing so bitter. I wish one could do something for him. No, I haven't seen him for years. It's no good trying to keep up old friendships. It's painful for both sides. The fact is, one grows out of people, and the only thing is to face it.'

But if he ran across Smith at some gathering like the private view of the Royal Academy no one could be more cordial. He wrung his hand and told him how delighted he was to see him. His face beamed. He shed good fellowship as the kindly sun its rays. Smith rejoiced in the glow of this wonderful vitality and it was damned decent of Roy to say he'd give his eye-teeth to have written a book half as good as Smith's last. On the other hand, if Roy thought Smith had not seen him, he looked the other way; but Smith *had* seen him, and Smith resented being cut. Smith was very acid. He said that in the old days Roy had been glad enough to share a steak with him in a shabby restaurant and spend a month's holiday in a fisherman's cottage at St Ives. Smith said that Roy was a time-server. He said he was a snob. He said he was a humbug.

Smith was wrong here. The most shining characteristic of Alroy Kear was his sincerity. No one can be a humbug for five-and-twenty years. Hypocrisy is the most difficult and nerve-racking vice that any man can pursue; it needs an un-ceasing vigilance and a rare detachment of spirit. It cannot, like adultery or gluttony, be practised at spare moments; it is a whole-time job. It needs also a cynical humour; although Roy laughed so much, I never thought he had a very quick sense of humour, and I am quite sure that he was incapable of cynicism. Though I have finished few of his novels, I have begun a good many, and to my mind his sincerity is stamped on every one of their multitudinous pages. This is clearly the chief ground of his stable popularity. Roy has always sincerely believed what everyone else believed at the moment. When he wrote novels about the aristocracy he sincerely believed that its members were dissipated and immoral, and yet had a certain nobility and an innate aptitude for governing the British Empire; when later he wrote of the middle classes he sincerely believed that they were the backbone of the country. His villains have always been villainous, his heroes heroic, and his maidens chaste.

When Roy asked the author of a flattering review to lunch it was because he was sincerely grateful to him for his good opinion, and when he asked the author of an unflattering one it was because he was sincerely concerned to improve himself. When unknown admirers from Texas or Western Australia came to London it was not only to cultivate his public that he took them to the National Gallery, it was because he was sincerely anxious to observe their reactions to art. You had only to hear him lecture to be convinced of his sincerity.

When he stood on the platform, in evening dress admirably worn, or in a loose, much used, but perfectly cut lounge suit if it better fitted the occasion, and faced his audience seriously, frankly, but with an engaging diffidence, you could not but realize that he was giving himself up to his task with complete earnestness. Though now and then he pretended to be at a loss for a word, it was only to make it more effective when he uttered it. His voice was full and manly. He told a story well. He was never dull. He was fond of lecturing upon the younger writers of England and America, and he explained their merits to his audience with an enthusiasm that attested his generosity. Perhaps he told almost too much, for when you had heard his lecture you felt that you really knew all you wanted to about them and it was quite unnecessary to read their books. I suppose that is why when Roy had lectured in some provincial town not a single copy of the books of the authors he had spoken of was ever asked for, but there was always a run on his own. His energy was prodigious. Not only did he make successful tours of the United States, but he lectured up and down Great Britain. No club was so small, no society for the self-improvement of its members so insignificant, that Roy disdained to give it an hour of his time. Now and then he revised his lectures and issued them in neat little books. Most people who are interested in these things have at least looked through the works entitled *Modern Novelists*, *Russian Fiction*, and *Some Writers*; and few can deny that they exhibit a real feeling for literature and a charming personality.

But this by no means exhausted his activities. He was an active member of the organizations that have been founded to further the interests of authors or to alleviate their hard lot when sickness or old age has brought them to penury. He was always willing to give his help when matters of copyright were the subject of legislation and he was never unprepared to take his place in those missions to a foreign country which are devised to establish amicable relations between writers of different nationalities. He could be counted on to reply for literature at a public dinner and he was invariably on the reception committee formed to give a proper welcome to a literary celebrity from overseas. No bazaar lacked an autographed copy of at least one of his books. He never refused to grant an interview. He justly said that no one knew better than he the hardships of the author's trade and if he could help a struggling journalist to earn a few guineas by having a pleasant chat with him he had not the inhumanity to refuse. He generally asked his interviewer to luncheon and seldom failed to make a good impression on him. The only stipulation he made was that he should see the article before it was published. He was never impatient with the persons who call up the celebrated on the telephone at inconvenient moments to ask them for the information of newspaper readers whether they believe in God or what they eat for breakfast. He figured in every symposium and the public knew what he thought of prohibi-

19

tion, vegetarianism, jazz, garlic, exercise, marriage, politics, and the place of women in the home.

His views on marriage were abstract, for he had successfully evaded the state which so many artists have found difficult to reconcile with the arduous pursuit of their calling. It was generally known that he had for some years cherished a hopeless passion for a married woman of rank, and though he never spoke of her but with chivalrous admiration, it was understood that she had treated him with harshness. The novels of his middle period reflected in their unwonted bitterness the strain to which he had been put. The anguish of spirit he had passed through then enabled him without offence to elude the advances of ladies of little reputation, frayed ornaments of a hectic circle, who were willing to exchange an uncertain present for the security of marriage with a successful novelist. When he saw in their bright eyes the shadow of the registry office he told them that the memory of his one great love would always prevent him from forming any permanent tie. His quixotry might exasperate, but could not affront, them. He sighed a little when he reflected that he must be for ever denied the joys of domesticity and the satisfaction of parenthood, but it was a sacrifice that he was prepared to make not only to his ideal, but also to the possible partner of his joys. He had noticed that people really do not want to be bothered with the wives of authors and painters. The artist who insisted on taking his wife wherever he went only made himself a nuisance and indeed was in consequence often not asked to places he would have liked to go to; and if he left his wife at home, he was on his return exposed to recriminations that shattered the repose so essential for him to do the best that was in him. Alroy Kear was a bachelor and now at fifty was likely to remain one.

He was an example of what an author can do, and to what heights he can rise, by industry, common sense, honesty, and the efficient combination of means and ends. He was a good fellow and none but a cross-grained carper could grudge him his success. I felt that to fall asleep with his image in my mind would ensure me a good night. I scribbled a note to Miss

Fellows, knocked the ashes out of my pipe, put out the light in my sitting-room, and went to bed.

chapter two

When I rang for my letters and the papers next morning a message was delivered to me, in answer to my note to Miss Fellows, that Mr Alroy Kear expected me at one-fifteen at his club in St James's Street; so a little before one I strolled round to my own and had the cocktail which I was pretty sure Roy would not offer me. Then I walked down St James's Street, looking idly at the shop windows, and since I had still a few minutes to spare (I did not want to keep my appointment too punctually) I went into Christie's to see if there was anything I liked the look of. The auction had already begun and a group of dark, small men were passing round to one another pieces of Victorian silver, while the auctioneer, following their gestures with bored eyes, muttered in a drone: 'Ten shillings offered, eleven, eleven and six' . . . It was a fine day, early in June, and the air in King Street was bright. It made the pictures on the walls of Christie's look very dingy. I went out. The people in the street walked with a kind of nonchalance, as though the ease of the day had entered into their souls and in the midst of their affairs they had a sudden and surprised inclination to stop and look at the picture of life.

Roy's club was sedate. In the ante-chamber were only an ancient porter and a page; and I had a sudden and melancholy feeling that the members were all attending the funeral of the head-waiter. The page, when I had uttered Roy's name, led me into an empty passage to leave my hat and stick and then into an empty hall hung with life-sized portraits of Victorian statesmen. Roy got up from a leather sofa and warmly greeted me.

'Shall we go straight up?' he said.

I was right in thinking that he would not offer me a cocktail and I commended my prudence. He led me up a noble flight of heavily carpeted stairs, and we passed nobody on the way; we entered the strangers' dining-room, and we were its only occupants. It was a room of some size, very clean and white, with an Adam window. We sat down by it and a demure waiter handed us the bill of fare. Beef, mutton, and lamb, cold salmon, apple tart, rhubarb tart, gooseberry tart. As my eye travelled down the inevitable list I sighed as I thought of the restaurants round the corner where there were French cooking, the clatter of life, and pretty, painted women in summer frocks.

'I can recommend the veal-and-ham pie,' said Roy.

'All right.'

'I'll mix the salad myself,' he told the waiter in an off-hand and yet commanding way, and then, casting his eye once more on the bill of fare, generously: 'And what about some asparagus to follow?'

'That would be very nice.'

His manner grew a trifle grander.

'Asparagus for two and tell the chef to choose them himself. Now what would you like to drink? What do you say to a bottle of hock? We rather fancy our hock here.'

When I had agreed to this he told the waiter to call the wine-steward. I could not but admire the authoritative and yet perfectly polite manner in which he gave his orders. You felt that thus would a well-bred king send for one of his field-marshals. The wine-steward, portly in black, with the silver chain of his office round his neck, bustled in with the wine-list in his hand. Roy nodded to him with curt familiarity.

'Hallo, Armstrong, we want some of the Liebfraumilch, the '21.'

'Very good, sir.'

'How's it holding up? Pretty well? We shan't be able to get any more of it, you know.'

'I'm afraid not, sir.'

'Well, it's no good meeting trouble half-way, is it, Armstrong?'

22

Roy smiled at the steward with breezy cordiality. The steward saw from his long experience of members that the remark needed an answer.

'No, sir.'

Roy laughed and his eye sought mine. Quite a character, Armstrong.

'Well, chill it, Armstrong; not too much, you know, but just right. I want my guest to see that we know what's what here.' He turned to me. 'Armstrong's been with us for eight and forty years.' And when the wine-steward had left us: 'I hope you don't mind coming here. It's quiet and we can have a good talk. It's ages since we did. You're looking very fit.'

This drew my attention to Roy's appearance.

'Not half so fit as you,' I answered.

'The result of an upright, sober, and godly life,' he laughed. 'Plenty of work. Plenty of exercise. How's the golf? We must have a game one of these days.'

I knew that Roy was scratch and that nothing would please him less than to waste a day with so indifferent a player as myself. But I felt I was quite safe in accepting so vague an invitation. He looked the picture of health. His curly hair was getting very grey, but it suited him and made his frank, sun-burned face look younger. His eyes, which looked upon the world with such a hearty candour, were bright and clear. He was not so slim as in his youth, and I was not surprised that when the waiter offered us rolls he asked for Ryvita. His slight corpulence only added to his dignity. It gave weight to his observations. Because his movements were a little more deliberate than they had been, you had a comfortable feeling of confidence in him; he filled his chair with so much solidity that you had almost the impression that he sat upon a monument.

I do not know whether, as I wished, I have indicated by my report of his dialogue with the waiter that his conversation was not as a rule brilliant or witty, but it was fluent and he laughed so much that you sometimes had the illusion that what he said was funny. He was never at a loss for a remark and he could discourse on the topics of the day with an ease

23

that prevented his hearers from experiencing any sense of strain.

Many authors from their preoccupation with words have the bad habit of choosing those they use in conversation too carefully. They form their sentences with unconscious care and say neither more nor less than they mean. It makes intercourse with them somewhat formidable to persons in the upper ranks of society whose vocabulary is limited by their simple spiritual needs, and their company consequently is sought only with hesitation. No constraint of this sort was ever felt with Roy. He could talk with a dancing guardee in terms that were perfectly comprehensible to him and with a racing countess in the language of her stable-boys. They said of him with enthusiasm and relief that he was not a bit like an author. No compliment pleased him better. The wise always use a number of ready-made phrases (at the moment I write 'nobody's business' is the most common), popular adjectives (like 'divine' or 'shy-making'), verbs that you only know the meaning of if you live in the right set (like 'dunch'), which give a homely sparkle to small talk and avoid the necessity of thought. The Americans, who are the most efficient people on the earth, have carried this device to such a height of perfection and have invented so wide a range of pithy and hackneyed phrases that they can carry on an amusing and animated conversation without giving a moment's reflection to what they are saying and so leave their minds free to consider the more important matters of big business and fornication. Roy's repertory was extensive and his scent for the word of the minute unerring; it peppered his speech, but aptly, and he used it each time with a sort of bright eagerness, as though his fertile brain had just minted it.

Now he talked of this and that, of our common friends and the latest books, of the opera. He was very breezy. He was always cordial, but today his cordiality took my breath away. He lamented that we saw one another so seldom and told me with the frankness that was one of his pleasantest characteristics how much he liked me and what a high opinion he had of me. I felt I must not fail to meet this friendliness half-way. He asked me about the book I was writing, I asked him about

24

the book he was writing. We told one another that neither of us had had the success he deserved. We ate the veal-and-ham pie and Roy told me how he mixed a salad. We drank the hock and smacked appreciative lips.

And I wondered when he was coming to the point.

I could not bring myself to believe that at the height of the London season Alroy Kear would waste an hour on a fellow writer who was not a reviewer and had no influence in any quarter whatever in order to talk of Matisse, the Russian Ballet, and Marcel Proust. Besides, at the back of his gaiety I vaguely felt a slight apprehension. Had I not known that he was in a prosperous state I should have suspected that he was going to borrow a hundred pounds from me. It began to look as though luncheon would end without his finding the opportunity to say what he had in mind. I knew he was cautious. Perhaps he thought that this meeting, the first after so long a separation, had better be employed in establishing friendly relations, and was prepared to look upon the pleasant, substantial meal merely as ground bait.

'Shall we go and have our coffee in the next room?' he said.

'If you like.'

'I think it's more comfortable.'

I followed him into another room, much more spacious, with great leather arm-chairs and huge sofas; there were papers and magazines on the tables. Two old gentlemen in a corner were talking in undertones. They gave us a hostile glance, but this did not deter Roy from offering them a cordial greeting.

'Hallo, General,' he cried, nodding breezily.

I stood for a moment at the window, looking at the gaiety of the day, and wished I knew more of the historical associations of St James's Street. I was ashamed that I did not even know the name of the club across the way and was afraid to ask Roy lest he should despise me for not knowing what every decent person knew. He called me back by asking me whether I would have a brandy with my coffee, and when I refused, insisted. The club's brandy was famous. We sat side by side on a sofa by the elegant fireplace and lit cigars.

25

'The last time Edward Driffield ever came to London he lunched with me here,' said Roy casually. 'I made the old man try our brandy and he was delighted with it. I was staying with his widow over last weekend.'

'Were you?'

'She sent you all sorts of messages.'

'That's very kind of her. I shouldn't have thought she remembered me.'

'Oh, yes, she does. You lunched there about six years ago, didn't you? She says the old man was so glad to see you.'

'I didn't think *she* was.'

'Oh, you're quite wrong. Of course she had to be very careful. The old man was pestered with people who wanted to see him and she had to husband his strength. She was always afraid he'd do too much. It's a wonderful thing if you come to think of it that she should have kept him alive and in possession of all his faculties to the age of eighty-four. I've been seeing a good deal of her since he died. She's awfully lonely. After all, she devoted herself to looking after him for twenty-five years. Othello's occupation, you know. I really feel sorry for her.'

'She's still comparatively young. I dare say she'll marry again.'

'Oh, no, she couldn't do that. That would be dreadful.'

There was a slight pause while we sipped our brandy.

'You must be one of the few persons still alive who knew Driffield when he was unknown. You saw quite a lot of him at one time, didn't you?'

'A certain amount. I was almost a small boy and he was a middle-aged man. We weren't boon companions, you know.'

'Perhaps not, but you must know a great deal about him that other people don't.'

'I suppose I do.'

'Have you ever thought of writing your recollections of him?'

'Good heavens, no!'

'Don't you think you ought to? He was one of the greatest novelists of our day. The last of the Victorians. He was an enormous figure. His novels have as good a chance of surviving

26

as any that have been written in the last hundred years.'

'I wonder. I've always thought them rather boring.'

Roy looked at me with eyes twinkling with laughter.

'How like you that is! Anyhow you must admit that you're in the minority. I don't mind telling you that I've read his novels not once or twice, but half a dozen times, and every time I read them I think they're finer. Did you read the articles that were written about him at his death?'

'Some of them.'

'The consensus of opinion was absolutely amazing. I read every one.'

'If they all said the same thing, wasn't that rather unnecessary?'

Roy shrugged his massive shoulders good-humouredly, but did not answer my question.

'I thought *The Times Lit. Sup.* was splendid. It would have done the old man good to read it. I hear that the *Quarterly* is going to have an article in its next number.'

'I still think his novels rather boring.'

Roy smiled indulgently.

'Doesn't it make you slightly uneasy to think that you disagree with everyone whose opinion matters?'

'Not particularly. I've been writing for thirty-five years now, and you can't think how many geniuses I've seen acclaimed, enjoy their hour or two of glory and vanish into obscurity. I wonder what's happened to them. Are they dead, are they shut up in mad-houses, are they hidden away in offices? I wonder if they furtively lend their books to the doctor and the maiden lady in some obscure village. I wonder if they are still great men in some Italian *pension.*'

'Oh, yes, they're the flash in the pans. I've known them.'

'You've even lectured about them.'

'One has to. One wants to give them a leg up if one can and one knows they won't amount to anything. Hang it all, one can afford to be generous. But after all, Driffield wasn't anything like that. The collected edition of his works is in thirty-seven volumes and the last set that came up at Sotheby's sold for seventy-eight pounds. That speaks for itself. His sales have increased steadily every year and last year was the best he ever had. You can take my word for that. Mrs Driffield showed me his accounts last time I was down there. Driffield has come to stay all right.'

'Who can tell?'

'Well, you think you can,' replied Roy acidly.

I was not put out. I knew I was irritating him and it gave me a pleasant sensation.

'I think the instinctive judgements I formed when I was a boy were right. They told me Carlyle was a great writer and I was ashamed that I found the *French Revolution* and *Sartor Resartus* unreadable. Can anyone read them now? I thought the opinions of others must be better than mine and I persuaded myself that I thought George Meredith magnificent. In my heart I found him affected, verbose, and insincere. A good many people think so too now. Because they told me that to admire Walter Pater was to prove myself a cultured young man, I admired Walter Pater, but heavens, how *Marius* bored me!'

'Oh, well, I don't suppose anyone reads Pater now, and, of course, Meredith has gone all to pot, and Carlyle was a pretentious windbag.'

'You don't know how secure of immortality they all looked thirty years ago.'

'And have you never made mistakes?'

'One or two. I didn't think half as much of Newman as I do now, and I thought a great deal more of the tinkling quatrains of Fitzgerald. I could not read Goethe's *Wilhelm Meister*; now I think it his masterpiece.'

'And what did you think much of then that you think much of still?'

'Well, *Tristram Shandy* and *Amelia* and *Vanity Fair*, *Madame Bovary*, *La Chartreuse de Parme*, and *Anna Karenina*. And Wordsworth and Keats and Verlaine.'

'If you don't mind my saying so, I don't think that's particularly original.'

'I don't mind your saying so at all. I don't think it is. But you asked me why I believed in my own judgement, and I was trying to explain to you that, whatever I said out of timidity and in deference to the cultured opinion of the day, I didn't really admire certain authors who were then thought admirable, and the event seems to show that I was right. And what I honestly and instinctively liked then has stood the test of time with me and with critical opinion in general.'

Roy was silent for a moment. He looked in the bottom of his cup, but whether to see if there were any more coffee in it or to find something to say, I did not know. I gave the clock on the chimney-piece a glance. In a minute it would be fitting for me to take my leave. Perhaps I had been wrong and Roy had invited me only that we might idly chat of Shakespeare and the musical glasses. I chid myself for the uncharitable thoughts I had had of him. I looked at him with concern. If that was his only object it must be that he was feeling tired or discouraged. If he was disinterested it could only be that for the moment at least the world was too much for him. But he caught my look at the clock and spoke.

'I don't see how you can deny that there must be something in a man who's able to carry on for sixty years, writing book after book, and who's able to hold an ever-increasing public. After all, at Ferne Court there are shelves filled with the translations of Driffield's books into every language of civilized people. Of course I'm willing to admit that a lot he wrote seems a bit old-fashioned nowadays. He flourished in a bad period and he was inclined to be long-winded. Most of his plots are melodramatic; but there's one quality you must allow him: beauty.'

'Yes?' I said.

'When all's said and done, that's the only thing that counts, and Driffield never wrote a page that wasn't instinct with beauty.'

'Yes?' I said.

'I wish you'd been there when we went down to present him with his portrait on his eightieth birthday. It really was a memorable occasion.'

'I read about it in the papers.'

'It wasn't only writers, you know, it was a thoroughly representative gathering – science, politics, business, art, the world; I think you'd have to go a long way to find gathered together such a collection of distinguished people as got out from that train at Blackstable. It was awfully moving when the P.M. presented the old man with the Order of Merit. He made a charming speech. I don't mind telling you there were tears in a good many eyes that day.'

'Did Driffield cry?'

'No, he was singularly calm. He was like he always was; rather shy, you know, and quiet, very well-mannered, grateful, of course, but a little dry. Mrs Driffield didn't want him to get over-tired and when we went in to lunch he stayed in his study, and she sent him something in on a tray. I slipped away while the others were having their coffee. He was smoking his pipe and looking at the portrait. I asked him what he thought of it. He wouldn't tell me, he just smiled a little. He asked me if I thought he could take his teeth out, and I said, No, the deputation would be coming in presently to say good-bye to him. Then I asked him if he didn't think it was a wonderful moment. "Rum," he said, "very rum." The fact is, I suppose, he was shattered. He was a messy eater in his later days and a messy smoker – he scattered the tobacco all over himself when he filled his pipe; Mrs Driffield didn't like people to see him when he was like that, but, of course, she didn't mind me; I tidied him up a bit, and then they all came in and shook hands with him, and we went back to town.'

I got up.

'Well, I really must be going. It's been awfully nice seeing you.'

'I'm just going along to the private view at the Leicester Galleries. I know the people there. I'll take you in if you like.'

'It's very kind of you, but they sent me a card. No, I don't think I'll come.'

We walked down the stairs and I got my hat. When we came out into the street and I turned towards Piccadilly, Roy said:

'I'll just walk up to the top with you.' He got into step with me. 'You knew his first wife, didn't you?'

'Whose?'

'Driffield's.'

'Oh!' I had forgotten him. 'Yes.'

'Well?'

'Fairly.'

'I suppose she was awful.'

'I don't recollect that.'

'She must have been dreadfully common. She was a bar-maid, wasn't she?'

'Yes.'

'I wonder why the devil he married her. I've always been given to understand that she was extremely unfaithful to him.'

'Extremely.'

'Do you remember at all what she was like?'

'Yes, very distinctly,' I smiled. 'She was sweet.'

Roy gave a short laugh.

'That's not the general impression.'

I did not answer. We had reached Piccadilly, and stopping I held out my hand to Roy. He shook it, but I fancied without his usual heartiness. I had the impression that he was disappointed with our meeting. I could not imagine why. Whatever he had wanted of me I had not been able to do, for the reason that he had given me no inkling of what it was, and as I strolled under the arcade of the Ritz Hotel and along the park railings till I came opposite Half Moon Street I wondered if my manner had been more than ordinarily forbidding. It was quite evident that Roy had felt the moment inopportune to ask me to grant him a favour.

I walked up Half Moon Street. After the gay tumult of Piccadilly it had a pleasant silence. It was sedate and respectable. Most of the houses let apartments, but this was not advertised by the vulgarity of a card; some had a brightly polished brass plate, like a doctor's, to announce the fact, and others the word *Apartments* neatly painted on the fanlight. One or two with an added discretion merely gave the name of the proprietor, so that if you were ignorant you might have thought it a tailor's or a money-lender's. There was none of the congested traffic of Jermyn Street, where also they let rooms, but here and there a smart car, unattended, stood outside a door and occasionally at another a taxi deposited a middle-aged lady. You had the feeling that the people who lodged here were not gay and a trifle disreputable as in Jermyn Street, racing men who rose in the morning with headaches and asked for a hair of the dog that bit them, but respectable women from the country who came up for six weeks for the London season and elderly gentlemen who belonged to exclusive clubs. You felt that they came year after year to the same house and perhaps had known the proprietor when he was still in private service. My own Miss Fellows had been cook in some very good places, but you would never have guessed it had you seen her walking along to do her shopping in Shepherd Market. She was not stout, red-faced, and blousy as one expects a cook to be; she was spare and very upright, neatly but fashionably dressed, a woman of middle age with determined features; her lips were rouged and she wore an eyeglass. She was businesslike, quiet, coolly cynical, and very expensive.

The rooms I occupied were on the ground floor. The parlour was papered with an old marbled paper and on the walls were water-colours of romantic scenes, cavaliers bidding good-bye to their ladies and knights of old banqueting in stately halls; there were large ferns in pots, and the arm-chairs were covered with faded leather. There was about the room an amusing air of the eighteen-eighties, and when I looked out of the window I expected to see a private hansom rather than a Chrysler. The curtains were of a heavy red rep.

chapter three

I had a good deal to do that afternoon, but my conversation with Roy and the impression of the day before yesterday, the sense of a past that still dwelt in the minds of men not yet old, that my room, I could not tell why, had given me even more strongly than usual as I entered it, inveigled my thoughts to saunter down the road of memory. It was as though all the people who had at one time and another inhabited my lodging pressed upon me with their old-fashioned ways and odd clothes, men with mutton-chop whiskers in frock-coats and women in bustles and flounced skirts. The rumble of London, which I did not know if I imagined or heard (my house was at the top of Half Moon Street), and the beauty of the sunny June day (*le vierge, le vivace et le bel aujourd'hui*), gave my reverie a poignancy which was not quite painful. The past I looked at seemed to have lost its reality and I saw it as though it were a scene in a play and I a spectator in the back row of a dark gallery. But it was all very clear as far as it went. It was not misty like life as one leads it, when the ceaseless throng of impressions seems to rob them of outline, but sharp and definite like a landscape painted in oils by a painstaking artist of the middle-Victorian era.

I fancy that life is more amusing now than it was forty years ago and I have a notion that people are more amiable. They may have been worthier then, possessed of more solid virtue as, I am told, they were possessed of more substantial knowledge; I do not know. I know they were more cantankerous; they ate too much, many of them drank too much, and they took too little exercise. Their livers were out of order and their digestions often impaired. They were irritable. I do not speak of London, of which I knew nothing till I was grown up, nor of grand people who hunted and shot, but of the countryside and of the modest persons, gentlemen of small means, clergymen, retired officers, and such-like who made up the local society. The dullness of their lives was almost incredible. There

33

were no golf links; at a few houses was an ill-kept tennis court, but it was only the very young who played; there was a dance once a year in the Assembly Rooms; carriage folk went for a drive in the afternoon; the others went for a 'constitutional'! You may say that they did not miss amusements they had never thought of, and that they created excitement for themselves from the small entertainment (tea when you were asked to bring your music and you sang the songs of Maude Valérie White and Tosti) which at infrequent intervals they offered one another; the days were very long; they were bored. People who were condemned to spend their lives within a mile of one another quarrelled bitterly, and, seeing each other every day in the town, cut one another for twenty years. They were vain, pig-headed, and odd. It was a life that perhaps formed queer characters; people were not so like one another as now and they acquired a small celebrity by their own idiosyncrasies, but they were not easy to get on with. It may be that we are flippant and careless, but we accept one another without the old suspicion; our manners, rough and ready, are kindly; we are more prepared to give and take and we are not so crabbed.

I lived with an uncle and aunt on the outskirts of a little Kentish town by the sea. It was called Blackstable and my uncle was the vicar. My aunt was a German. She came of a very noble but impoverished family, and the only portion she brought her husband was a marquetry writing-desk, made for an ancestor in the seventeenth century, and a set of tumblers. Of these only a few remained when I entered upon the scene, and they were used as ornaments in the drawing-room. I liked the grand coat-of-arms with which they were heavily engraved. There were I don't know how many quarterings, which my aunt used demurely to explain to me, and the supporters were fine and the crest emerging from a crown incredibly romantic. She was a simple old lady, of a meek and Christian disposition, but she had not, though married for more than thirty years to a modest parson with very little income beyond his stipend, forgotten that she was *hochwohlgeboren*. When a rich banker from London, with a name that in these days is famous in financial circles, took a neighbouring house for the summer holidays, though my uncle called on him (chiefly, I surmise, to get a subscription to the Additional Curates Society), she refused to do so because he was in trade. No one thought her a snob. It was accepted as perfectly reasonable. The banker had a little boy of my own age, and, I forget how, I became acquainted with him. I still remember the discussion that ensued when I asked if I might bring him to the vicarage; permission was reluctantly given me, but I was not allowed to go in return to his house. My aunt said I'd be wanting to go to the coal merchant's next, and my uncle said:

'Evil communications corrupt good manners.'

The banker used to come to church every Sunday morning, and he always put half a sovereign in the plate, but if he thought his generosity made a good impression he was much mistaken. All Blackstable knew, but only thought him purse-proud.

Blackstable consisted of a long winding street that led to the sea, with little two-storey houses, many of them residential but with a good many shops; and from this ran a certain number of short streets, recently built, that ended on one side in the country and on the other in the marshes. Round about the harbour was a congeries of narrow winding alleys. Colliers brought coal from Newcastle to Blackstable and the harbour was animated. When I was old enough to be allowed out by myself I used to spend hours wandering about there looking at the rough grimy men in their jerseys and watching the coal being unloaded.

It was at Blackstable that I first met Edward Driffield. I was fifteen and had just come back from school for the summer holidays. The morning after I got home I took a towel and bathing drawers and went down to the beach. The sky was unclouded and the air hot and bright, but the North Sea gave it a pleasant tang so that it was a delight just to live and breathe. In winter the natives of Blackstable walked down the empty street with hurried gait, screwing themselves up in order to expose as little surface as possible to the bitterness of the east wind, but now they dawdled; they stood about in groups in the little space between the Duke of Kent and the Bear and

Key. You heard a hum of their East Anglian speech, drawling a little with an accent that may be ugly, but in which from old association I still find a leisurely charm. They were fresh-complexioned, with blue eyes and high cheekbones, and their hair was light. They had a clean, honest, and ingenuous look. I do not think they were very intelligent, but they were guileless. They looked healthy, and, though not tall, for the most part were strong and active. There was little wheeled traffic in Blackstable in those days and the groups that stood about the road chatting seldom had to move for anything but the doctor's dogcart or the baker's trap.

Passing the bank, I called in to say how-do-you-do to the manager, who was my uncle's churchwarden, and when I came out met my uncle's curate. He stopped and shook hands with me. He was walking with a stranger. He did not introduce me to him. He was a smallish man with a beard and he was dressed rather loudly in a bright brown knickerbocker suit, the breeches very tight, with navy-blue stockings, black boots, and a billy-cock hat. Knickerbockers were uncommon then, at least in Blackstable, and being young and fresh from school I immediately set the fellow down as a cad. But while I chatted with the curate he looked at me in a friendly way, with a smile in his pale blue eyes. I felt that for two pins he would have joined in the conversation and I assumed a haughty demeanour. I was not going to run the risk of being spoken to by a chap who wore knickerbockers like a gamekeeper, and I resented the familiarity of his good-humoured expression. I was myself faultlessly dressed in white flannel trousers, a blue blazer with the arms of my school on the breast pocket, and a black-and-white straw hat with a very wide brim. The curate said that he must be getting on (fortunately, for I never knew how to break away from a meeting in the street and would endure agonies of shyness while I looked in vain for an opportunity), but said that he would be coming up to the vicarage that afternoon and would I tell my uncle. The stranger nodded and smiled as we parted, but I gave him a stony stare. I supposed he was a summer visitor, and in Blackstable we did not mix with the summer visitors. We thought London people vulgar. We said it was horrid to have all that rag-tag and bob-tail down from town every year, but of course it was all right for the tradespeople. Even they, however, gave a faint sigh of relief when September came to an end and Blackstable sank back into its usual peace.

When I went home to dinner, my hair insufficiently dried and clinging dankly to my head, I remarked that I had met the curate and he was coming up that afternoon.

'Old Mrs Shepherd died last night,' said my uncle in explanation.

The curate's name was Galloway; he was a tall, thin, un-gainly man with untidy black hair and a small, sallow dark face. I suppose he was quite young, but to me he seemed middle-aged. He talked very quickly and gesticulated a great deal. This made people think him rather queer and my uncle would not have kept him but that he was very energetic, and my uncle, being extremely lazy, was glad to have someone to take so much work off his shoulders. After he had finished the business that had brought him to the vicarage Mr Galloway came in to say how-do-you-do to my aunt, and she asked him to stay to tea.

'Who was that you were with this morning?' I asked him as he sat down.

'Oh, that was Edward Driffield. I didn't introduce him. I wasn't sure if your uncle would wish you to know him.'

'I think it would be most undesirable,' said my uncle.

'Why, who is he? He's not a Blackstable man, is he?'

'He was born in the parish,' said my uncle. 'His father was old Miss Wolfe's bailiff at Ferne Court. But they were chapel people.'

'He married a Blackstable girl,' said Mr Galloway.

'In church, I believe,' said my aunt. 'Is it true that she was a barmaid at the Railway Arms?'

'She looks as if she might have been something like that,' said Mr Galloway with a smile.

'Are they going to stay long?'

'Yes, I think so. They've taken one of those houses in that street where the Congregational Chapel is,' said the curate.

At that time in Blackstable, though the new streets doubtless had names, nobody knew or used them.

'Is he coming to church?' asked my uncle.

'I haven't actually talked to him about it yet,' answered Mr Galloway. 'He's quite an educated man, you know.'

'I can hardly believe that,' said my uncle.

'He was at Haversham School, I understand, and he got any number of scholarships and prizes. He got a scholarship to Wadham, but he ran away to sea instead.'

'I'd heard he was rather a harum-scarum,' said my uncle.

'He doesn't look much like a sailor,' I remarked.

'Oh, he gave up the sea many years ago. He's been all sorts of things since then.'

'Jack of all trades and master of none,' said my uncle.

'Now, I understand, he's a writer.'

'That won't last long,' said my uncle.

I had never known a writer before; I was interested.

'What does he write?' I asked. 'Books?'

'I believe so,' said the curate, 'and articles. He had a novel published last spring. He's promised to lend it me.'

'I wouldn't waste my time on rubbish in your place,' said my uncle, who never read anything but *The Times* and the *Guardian*.

'What's it called?' I asked.

'He told me the title, but I forget it.'

'Anyhow, it's quite unnecessary that you should know,' said my uncle. 'I should very much object to your reading trashy novels. During your holidays the best thing you can do is to keep out in the open air. And you have a holiday task, I presume?'

I had. It was *Ivanhoe*. I had read it when I was ten, and the notion of reading it again and writing an essay on it bored me to distraction.

When I consider the greatness that Edward Driffield afterward achieved I cannot but smile as I remember the fashion in which he was discussed at my uncle's table. When he died a little while ago and an agitation arose among his admirers to have him buried in Westminster Abbey, the present incumbent at Blackstable, my uncle's successor twice removed, wrote to the *Daily Mail* pointing out that Driffield was born in the parish and not only had passed long years, especially the last twenty-five of his life, in the neighbourhood, but had laid there the scene of some of his most famous books; it was only becoming, then, that his bones should rest in the churchyard where under the Kentish elms his father and mother dwelt in peace. There was relief in Blackstable when, the Dean of Westminster having somewhat curtly refused the abbey, Mrs Driffield sent a dignified letter to the Press in which she expressed her confidence that she was carrying out the dearest wishes of her dead husband in having him buried among the simple people he knew and loved so well. Unless the notabilities of Blackstable have very much changed since my day, I do not believe they vastly liked that phrase about 'simple people', but, as I afterward learnt, they had never been able to 'abide' the second Mrs Driffield.

chapter four

To my surprise, two or three days after I lunched with Alroy Kear I received a letter from Edward Driffield's widow. It ran as follows:

Dear Friend,

I hear that you had a long talk with Roy last week about Edward Driffield and I am so glad to know that you spoke of him so nicely. He often talked to me of you. He had the greatest admiration for your talent and he was so very pleased to see you when you came to lunch with us. I wonder if you have in your possession any letters that he wrote to you, and if so whether you would let me have copies of them. I should be very pleased if I could persuade you to come down for two or three days and stay with me. I live very quietly now and have no one here, so please choose your own time. I shall be delighted to see you again and have a talk of old times. I have a particular service I want you to do me, and I am sure that for the sake of my dear dead husband you will not refuse.

Yours ever sincerely,
Amy Driffield

I had seen Mrs Driffield only once and she but mildly interested me; I do not like being addressed as 'dear friend'; that alone would have been enough to make me decline her invitation; and I was exasperated by its general character which, however ingenious an excuse I invented, made the reason I did not go quite obvious, namely, that I did not want to. I had no letters of Driffield's. I suppose years ago he had written to me several times, brief notes, but he was then an obscure scribbler and even if I ever kept letters it would never have occurred to me to keep his. How was I to know that he was going to be acclaimed as the greatest novelist of our day? I hesitated only because Mrs Driffield said she wanted me to do something for her. It would certainly be a nuisance, but it would be churlish not to do it if I could, and after all, her husband was a very distinguished man.

The letter came by the first post, and after breakfast I rang up Roy. As soon as I mentioned my name I was put through to him by his secretary. If I were writing a detective story I should immediately have suspected that my call was awaited, and Roy's virile voice calling hallo would have confirmed my suspicion. No one could naturally be quite so cheery so early in the morning.

'I hope I didn't wake you,' I said.

'Good God, no!' His healthy laugh rippled along the wires. 'I've been up since seven. I've been riding in the park. I'm just going to have breakfast. Come along and have it with me.'

'I have a great affection for you, Roy,' I answered, 'but I don't think you're the sort of person I'd care to have breakfast with. Besides, I've already had mine. Look here, I've just had a letter from Mrs Driffield asking me to go down and stay.'

'Yes, she told me she was going to ask you. We might go down together. She's got quite a good grass court and she does one very well. I think you'd like it.'

'What is it that she wants me to do?'

'Ah, I think she'd like to tell you that herself.'

There was a softness in Roy's voice such as I imagined he would use if he were telling a prospective father that his wife was about to gratify his wishes. It cut no ice with me.

'Come off it, Roy,' I said. 'I'm too old a bird to be caught with chaff. Spit it out.'

There was a moment's pause at the other end of the telephone. I felt that Roy did not like my expression.

'Are you busy this morning?' he asked suddenly. 'I'd like to come and see you.'

'All right, come on. I shall be in till one.'

'I'll be round in about an hour.'

I replaced the receiver and relit my pipe. I gave Mrs Driffield's letter a second glance.

I remembered vividly the luncheon to which she referred. I happened to be staying for a long weekend not far from Tercanbury with a certain Lady Hodmarsh, the clever and handsome American wife of a sporting baronet with no intelligence and charming manners. Perhaps to relieve the tedium of domestic life she was in the habit of entertaining persons connected with the arts. Her parties were mixed and gay. Members of the nobility and gentry mingled with astonishment and an uneasy awe with painters, writers, and actors. Lady Hodmarsh neither read the books nor looked at the pictures of the people to whom she offered hospitality, but she liked their company and enjoyed the feeling it gave her of being in the artistic know. When on this occasion the conversation happened to dwell for a moment on Edward Driffield, her most celebrated neighbour, and I mentioned that I had at one time known him very well, she proposed that we should go over and lunch with him on Monday when a number of her guests were going back to London. I demurred, for I had not seen Driffield for five and thirty years and I could not believe that he would remember me; and if he did (though this I kept to myself) I could not believe that it would be with pleasure. But there was a young peer there, a certain Lord Scallion, with literary inclinations so violent that, instead of ruling this country as the laws of man and nature have decreed, he devoted his energy to the composition of detective novels. His curiosity to see Driffield was boundless, and the moment Lady Hodmarsh made her suggestion he said it would be too divine. The star guest of the party was a big young fat duchess, and it appeared that her admiration for the famous writer was so intense that she was prepared to cut an engagement in London and not go up till the afternoon.

'That would make four of us,' said Lady Hodmarsh. 'I don't think they could manage more than that. I'll wire to Mrs Driffield at once.'

I could not see myself going to see Driffield in that company and tried to throw cold water on the scheme.

'It'll only bore him to death,' I said. 'He'll hate having a lot of strangers barging in on him like this. He's a very old man.'

'That's why if they want to see him they'd better see him now. He can't last much longer. Mrs Driffield says he likes to meet people. They never see anyone but the doctor and the parson and it's a change for them. Mrs Driffield said I could always bring anyone interesting. Of course she has to be very careful. He's pestered by all sorts of people who want to see him just out of idle curiosity, and interviewers and authors who want him to read their books, and silly hysterical women. But Mrs Driffield is wonderful. She keeps everyone away from him but those she thinks he ought to see. I mean, he'd be dead in a week if he saw everyone who wants to see him. She has to think of his strength. Naturally we're different.'

Of course I thought I was; but as I looked at them I perceived that the duchess and Lord Scallion thought they were too; so it seemed best to say no more.

We drove over in a bright yellow Rolls. Ferne Court was three miles from Blackstable. It was a stucco house built, I suppose, about 1840, plain and unpretentious, but substantial; it was the same back and front, with two large bows on each side of a flat piece in which was the front door and there were two large bows on the first floor. A plain parapet hid the low roof. It stood in about an acre of garden, somewhat overgrown with trees, but neatly tended, and from the drawing-room window you had a pleasant view of woods and green downland. The drawing-room was furnished so exactly as you felt a drawing-room in a country house of modest size should be furnished, that it was slightly disconcerting. Clean, bright chintzes covered the comfortable chairs and the large sofa, and the curtains were of the same bright clean chintz. On little Chippendale tables stood large Oriental bowls filled with pot-pourri. On the cream-coloured walls were pleasant water-colours by painters well known at the beginning of this century. There were great masses of flowers charmingly arranged, and on the grand piano, in silver frames, photographs of celebrated actresses, deceased authors, and minor royalties.

It was no wonder that the duchess cried out that it was a lovely room. It was just the kind of room in which a distin-guished writer should spend the evening of his days. Mrs Driffield received us with modest assurance. She was a woman of about five and forty, I judged, with a small sallow face and neat sharp features. She had a black cloche hat pressed tight down on her head and wore a grey coat and skirt. Her figure was slight and she was neither tall nor short, and she looked trim, competent and alert. She might have been the squire's widowed daughter, who ran the parish and had a peculiar gift for organization. She introduced us to a clergyman and a lady, who got up as we were shown in. They were the Vicar of Blackstable and his wife. Lady Hodmarsh and the duchess immediately assumed the cringing affability that persons of rank assume with their inferiors in order to show them that they are not in the least conscious of any difference in station between them.

Then Edward Driffield came in. I had seen portraits of him from time to time in the illustrated papers, but it was with dismay that I saw him in the flesh. He was smaller than I remembered and very thin, his head was barely covered with fine silvery hair, he was clean-shaven, and his skin was almost transparent. His blue eyes were very pale and the rims of his eyelids red. He looked an old, old man, hanging on to mortality by a thread; he wore very white false teeth and they made his smile seem forced and stiff. I had never seen him but bearded, and his lips were thin and pallid. He was dressed in a new, well-cut suit of blue serge, and his low collar, two or three sizes too large for him, showed a wrinkled, scraggy neck. He wore a neat black tie with a pearl in it. He looked a little like a dean in mufti on his summer holiday in Switzerland.

Mrs Driffield gave him a quick glance as he came in and smiled encouragingly; she must have been satisfied with the neatness of his appearance. He shook hands with his guests and to each said something civil. When he came to me he said:

'It's very good of a busy and successful man like you to come all this way to see an old fogy.'

I was a trifle taken aback, for he spoke as though he had never seen me before, and I was afraid my friends would think I had been boasting when I claimed at one time to have known him intimately. I wondered if he had completely forgotten me.

'I don't know how many years it is since we last met,' I said, trying to be hearty.

He looked at me for what I suppose was no more than a few seconds, but for what seemed to me quite a long time, and then I had a sudden shock; he gave me a little wink. It was so quick that nobody but I could have caught it, and so unexpected in that distinguished old face that I could hardly believe my eyes. In a moment his face was once more composed, intelligently benign, and quietly observant. Luncheon was announced and we trooped into the dining-room.

This also was in what can only be described as the acme of good taste. On the Chippendale sideboard were silver candlesticks. We sat on Chippendale chairs and ate off a Chippendale table. In a silver bowl in the middle were roses, and round this were silver dishes with chocolates in them and peppermint creams; the silver salt-cellars were brightly polished and evidently Georgian. On the cream-coloured walls were mezzotints of ladies painted by Sir Peter Lely and on the chimneypiece a garniture of blue delf. The service was conducted by two maids in brown uniform and Mrs Driffield in the midst of her fluent conversation kept a wary eye on them. I wondered how she had managed to train these buxom Kentish girls (their healthy colour and high cheek-bones betrayed the fact that they were 'local') to such a pitch of efficiency. The lunch was

44

just right for the occasion, smart but not showy, fillets of sole rolled up and covered with a white sauce, roast chicken, with new potatoes and green peas, asparagus, and gooseberry fool. It was the dining-room and the lunch and the manner which you felt exactly fitted a literary gent of great celebrity but moderate wealth.

Mrs Driffield, like the wives of most men of letters, was a great talker and she did not let the conversation at her end of the table flag; so that, however much we might have wanted to hear what her husband was saying at the other, we had no opportunity. She was gay and sprightly. Though Edward Driffield's indifferent health and great age obliged her to live most of the year in the country, she managed notwithstanding to run up to town often enough to keep abreast of what was going on, and she was soon engaged with Lord Scallion in an animated discussion of the plays in the London theatres and the terrible crowd at the Royal Academy. It had taken her two visits to look at all the pictures, and even then she had not had time to see the water-colours. She liked water-colours so much; they were unpretentious; she hated things to be pretentious.

So that host and hostess should sit at the head and foot of the table, the vicar sat next to Lord Scallion and his wife next to the duchess. The duchess engaged her in conversation on the subject of working-class dwellings, a subject on which she seemed to be much more at home than the parson's lady, and my attention being thus set free I watched Edward Driffield. He was talking to Lady Hodmarsh. She was apparently telling him how to write a novel, and giving him a list of a few that he really ought to read. He listened to her with what looked like polite interest, putting in now and then a remark in a voice too low for me to catch, and when she made a jest (she made them frequently and often good ones) he gave a little chuckle and shot her a quick look that seemed to say: this woman isn't such a damned fool after all. Remembering the past, I asked myself curiously what he thought of this grand company, his neatly-turned-out wife, so competent and discreetly managing, and the elegant surroundings in which he lived. I wondered if he regretted his early days of adventure. I wondered if all this amused him or if the amiable civility of his manner masked a hideous boredom. Perhaps he felt my eyes upon him, for he raised his. They rested on me for a while with a thoughtful look, mild and yet oddly scrutinizing, and then suddenly, unmistakably this time, he gave me another wink. The frivolous gesture in that old, withered face was more than startling, it was embarrassing; I did not know what to do. My lips outlined a dubious smile.

But the duchess joining in the conversation at the head of that table, the vicar's wife turned to me.

'You knew him many years ago, didn't you?' she asked me in a low tone.

'Yes.'

She gave the company a glance to see that no one was attending to us.

'His wife is anxious that you shouldn't call up old memories that might be painful to him. He's very frail, you know, and the least thing upsets him.'

'I'll be very careful.'

'The way she looks after him is simply wonderful. Her devotion is a lesson to all of us. She realizes what a precious charge it is. Her unselfishness is beyond words.' She lowered her voice a little more. 'Of course he's a very old man, and old men sometimes are a little trying; I've never seen her out of patience. In her way she's just as wonderful as he is.'

These were the sort of remarks to which it was difficult to find a reply, but I felt that one was expected of me.

'Considering everything I think he looks very well,' I murmured.

'He owes it all to her.'

At the end of luncheon we went back into the drawing-room, and after we had been standing about for two or three minutes Edward Driffield joined me. I was talking with the vicar, and for want of anything better to say was admiring the charming view. I turned to my host.

'I was just saying how picturesque that little row of cottages is down there.'

'From here.' Driffield looked at their broken outline and an ironic smile curled his thin lips. 'I was born in one of them. Rum, isn't it?'

But Mrs Driffield came up to us with bustling geniality. Her voice was brisk and melodious.

'Oh, Edward, I'm sure the duchess would like to see your writing-room. She has to go almost immediately.'

'I'm so sorry, but I must catch the three-eighteen from Tercanbury,' said the duchess.

We filed into Driffield's study. It was a large room on the other side of the house, looking out on the same view as the dining-room, with a bow window. It was the sort of room that a devoted wife would evidently arrange for her literary husband. It was scrupulously tidy and large bowls of flowers gave it a feminine touch.

'This is the desk at which he's written all his later works,' said Mrs Driffield, closing a book that was open face downward on it. 'It's the frontispiece in the third volume of the *edition de luxe*. It's a period piece.'

We all admired the writing-table, and Lady Hodmarsh, when she thought no one was looking, ran her fingers along its under edge to see if it was genuine. Mrs Driffield gave us a quick, bright smile.

'Would you like to see one of his manuscripts?'

'I'd love to,' said the duchess, 'and then I simply must bolt.'

Mrs Driffield took from a shelf a manuscript bound in blue morocco, and while the rest of the party reverently examined it I had a look at the books with which the room was lined. As authors will, I ran my eye round quickly to see if there were any of mine, but could not find one; I saw, however, a complete set of Alroy Kear's and a great many novels in bright bindings, which looked suspiciously unread; I guessed that they were the works of authors who had sent them to the master in homage to his talent and perhaps the hope of a few words of eulogy that could be used in the publisher's advertisements. But all the books were so neatly arranged, they were so clean, that I had the impression they were very seldom read. There was the Oxford Dictionary and there were standard editions in grand bindings of most of the English classics, Fielding, Boswell, Hazlitt, and so on, and there were a great many books on the sea; I recognized the variously coloured, untidy volumes of the sailing directions issued by the Admiralty, and there were a number of works on gardening. The room had the look not of a writer's workshop, but of a memorial to a great name, and you could almost see already the desultory tripper wandering in for want of something better to do and smell the rather musty, close smell of a museum that few visited. I had a suspicion that nowadays if Driffield read anything at all it was the *Gardener's Chronicle* or the *Shipping Gazette*, of which I saw a bundle on a table in the corner.

When the ladies had seen all they wanted we bade our hosts farewell. But Lady Hodmarsh was a woman of tact, and it must have occurred to her that I, the excuse for the party, had scarcely had a word with Edward Driffield, for at the door, enveloping me with a friendly smile, she said to him:

'I was so interested to hear that you and Mr Ashenden had known one another years and years ago. Was he a nice little boy?'

Driffield looked at me for a moment with that level, ironic gaze of his. I had the impression that if there had been nobody there he would have put his tongue out at me.

'Shy,' he replied. 'I taught him to ride a bicycle.'

We got once more into the huge yellow Rolls and drove off.

'He's too sweet,' said the duchess. 'I'm so glad we went.'

'He has such nice manners, hasn't he?' said Lady Hodmarsh.

'You didn't really expect him to eat his peas with a knife, did you?' I asked.

'I wish he had,' said Scallion. 'It would have been so picturesque.'

'I believe it's very difficult,' said the duchess. 'I've tried over and over again and I can never get them to stay on.'

'You have to spear them,' said Scallion.

'Not at all,' retorted the duchess. 'You have to balance them on the flat, and they roll like the devil.'

'What did you think of Mrs Driffield?' asked Lady Hodmarsh.

'I suppose she serves her purpose,' said the duchess.

'He's so old, poor darling, he must have someone to look after him. You know she was a hospital nurse?'

'Oh, was she?' said the duchess. 'I thought perhaps she'd been his secretary or typist or something.'

'She's quite nice,' said Lady Hodmarsh, warmly defending a friend.

'Oh, quite.'

'He had a long illness about twenty years ago, and she was his nurse then, and after he got well he married her.'

'Funny how men will do that. She must have been years younger than him. She can't be more than – what? – forty or forty-five.'

'No, I shouldn't think so. Forty-seven, say. I'm told she's done a great deal for him. I mean, she's made him quite presentable. Alroy Kear told me that before that he was almost too Bohemian.'

'As a rule authors' wives are odious.'

'It's such a bore having to have them, isn't it?'

'Crashing. I wonder they don't see that themselves.'

'Poor wretches, they often suffer from the delusion that people find them interesting,' I murmured.

We reached Tercanbury, dropped the duchess at the station and drove on.

chapter five

It was true that Edward Driffield had taught me to bicycle. That was indeed how I first made his acquaintance. I do not know how long the safety bicycle had been invented, but I know that it was not common in the remote part of Kent in which I lived, and when you saw someone speeding along on solid tyres you turned round and looked till he was out of sight. It was still a matter for jocularity on the part of middle-aged gentlemen who said Shank's pony was good enough for them, and for trepidation on the part of elderly ladies who made a dash for the side of the road when they saw one coming. I had been for some time filled with envy of the boys whom I saw riding into the school grounds on their bicycles. It gave a pretty opportunity for showing off when you entered the gateway without holding on to the handles. I had persuaded my uncle to let me have one at the beginning of the summer holidays, and though my aunt was against it, since she said I should only break my neck, he had yielded to my pertinacity more willingly because I was, of course, paying for it out of my own money. I ordered it before school broke up, and a few days later the carrier brought it over from Tercanbury.

I was determined to learn to ride it by myself, and chaps at school had told me that they had learned in half an hour. I tried and tried, and at last came to the conclusion that I was abnormally stupid, but even after my pride was sufficiently humbled for me to allow the gardener to hold me up I seemed at the end of the first morning no nearer to being able to get on by myself than at the beginning. Next day, however, thinking that the carriage drive at the vicarage was too winding to give a fellow a proper chance, I wheeled the bicycle to a road not far away which I knew was perfectly flat and straight, and so solitary that no one would see me making a fool of myself. I tried several times to mount, but fell off each time. I barked my shins against the pedals, and got very hot and bothered. After I had been doing this for about an hour, though I began to think that God did not intend me to ride a bicycle, but was determined (unable to bear the thought of the sarcasms of my uncle, his representative at Blackstable) to do so all the same, to my disgust I saw two people on bicycles coming along the deserted road. I immediately wheeled my machine to the side and sat down on a stile, looking out to sea in a nonchalant way, as though I had been for a ride and were just sitting there wrapped in contemplation of the vasty ocean. I kept my eyes dreamily averted from the two persons who were advancing toward me, but I felt that they were coming nearer, and through the corner of my eye I saw that they were a man and a woman. As they passed me the woman swerved violently to my side of the road and, crashing against me, fell to the ground.

'Oh, I'm sorry,' she said. 'I knew I should fall off the moment I saw you.'

It was impossible under the circumstances to preserve my appearance of abstraction and, blushing furiously, I said that it didn't matter at all.

The man had got off as she fell.

'You haven't hurt yourself?' he asked.

'Oh, no.'

I recognized him then as Edward Driffield, the author I had seen walking with the curate a few days before.

'I'm just learning to ride,' said his companion. 'And I fall off whenever I see anything in the road.'

'Aren't you the vicar's nephew?' said Driffield. 'I saw you the other day. Galloway told me who you were. This is my wife.'

She held out her hand with an oddly frank gesture, and when I took it gave mine a warm and hearty pressure. She smiled with her lips and with her eyes, and there was in her smile something that even then I recognized as singularly pleasant. I was confused. People I did not know made me dreadfully self-conscious, and I could not take in any of the details of her appearance. I just had an impression of a rather large blonde woman. I do not know if I noticed then or only remembered afterward that she wore a full skirt of blue serge, a pink shirt with a starched front and a starched collar, and a straw hat, called in those days, I think, a boater, perched on the top of a lot of golden hair.

'I think bicycling's lovely, don't you?' she said, looking at my beautiful new machine which leaned against the stile. 'It must be wonderful to be able to ride well.'

I felt that this inferred an admiration for my proficiency.

'It's only a matter of practice,' I said.

'This is only my third lesson. Mr Driffield says I'm coming on wonderfully, but I feel so stupid I could kick myself. How long did it take you before you could ride?'

I blushed to the roots of my hair. I could hardly utter the shameful words.

'I can't ride,' I said. 'I've only just got this bike, and this is the first time I've tried.'

I equivocated a trifle there, but I made it all right with my conscience by adding the mental reservation: except yesterday at home in the garden.

'I'll give you a lesson if you like,' said Driffield in his good-humoured way. 'Come on.'

'Oh, no,' I said. 'I wouldn't dream of it.'

'Why not?' asked his wife, her blue eyes still pleasantly smiling. 'Mr Driffield would like to and it'll give me a chance to rest.'

Driffield took my bicycle, and I, reluctant but unable to withstand his friendly violence, clumsily mounted. I swayed from side to side, but he held me with a firm hand.

'Faster,' he said.

I pedalled and he ran by me as I wobbled from side to side. We were both very hot when, notwithstanding his efforts, I at last fell off. It was very hard under such circumstances to preserve the standoffishness befitting the vicar's nephew with the son of Miss Wolfe's bailiff, and when I started back again and for thirty or forty thrilling yards actually rode by myself and Mrs Driffield ran into the middle of the road with her arms akimbo shouting: 'Go it, go it, two to one on the favourite,' I was laughing so much that I positively forgot all about my social status. I got off of my own accord, my face no doubt wearing an air of immodest triumph, and received without embarrassment the Driffields' congratulation on my cleverness in riding a bicycle the very first day I tried.

'I want to see if I can get on by myself,' said Mrs Driffield, and I sat down again on the stile while her husband and I watched her unavailing struggles.

Then, wanting to rest again, disappointed but cheerful, she sat down beside me. Driffield lit his pipe. We chatted. I did not, of course, realize it then, but I know now that there was a disarming frankness in her manner that put one at one's ease. She talked with a kind of eagerness, like a child bubbling over with the zest of life, and her eyes were lit all the time by her engaging smile. I did not know why I liked it. I should say it was a little sly, if slyness were not a displeasing quality; it was too innocent to be sly. It was mischievous rather, like that of a child who has done something that he thinks funny but is quite well aware that you will think rather naughty; he knows all the same that you won't be really cross and if you don't find out about it quickly he'll come and tell you himself. But of course then I only knew that her smile made me feel at home.

Presently Driffield, looking at his watch, said that they must be going and suggested that we should all ride back together in style. It was just the time that my aunt and uncle would be coming home from their daily walk down the town and I did not like to run the risk of being seen with people whom they would not at all approve of; so I asked them to go on first, as they would go more quickly than I. Mrs Driffield would not hear of it, but Driffield gave me a funny, amused little look, which made me think that he saw through my excuse, so that I blushed scarlet and he said:

'Let him go by himself, Rosie. He can manage better alone.'

'All right. Shall you be here tomorrow? We're coming.'

'I'll try to,' I answered.

They rode off, and in a few minutes I followed. Feeling very much pleased with myself, I rode all the way to the vicarage gates without falling. I think I boasted a good deal at dinner, but I did not say that I had met the Driffields.

Next day at about eleven I got my bicycle out of the coachhouse. It was so called though it held not even a pony trap and

53

was used by the gardener to keep the mower and the roller, and by Mary-Ann for her sack of meal for the chickens. I wheeled it down to the gate and, mounting none too easily, rode along the Tercanbury Road till I came to the old turnpike and turned into Joy Lane.

The sky was blue and the air, warm and yet fresh, crackled, as it were, with the heat. The light was brilliant without harshness. The sun's beams seemed to hit the white road with a directed energy and bounce back like a rubber ball.

I rode backward and forward, waiting for the Driffields, and presently saw them come. I waved to them and turned round (getting off to do so) and we pedalled along together. Mrs Driffield and I complimented one another on our progress. We rode anxiously, clinging like grim death to the handle-bars, but exultant, and Driffield said that as soon as we felt sure of ourselves we must go for rides all over the county.

'I want to get rubbings of one or two brasses in the neighbourhood,' he said.

I did not know what he meant, but he would not explain.

'Wait and I'll show you,' he said. 'Do you think you could ride fourteen miles tomorrow, seven there and seven back?'

'Rather,' I said.

'I'll bring a sheet of paper for you and some wax and you can make a rubbing. But you'd better ask your uncle if you can come.'

'I needn't do that.'

'I think you'd better, all the same.'

Mrs Driffield gave me that peculiar look of hers, mischievous and yet friendly, and I blushed scarlet. I knew that if I asked my uncle he would say no. It would be much better to say nothing about it. But as we rode along I saw coming toward us the doctor in his dogcart. I looked straight in front of me as he passed, in the vain hope that if I did not look at him he would not look at me. I was uneasy. If he had seen me the fact would quickly reach the ears of my uncle or my aunt, and I considered whether it would not be safer to disclose myself a secret that could no longer be concealed. When we parted at the vicarage gates (I had not been able to avoid riding as far as this in their company) Driffield said that if I found I could come with them next day I had better call for them as early as I could.

'You know where we live, don't you? Next door to the Congregational Church. It's called Lime Cottage.'

When I sat down to dinner I looked for an opportunity to slip in casually the information that I had by accident run across the Driffields; but news travelled fast in Blackstable.

'Who were those people you were bicycling with this morning?' asked my aunt. 'We met Dr Anstey in the town and he said he'd seen you.'

My uncle, chewing his roast beef with an air of disapproval, looked sullenly at his plate.

'The Driffields,' I said with nonchalance. 'You know, the author. Mr Galloway knows them.'

'They're most disreputable people,' said my uncle. 'I don't wish you to associate with them.'

'Why not?' I asked.

'I'm not going to give you my reasons. It's enough that I don't wish it.'

'How did you ever get to know them?' asked my aunt.

'I was just riding along, and they were riding along, and they asked me if I'd like to ride with them,' I said, distorting the truth a little.

'I call it very pushing,' said my uncle.

I began to sulk. And to show my indignation, when the sweet was put on the table, though it was raspberry tart, which I was extremely fond of, I refused to have any. My aunt asked me if I was not feeling very well.

'Yes,' I said, as haughtily as I could, 'I'm feeling all right.'

'Have a little bit,' said my aunt.

'I'm not hungry,' I answered.

'Just to please me.'

'He must know when he's had enough,' said my uncle.

I gave him a bitter look.

'I don't mind having a small piece,' I said.

My aunt gave me a generous helping, which I ate with the air of one who, impelled by a stern sense of duty, performs an act that is deeply distasteful to him. It was a beautiful rasp-berry tart. Mary-Ann made short pastry that melted in the mouth. But when my aunt asked me whether I could not manage a little more I refused with cold dignity. She did not insist. My uncle said grace, and I carried my outraged feelings into the drawing-room.

But when I reckoned that the servants had finished their dinner I went into the kitchen. Emily was cleaning the silver in the pantry. Mary-Ann was washing-up.

'I say, what's wrong with the Driffields?' I asked her.

Mary-Ann had come to the vicarage when she was eighteen. She had bathed me when I was a small boy, given me powders in plum jam when I needed them, packed my box when I went to school, nursed me when I was ill, read to me when I was bored, and scolded me when I was naughty. Emily, the house-maid, was a flighty young thing, and Mary-Ann didn't know whatever would become of me if *she* had the looking after me. Mary-Ann was a Blackstable girl. She had never been to London in her life, and I do not think she had been to Tercan-bury more than three or four times. She was never ill. She never had a holiday. She was paid twelve pounds a year. One evening a week she went down the town to see her mother, who did the vicarage washing; and on Sunday evenings she went to church. But Mary-Ann knew everything that went on in Blackstable. She knew who everybody was, who had married whom, what anyone's father had died of, and how many children, and what they were called, any woman had had.

I asked Mary-Ann my question, and she slopped a wet clout noisily into the sink.

'I don't blame your uncle,' she said. 'I wouldn't let you go about with them, not if you was my nephew. Fancy their askin' you to ride your bicycle with them. Some people will do anything.'

I saw that the conversation in the dining-room had been repeated to Mary-Ann.

'I'm not a child,' I said.

'That makes it all the worse. The impudence of their comin' 'ere at all!' Mary-Ann dropped her aitches freely. 'Takin' a house and pretendin' to be ladies and gentlemen. Now leave that pie alone.'

The raspberry tart was standing on the kitchen table, and I broke off a piece of crust with my fingers and put it in my mouth.

'We're goin' to eat that for our supper. If you'd wanted a second 'elpin' why didn't you 'ave one when you was 'avin' your dinner? Ted Driffield never could stick to anything. He 'ad a good education, too. The one I'm sorry for is his mother. He's been a trouble to 'er from the day he was born. And then to go an' marry Rosie Gann. They tell me that when he told his mother what he was goin' to do she took to 'er bed and stayed there for three weeks, and wouldn't talk to anybody.'

'Was Mrs Driffield Rosie Gann before she married? Which Ganns were those?'

Gann was one of the commonest names at Blackstable. The churchyard was thick with their graves.

'Oh, you wouldn't 'ave known them. Old Josiah Gann was her father. He was a wild one, too. He went for a soldier, and when he came back he 'ad a wooden leg. He used to go out doing painting, but he was out of work more often than not. They lived in the next 'ouse to us in Rye Lane. Me an' Rosie used to go to Sunday school together.'

'But she's not as old as you are,' I said, with the bluntness of my age.

'She'll never see thirty again.'

Mary-Ann was a little woman with a snub nose and decayed teeth, but fresh-coloured, and I do not suppose she could have been more than thirty-five.

'Rosie ain't more than four or five years younger than me, whatever she may pretend she is. They tell me you wouldn't know her now all dressed up and everything.'

'Is it true that she was a barmaid?' I asked.

'Yes, at the Railway Arms and then at the Prince of Wales's Feathers at Haversham. Mrs Reeves 'ad 'er to 'elp in the bar at the Railway Arms, but it got so bad she had to get rid of her.'

The Railway Arms was a very modest little public-house just opposite the station of the London, Chatham and Dover

Railway. It had a sort of sinister gaiety. On a winter's night as you passed by you saw through the glass doors men lounging about the bar. My uncle very much disapproved of it, and had for years been trying to get its licence taken away. It was frequented by the railway porters, colliers, and farm labourers. The respectable residents of Blackstable would have disdained to enter it and, when they wanted a glass of bitter, went to the Bear and Key or the Duke of Kent.

'Why, what did she do?' I asked, my eyes popping out of my head.

'What didn't she do?' said Mary-Ann. 'What d'you think your uncle would say if he caught me tellin' you things like that? There wasn't a man who come in to 'ave a drink what she didn't carry on with. No matter who they was. She couldn't stick to anybody, it was just one man after another. They tell me it was simply 'orrible. That was when it begun with Lord George. It wasn't the sort of place he was likely to go to, he was too grand for that, but they say he went in accidental like one day when his train was late, and he saw her. And after that he was never out of the place, mixin' with all them common rough people, and, of course, they all knew what he was there for, and him with a wife and three children. Oh, I was sorry for her! And the talk it made. Well, it got so Mrs Reeves said she wasn't going to put up with it another day and she give her her wages and told her to pack her box and go. Good riddance to bad rubbish, that's what I said.'

I knew Lord George very well. His name was George Kemp and the title by which he was always known had been given him ironically owing to his grand manner. He was our coal merchant, but he also dabbled in house property, and he owned a share in one or two collieries. He lived in a new brick house that stood in its own grounds and he drove his own trap. He was a stoutish man with a pointed beard, florid, with a high colour and bold blue eyes. Remembering him, I think he must have looked like some jolly rubicund merchant in an old Dutch picture. He was always very flashily dressed, and when you saw him driving at a smart pace down the middle of the High Street in a fawn-coloured covert-coat with large buttons, his brown bowler on the side of his head and a red rose in his buttonhole, you could not but look at him. On Sunday he used to come to church in a lustrous topper and a frock-coat. Everyone knew that he wanted to be made churchwarden, and it was evident that his energy would have made him useful, but my uncle said not in his time, and though Lord George as a protest went to chapel for a year my uncle remained obdurate. He cut him dead when he met him in the town. A reconciliation was effected and Lord George came to church again, but my uncle only yielded so far as to appoint him sidesman. The gentry thought him vulgar and I have no doubt that he was vain and boastful. They complained of his loud voice and his strident laugh – when he was talking to somebody on one side of the street you heard every word he said from the other – and they thought his manners dreadful. He was much too friendly; when he talked to them it was as though he were not in trade at all; they said he was very pushing. But if he thought his hail-fellow-well-met air, his activity in public works, his open purse when subscriptions were needed for the annual regatta or for the harvest festival, his willingness to do anyone a good turn were going to break the barriers at Blackstable he was mistaken. His efforts at sociability were met with blank hostility.

I remember once that the doctor's wife was calling on my aunt and Emily came in to tell my uncle that Mr George Kemp would like to see him.

'But I heard the front door ring, Emily,' said my aunt.

'Yes'm, he came to the front door.'

There was a moment's awkwardness. Everyone was at a loss to know how to deal with such an unusual occurrence, and even Emily, who knew who should come to the front door, who should go to the side door, and who to the back, looked a trifle flustered. My aunt, who was a gentle soul, I think felt honestly embarrassed that anyone should put himself in such a false position; but the doctor's wife gave a little sniff of contempt. At last my uncle collected himself.

'Show him into the study, Emily,' he said. 'I'll come as soon as I've finished my tea.'

But Lord George remained exuberant, flashy, loud, and boisterous. He said the town was dead and he was going to wake it up. He was going to get the company to run excursion trains. He didn't see why it shouldn't become another Margate. And why shouldn't they have a mayor? Ferne Bay had one.

'I suppose he thinks he'd be mayor himself,' said the people of Blackstable. They pursed their lips. 'Pride goeth before a fall,' they said.

And my uncle remarked that you could take a horse to the water but you couldn't make him drink.

I should add that I looked upon Lord George with the same scornful derision as everyone else. It outraged me that he should stop me in the street and call me by my Christian name and talk to me as though there were no social difference between us. He even suggested that I should play cricket with his sons, who were of about the same age as myself. But they went to the grammar school at Haversham and of course I couldn't possibly have anything to do with them.

I was shocked and thrilled by what Mary-Ann told me, but I had difficulty in believing it. I had read too many novels and had learnt too much at school not to know a good deal about love, but I thought it was a matter that only concerned young people. I could not conceive that a man with a beard, who had sons as old as I, could have any feelings of that sort. I thought when you married all that was finished. That people over thirty should make love seemed to me rather disgusting.

'You don't mean to say they did anything?' I asked Mary-Ann.

'From what I hear there's very little that Rosie Gann didn't do. And Lord George wasn't the only one.'

'But, look here, why didn't she have a baby?'

In the novels I had read whenever lovely woman stooped to folly she had a baby. The cause was put with infinite precaution, sometimes indeed suggested only by a row of asterisks, but the result was inevitable.

'More by good luck than by good management, I lay,' said Mary-Ann. Then she recollected herself and stopped drying the plates she was busy with. 'It seems to me you know a lot more than you ought to,' she said.

'Of course I know,' I said importantly. 'Hang it all, I'm practically grown up, aren't I?'

'All I can tell you,' said Mary-Ann, 'is that when Mrs Reeves give her the sack Lord George got her a job at the Prince of Wales's Feathers at Haversham, and he was always poppin' over there in his trap. You can't tell me the ale's any different over there from what it is here.'

'Then why did Ted Driffield marry her?' I asked.

'Ask me another,' said Mary-Ann. 'It was at the Feathers he saw her. I suppose he couldn't get no one else to marry him. No respectable girl would 'ave 'ad 'im.'

'Did he know about her?'

'You'd better ask him.'

I was silent. It was all very puzzling.

'What does she look like now?' asked Mary-Ann. 'I never seen her since she married. I never even speak to 'er after I 'eard what was goin' on at the Railway Arms.'

'She looks all right,' I said.

'Well, you ask her if she remembers me and see what she says.'

chapter six

I had quite made up my mind that I was going out with the Driffields next morning, but I knew that it was no good asking my uncle if I might. If he found out that I had been and made a row it couldn't be helped, and if Ted Driffield asked me whether I had got my uncle's permission I was quite prepared to say I had. But I had after all no need to lie. In the afternoon, the tide being high, I walked down to the beach to bathe, and my uncle, having something to do in the town, walked part of the way with me. Just as we were passing the Bear and Key Ted Driffield stepped out of it. He saw us and came straight up to my uncle. I was startled at his coolness.

'Good afternoon, vicar,' he said. 'I wonder if you remember me. I used to sing in the choir when I was a boy. Ted Driffield. My old governor was Miss Wolfe's bailiff.'

My uncle was a very timid man, and he was taken aback.

'Oh, yes, how do you do? I was sorry to hear your father died.'

'I've made the acquaintance of your young nephew. I was wondering if you'd let him come for a ride with me tomorrow. It's rather dull for him riding alone, and I'm going to do a rubbing of one of the brasses at Ferne Church.'

'It's very kind of you but –'

My uncle was going to refuse, but Driffield interrupted him.

'I'll see he doesn't get up to any mischief. I thought he might like to make a rubbing himself. It would be an interest for him. I'll give him some paper and wax so that it won't cost him anything.'

My uncle had not a consecutive mind, and the suggestion that Ted Driffield should pay for my paper and wax offended him so much that he quite forgot his intention to forbid me to go at all.

'He can quite well get his own paper and wax,' he said. 'He has plenty of pocket-money, and he'd much better spend it on something like that than on sweets and make himself sick.'

'Well, if he goes to Hayward, the stationer's, and says he wants the same paper as I got and the wax, they'll let him have it.'

'I'll go now,' I said, and to prevent any change of mind on my uncle's part dashed across the road.

chapter seven

I do not know why the Driffields bothered about me unless it was from pure kindness of heart. I was a dull little boy, not very talkative, and if I amused Ted Driffield at all it must have been unconsciously. Perhaps he was tickled by my attitude of superiority. I was under the impression that it was condescension on my part to consort with the son of Miss Wolfe's bailiff, and he what my uncle called a penny-a-liner; and when, perhaps with a trace of superciliousness, I asked him to lend me one of his books, and he said it wouldn't interest me, I took him at his word and did not insist. After my uncle had once consented to my going out with the Driffields he made no further objection to my association with them. Sometimes we went for sails together, sometimes we went to some picturesque spot and Driffield painted a little water-colour. I do not know if the English climate was better in those days or if it is only an illusion of youth, but I seem to remember that all through that summer the sunny days followed one another in an unbroken line. I began to feel a curious affection for the undulating, opulent, and gracious country. We went far afield, to one church after another, taking rubbings of brasses, knights in armour, and ladies in stiff farthingales. Ted Driffield fired me with his own enthusiasm for this simple pursuit, and I rubbed with passion. I showed my uncle proudly the results of my industry, and I suppose he thought that whatever my company, I could not come to much harm when I was occupied in church. Mrs Driffield used to remain in the churchyard while we were at work, not reading or sewing, but just mooning about; she seemed able to do nothing for an indefinite time without feeling bored. Sometimes I would go out and sit with her for a little on the grass. We chattered about my school, my friends there, and my masters, about the people at Blackstable, and about nothing at all. She gratified me by calling me Mr Ashenden. I think she was the first person who had ever done so, and it made me feel grown up. I resented it vastly when people called me Master Willie. I thought it a ridiculous name for anyone to have. In fact, I did not like either of my names, and spent much time inventing others that would have suited me better. The ones I preferred were Roderic Ravensworth and I covered sheets of paper with this signature in a suitably dashing hand. I did not mind Ludovic Montgomery either.

I could not get over what Mary-Ann had told me about Mrs Driffield. Though I knew theoretically what people did when they were married, and was capable of putting the facts in the bluntest language, I did not really understand it. I thought it indeed rather disgusting, and I did not quite, quite believe it. After all, I was aware that the earth was round, but I *knew* it was flat. Mrs Driffield seemed so frank, her laugh was so open, there was in her demeanour something so young and childlike, that I could not see her 'going with' sailors, and above all anyone so gross and horrible as Lord George. She was not at all the type of the wicked woman I had read of in novels. Of course I knew she wasn't 'good form', and she spoke with the Blackstable accent, she dropped an aitch now and then, and sometimes her grammar gave me a shock, but I couldn't help liking her. I came to the conclusion that what Mary-Ann had told me was a pack of lies.

One day I happened to tell her that Mary-Ann was our cook. 'She says she lived next door to you in Rye Lane,' I added, quite prepared to hear Mrs Driffield say that she had never even heard of her.

But she smiled and her blue eyes gleamed.

'That's right. She used to take me to Sunday school. She used to have a rare job keeping me quiet. I heard she'd gone to service at the vicarage. Fancy her being there still! I haven't seen her for donkey's years. I'd like to see her again and have a chat about old days. Remember me to her, will you, and ask her to look in on her evening out. I'll give her a cup of tea.'

I was taken aback at this. After all, the Driffields lived in a house that they were talking of buying and they had a 'general'. It wouldn't be at all the thing for them to have Mary-Ann to tea, and it would make it very awkward for me. They

64

seemed to have no sense of the things one could do, and the things one simply couldn't. It never ceased to embarrass me, the way in which they talked of incidents in their past that I should have thought they would not dream of mentioning. I do not know that the people I lived among were pretentious in the sense of making themselves out to be richer or grander than they really were, but looking back it does seem to me that they lived a life full of pretences. They dwelt behind a mask of respectability. You never caught them in their shirtsleeves with their feet on the table. The ladies put on afternoon dresses, and were not visible till then; they lived privately with rigid economy so that you could not drop in for a casual meal, but when they entertained their tables groaned with food. Though catastrophe overwhelmed the family they held their heads high and ignored it. One of the sons might have married an actress, but they never referred to the calamity, and though the neighbours said it was dreadful, they took ostentatious care not to mention the theatre in the presence of the afflicted. We all knew that the wife of Major Greencourt who had taken the Three Gables was connected with trade, but neither she nor the major ever so much as hinted at the discreditable secret; and though we sniffed at them behind their backs, we were too polite even to mention crockery (the source of Mrs Greencourt's adequate income) in their presence. It was still not unheard of for an angry parent to cut off his son with a shilling, or to tell his daughter (who like my own mother had married a solicitor) never to darken his doors again. I was used to all this, and it seemed to me natural. What did shock me was to hear Ted Driffield speak of being a waiter in a restaurant in Holborn as though it were the most ordinary thing in the world. I knew he had run away to sea: that was romantic; I knew that boys, in books at all events, often did this and had thrilling adventures before they married a fortune and an earl's daughter; but Ted Driffield had driven a cab at Maidstone and had been clerk in a booking-office at Birmingham. Once when we bicycled past the Railway Arms, Mrs Driffield mentioned quite casually, as though it were something that anyone might have done, that she had worked there for three years.

'It was my first place,' she said. 'After that I went to the Feathers at Haversham. I only left there to get married.'

She laughed as though she enjoyed the recollection. I did not know what to say; I did not know which way to look; I blushed scarlet. Another time when we were going through Ferne Bay on our way back from a long excursion, it being a hot day, and all of us thirsty, she suggested that we should go into the Dolphin and have a glass of beer. She began talking to the girl behind the bar, and I was horrified to hear her remark that she had been in the business herself for five years. The landlord joined us, and Ted Driffield offered him a drink, and Mrs Driffield said that the barmaid must have a glass of port, and for some time they all chatted amiably about trade and tied houses, and how the price of everything was going up. Meanwhile, I stood, hot and cold all over, and not knowing what to do with myself. As we went out Mrs Driffield remarked:

'I took quite a fancy to that girl, Ted. She ought to do well for herself. As I said to her, it's a hard life but a merry one. You do see a bit of what's going on and if you play your cards right you ought to marry well. I noticed she had an engagement ring on, but she told me she just wore that because it gave the fellows a chance to tease her.'

Driffield laughed. She turned to me.

'I had a rare old time when I was a barmaid, but of course you can't go on for ever. You have to think of your future.'

But a greater jolt awaited me. It was half-way through September and my holidays were drawing to an end. I was very full of the Driffields, but my desire to talk about them at home was snubbed by my uncle.

'We don't want your friends pushed down our throats all day long,' said he. 'There are other topics of conversation that are more suitable. But I do think that, as Ted Driffield was born in the parish and is seeing you almost every day, he might come to church occasionally.'

One day I told Driffield: 'My uncle wants you to come to church.'

'All right. Let's go to church next Sunday night, Rosie.'

'I don't mind,' she said.

I told Mary-Ann they were going. I sat in the vicarage pew just behind the squire's and I could not look round, but I was conscious by the behaviour of my neighbours on the other side of the aisle that they were there, and as soon as I had a chance next day I asked Mary-Ann if she had seen them.

'I see 'er all right,' said Mary-Ann grimly.

'Did you speak to her afterwards?'

'Me?' She suddenly burst into anger. 'You get out of my kitchen. What d'you want to come bothering me all day long? How d'you expect me to do my work with you getting in my way all the time?'

'All right,' I said. 'Don't get in a wax.'

'I don't know what your uncle's about lettin' you go all over the place with the likes of them. All them flowers in her 'at. I wonder she ain't ashamed to show her face. Now run along, I'm busy.'

I did not know why Mary-Ann was so cross. I did not mention Mrs Driffield again. But two or three days later I happened to go into the kitchen to get something I wanted. There were two kitchens at the vicarage, a small one in which the cooking was done and a large one, built, I suppose, for a time when country clergymen had large families and gave grand dinners to the surrounding gentry, where Mary-Ann sat and sewed when her day's work was over. We had cold supper at eight so that after tea she had little to do. It was getting on for seven and the day was drawing in. It was Emily's evening out and I expected to find Mary-Ann alone, but as I went along the passage I heard voices and the sound of laughter. I supposed Mary-Ann had someone in to see her. The lamp was lit, but it had a thick green shade and the kitchen was almost in darkness. I saw a teapot and cups on the table. Mary-Ann was having a late cup of tea with her friend. The conversation stopped as I opened the door, then I heard a voice:

'Good evening.'

With a start I saw that Mary-Ann's friend was Mrs Driffield. Mary-Ann laughed a little at my surprise.

'Rosie Gann dropped in to have a cup of tea with me,' she said. 'We've been having a talk about old times.'

Mary-Ann was a little shy at my finding her thus, but not half so shy as I. Mrs Driffield gave me that childlike, mischievous smile of hers; she was perfectly at her ease. For some reason I noticed her dress, I suppose because I had never seen her so grand before. It was of pale blue cloth, very tight at the waist, with high sleeves and a long skirt with a flounce at the bottom. She wore a large, black, straw hat with a great quantity of roses and leaves and bows on it. It was evidently the hat she had worn in church on Sunday.

'I thought if I went on waiting till Mary-Ann came to see me I'd have to wait till Doomsday, so I thought the best thing I could do was to come and see her myself.'

Mary-Ann grinned self-consciously, but did not look displeased. I asked for whatever it was I wanted and, as quickly as I could, left them. I went out into the garden and wandered about aimlessly. I walked down to the road and looked over the gate. The night had fallen. Presently I saw a man strolling along. I paid no attention to him, but he passed backward and forward and it looked as though he were waiting for someone. At first I thought it might be Ted Driffield and I was on the point of going out when he stopped and lit a pipe; I saw it was Lord George. I wondered what he was doing there and at the same moment it struck me that he was waiting for Mrs Driffield. My heart began to beat fast, and though I was hidden by the darkness I withdrew into the shade of the bushes. I waited a few minutes longer, then I saw the side door open and Mrs Driffield let out by Mary-Ann. I heard her footsteps on the gravel. She came to the gate and opened it. It opened with a little click. At the sound Lord George stepped across the road and before she could come out slipped in. He took her in his arms and gave her a great hug. She gave a little laugh.

'Take care of my hat,' she whispered.

I was not more than three feet away from them and I was terrified lest they should notice me. I was so ashamed for them. I was trembling with agitation. For a minute he held her in his arms.

68

'What about the garden?' he said, still in a whisper.

'No; there's that boy. Let's go in the fields.'

They went out by the gate, he with his arm round her waist, and were lost in the night. Now I felt my heart pounding against my chest so that I could hardly breathe. I was so astonished at what I had seen that I could not think sensibly. I would have given anything to be able to tell someone, but it was a secret and I must keep it. I was thrilled with the importance it gave me. I walked slowly up to the house and let myself in by the side door. Mary-Ann, hearing it open, called me.

'Is that you, Master Willie?'

'Yes.'

I looked in the kitchen. Mary-Ann was putting the supper on a tray to take it into the dining-room.

'I wouldn't say anything to your uncle about Rosie Gann 'avin' been here,' she said.

'Oh, no.'

'It was a surprisement to me. When I 'eard a knock at the side door and opened it and saw Rosie standing there, you could 'ave knocked me down with a feather. "Mary-Ann," she says, an' before I knew what she was up to she was kissing me all over me face. I couldn't but ask 'er in and when she was in I couldn't but ask her to 'ave a nice cup of tea.'

Mary-Ann was anxious to excuse herself. After all she had said of Mrs Driffield it must seem strange to me that I should find them sitting there together chatting away and laughing. I did not want to crow.

'She's not so bad, is she?' I said.

Mary-Ann smiled. Notwithstanding her black decayed teeth her smile was sweet and touching.

'I don't 'ardly know what it is, but there's somethin' you can't 'elp likin' about her. She was 'ere the best part of an hour and I will say that for 'er, she never once give 'erself airs. And she told me with 'er own lips the material of that dress she 'ad on cost thirteen and eleven a yard and I believe it. She remembers everything, how I used to brush her 'air for her when she was a tiny tot and how I used to make her wash her little 'ands before tea. You see, sometimes her mother used to send 'er in to 'ave her tea with us. She was as pretty as a picture in them days.'

Mary-Ann looked back into the past and her funny crumpled face grew wistful.

'Oh, well,' she said after a pause, 'I dare say she's been no worse than plenty others if the truth was only known. She 'ad more temptation than most, and I dare say a lot of them as blame her would 'ave been no better than what she was if they'd 'ad the opportunity.'

chapter eight

The weather broke suddenly; it grew chilly, and heavy rain fell. It put an end to our excursions. I was not sorry, for I did not know how I could look Mrs Driffield in the face now that I had seen her meeting with George Kemp. I was not so much shocked as astonished. I could not understand how it was possible for her to like being kissed by an old man, and the fantastic notion passed through my mind, filled with the novels I had read, that somehow Lord George held her in his power and forced her by his knowledge of some fearful secret to submit to his loathsome embraces. My imagination played with terrible possibilities. Bigamy, murder, and forgery. Very few villains in books failed to hold the threat of exposure of one of these crimes over some hapless female. Perhaps Mrs Driffield had backed a bill; I never could quite understand what this meant, but I knew that the consequences were disastrous. I toyed with the fancy of her anguish (the long sleepless nights when she sat at her window in her nightdress, her fair hair hanging to her knees, and watched hopelessly for the dawn) and saw myself (not a boy of fifteen with sixpence a week pocket-money, but a tall man with a waxed moustache and muscles of steel, in faultless evening dress) with a happy blend of heroism and dexterity rescuing her from the toils of the rascally blackmailer. On the other hand, it had not looked as though she had yielded quite unwillingly to Lord George's fondling and I could not get out of my ears the sound of her laugh. It had a note that I had never heard before. It gave me a queer feeling of breathlessness.

During the rest of my holidays I only saw the Driffields once more. I met them by chance in the town and they stopped and spoke to me. I suddenly felt very shy again, and when I looked at Mrs Driffield I could not help blushing with embarrassment, for there was nothing in her countenance that indicated a guilty secret. She looked at me with those soft blue eyes of hers in which there was a child's playful naughtiness. She often held her mouth a little open, as though it were just going to break into a smile, and her lips were full and red. There was honesty and innocence in her face and an ingenuous frankness, and though then I could not have expressed this, I felt it quite strongly. If I had put it into words at all I think I should have said: she looks as straight as a die. It was impossible that she could be 'carrying on' with Lord George. There must be an explanation; I did not believe what my eyes had seen.

Then the day came when I had to go back to school. The carter had taken my trunk and I walked to the station by myself. I had refused to let my aunt see me off, thinking it more manly to go alone, but I felt rather low as I walked down the street. It was a small branch line to Tercanbury and the station was at the other end of the town near the beach. I took my ticket and settled myself in the corner of a third-class carriage. Suddenly I heard a voice: 'There he is'; and Mr and Mrs Driffield bustled gaily up.

'We thought we must come and see you off,' she said. 'Are you feeling miserable?'

'No, of course not.'

'Oh, well, it won't last long. We'll have no end of a time when you come back for Christmas. Can you skate?'

'No.'

'I can. I'll teach you.'

Her high spirits cheered me, and at the same time the thought that they had come to the station to say good-bye to me gave me a lump in my throat. I tried hard not to let the emotion I felt appear on my face.

'I expect I shall be playing a lot of rugger this term,' I said. 'I ought to get into the second fifteen.'

She looked at me with kindly shining eyes, smiling with her full red lips. There was something in her smile I had always rather liked, and her voice seemed almost to tremble with a laugh or a tear. For one horrible moment I was afraid that she was going to kiss me. I was scared out of my wits. She talked on, she was mildly facetious as grown-up people are with schoolboys, and Driffield stood there without saying anything. He looked at me with a smile in his eyes and pulled his beard. Then the guard blew a cracked whistle and waved a flag. Mrs Driffield took my hand and shook it. Driffield came forward.

'Good-bye,' he said. 'Here's something for you.'

He pressed a tiny packet into my hand and the train steamed off. When I opened it I found two half-crowns wrapped in a piece of toilet-paper. I blushed to the roots of my hair. I was glad enough to have an extra five shillings, but the thought that Ted Driffield had dared to give me a tip filled me with rage and humiliation. I could not possibly accept anything from him. It was true that I had bicycled with him and sailed with him, but he wasn't a sahib (I had got that from Major Greencourt) and it was an insult to give me five shillings. At first I thought of returning the money without a word, showing by my silence how outraged I was at the solecism he had committed, then I composed in my head a dignified and frigid letter, in which I thanked him for his generosity, but said that he must see how impossible it was for a gentleman to accept a tip from someone who was practically a stranger. I thought it over for two or three days, and every day it seemed more difficult to part with the two half-crowns. I felt sure that Driffield had meant it kindly, and of course he was very bad form, and didn't know about things; it would be rather hard to hurt his feelings by sending the money back, and finally I spent it. But I assuaged my wounded pride by not writing to thank Driffield for his gift.

When Christmas came, however, and I went back to Blackstable for the holidays, it was the Driffields I was most eager to see. In that stagnant little place they alone seemed to have a connexion with the outside world which already was beginning to touch my daydreams with anxious curiosity. But I could not overcome my shyness enough to go to their house and call, and I hoped that I should meet them in the town. But the weather was dreadful, a boisterous wind whistled down the street, piercing you to the bone, and the few women who had an errand were swept along by their full skirts like fishing boats in half a gale. The cold rain scudded in sudden squalls, and the sky, which in summer had enclosed the friendly country so snugly, now was a great pall that pressed upon the earth with awful menace. There was small hope of meeting the Driffields by chance, and at last I took my courage in both hands and one day after tea slipped out. As far as the station the road was pitch dark, but there the street lamps, few and dim, made it easier to keep to the pavement. The Driffields lived in a little two-storey house in a side street; it was of dingy yellow brick, and had a bow window. I knocked, and presently a little maid opened the door; I asked if Mrs Driffield was in. She gave me an uncertain look, and, saying she would go and see, left me standing in the passage. I had already heard voices in the next room, but they were stilled as she opened the door and, entering, shut it behind her. I had a faint impression of mystery; in the houses of my uncle's friends, even if there was no fire and the gas had to be lit as you went in, you were shown into the drawing-room when you called. But the door was opened and Driffield came out. There was only a speck of light in the passage, and at first he could not see who it was; but in an instant he recognized me.

'Oh, it's you. We wondered when we were going to see you.' Then he called out: 'Rosie, it's young Ashenden.'

There was a cry, and before you could say knife Mrs

Driffield had come into the passage and was shaking my hands.

'Come in, come in. Take off your coat. Isn't it awful, the weather? You must be perishing.'

She helped me with my coat and took off my muffler and snatched my cap out of my hand and drew me into the room. It was hot and stuffy, a tiny room full of furniture, with a fire burning in the grate; they had gas there, which we hadn't at the vicarage, and the three burners in round globes of frosted glass filled the room with harsh light. The air was grey with tobacco smoke. At first, dazzled and then taken aback by my effusive welcome, I did not see who the two men were who got up as I came in. Then I saw they were the curate, Mr Galloway, and Lord George Kemp. I fancied that the curate shook my hand with constraint.

'How are you? I just came in to return some books that Mr Driffield had lent me, and Mrs Driffield very kindly asked me to stay to tea.'

I felt rather than saw the quizzical look that Driffield gave him. He said something about the mammon of unrighteousness, which I recognized as a quotation, but did not gather the sense of. Mr Galloway laughed.

'I don't know about that,' he said. 'What about the publicans and sinners?'

I thought the remark in very bad taste, but I was immediately seized upon by Lord George. There was no constraint about him.

'Well, young fellow, home for the holidays? My word, what a big chap you're growing.'

I shook hands with him rather coldly. I wished I had not come.

'Let me give you a nice strong cup of tea,' said Mrs Driffield.

'I've already had tea.'

'Have some more,' said Lord George, speaking as though he owned the place (that was just like him). 'A big fellow like you can always tuck away another piece of bread and butter and jam, and Mrs D. will cut you a slice with her own fair hands.'

The tea things were still on the table and they were sitting round it. A chair was brought up for me and Mrs Driffield gave me a piece of cake.

'We were just trying to persuade Ted to sing us a song,' said Lord George. 'Come on, Ted.'

'Sing *All through stickin' to a Soljer*, Ted,' said Mrs Driffield. 'I love that.'

'No, sing *First we mopped the Floor with him*.'

'I'll sing 'em both if you're not careful,' said Driffield.

He took his banjo, which was lying on the top of the cottage piano, tuned it and began to sing. He had a rich baritone voice. I was quite used to people singing songs. When there was a tea party at the vicarage, or I went to one at the major's or the doctor's, people always brought their music with them. They left it in the hall, so that it should not seem that they wanted to be asked to play or sing; but after tea the hostess asked them if they had brought it. They shyly admitted that they had, and if it was at the vicarage I was sent to fetch it. Sometimes a young lady would say that she had quite given up playing and hadn't brought anything with her, and then her mother would break in and say that *she* had brought it. But when they sang it was not comic songs; it was *I'll sing thee Songs of Araby*, or *Good-night, Beloved*, or *Queen of my Heart*. Once at the annual concert at the Assembly Rooms, Smithson, the draper, had sung a comic song, and though the people at the back of the hall had applauded a great deal, the gentry had seen nothing funny in it. Perhaps there wasn't. Anyhow, before the next concert he was asked to be a little more careful about what he sang ('Remember there are ladies present, Mr Smithson') and so gave *The Death of Nelson*. The next ditty that Driffield sang had a chorus and the curate and Lord George joined in lustily. I heard it a good many times afterwards, but I can only remember four lines.

First we mopped the floor with him;
    Dragged him up and down the stairs.
Then we lugged him round the room,
    Under tables, over chairs.

When it was finished, assuming my best company manners, I turned to Mrs Driffield.

'Don't you sing?' I asked.

'I do, but it always turns the milk, so Ted doesn't encourage me.'

Driffield put down his banjo and lit a pipe.

'Well, how's the old book getting along, Ted?' said Lord George heartily.

'Oh, all right. I'm working away, you know.'

'Good old Ted and his books,' Lord George laughed. 'Why don't you settle down and do something respectable for a change? I'll give you a job in my office.'

'Oh, I'm all right.'

'You let him be, George,' said Mrs Driffield. 'He likes writing, and what I say is, as long as it keeps him happy, why shouldn't he?'

'Well, I don't pretend to know anything about books,' began George Kemp.

'Then don't talk about them,' interrupted Driffield with a smile.

'I don't think anyone need be ashamed to have written *Fairhaven*,' said Mr Galloway, 'and I don't care what the critics said.'

'Well, Ted, I've known you since I was a boy and *I* couldn't read it, try as I would.'

'Oh, come on, we don't want to start talking about books,' said Mrs Driffield. 'Sing us another song, Ted.'

'I must be going,' said the curate. He turned to me. 'We might walk along together. Have you got anything for me to read, Driffield?'

Driffield pointed to a pile of new books that were heaped up on a table in the corner.

'Take your pick.'

'By Jove, what a lot!' I said, looking at them greedily.

'Oh, it's all rubbish. They're sent down for review.'

'What d'you do with them?'

'Take 'em into Tercanbury and sell 'em for what they'll fetch. It all helps to pay the butcher.'

When we left, the curate and I, he with several books under his arm, he asked me:

'Did you tell your uncle you were coming to see the Driffields?'

'No, I just went out for a walk and it suddenly occurred to me that I might look in.'

This of course was some way from the truth, but I did not care to tell Mr Galloway that, though I was practically grown up, my uncle realized the fact so little that he was capable of trying to prevent me from seeing people he objected to.

'Unless you have to I wouldn't say anything about it in your place. The Driffields are perfectly all right, but your uncle doesn't quite approve of them.'

'I know,' I said. 'It's such rot.'

'Of course they're rather common, but he doesn't write half badly, and when you think what he came from it's wonderful that he writes at all.'

I was glad to know how the land lay. Mr Galloway did not wish my uncle to know that he was on friendly terms with the Driffields. I could feel sure at all events that he would not give me away.

The patronizing manner in which my uncle's curate spoke of one who has been now so long recognized as one of the greatest of the later Victorian novelists must arouse a smile; but it was the manner in which he was generally spoken of at Blackstable. One day we went to tea at Mrs Greencourt's, who had staying with her a cousin, the wife of an Oxford don, and we had been told that she was very cultivated. She was a Mrs Encombe, a little woman with an eager wrinkled face; she surprised us very much because she wore her grey hair short and a black serge skirt that only just came down below the tops of her square-toed boots. She was the first example of the New Woman that had ever been seen in Blackstable. We were staggered and immediately on the defensive, for she looked intellectual, and it made us feel shy. (Afterward we all scoffed at her, and my uncle said to my aunt: 'Well, my dear, I'm thankful you're not clever, at least I've been spared that'; and my aunt in a playful mood put my uncle's slippers which were warming for him by the fire over her boots and said: 'Look, I'm the new woman.' And then we all said: 'Mrs Greencourt is very funny; you never know what she'll do next. But of course she isn't quite quite.' We could hardly forget that her father made china and that her grandfather had been a factory hand.)

But we all found it very interesting to hear Mrs Encombe talk of the people she knew. My uncle had been at Oxford, but everyone he asked about seemed to be dead. Mrs Encombe knew Mrs Humphry Ward, and admired *Robert Elsmere*. My uncle considered it a scandalous work, and he was surprised that Mr Gladstone, who at least called himself a Christian, had found a good word to say for it. They had quite an argument about it. My uncle said he thought it would unsettle people's opinions and give them all sorts of ideas that they were much better without. Mrs Encombe answered that he wouldn't think that if he knew Mrs Humphry Ward. She was a woman of the very highest character, a niece of Mr Matthew Arnold, and whatever you might think of the book itself (and she, Mrs Encombe, was quite willing to admit that there were parts which had better have been omitted) it was quite certain that she had written it from the very highest motives. Mrs Encombe knew Miss Broughton too. She was of very good family and it was strange that she wrote the books she did.

'I don't see any harm in them,' said Mrs Hayforth, the doctor's wife. 'I enjoy them, especially *Red as a Rose is She*.'

'Would you like your girls to read them?' asked Mrs Encombe.

'Not just yet perhaps,' said Mrs Hayforth. 'But when they're married I should have no objection.'

'Then it might interest you to know,' said Mrs Encombe, 'that when I was in Florence last Easter I was introduced to Ouida.'

'That's quite another matter,' returned Mrs Hayforth. 'I can't believe that any lady would read a book by Ouida.'

'I read one out of curiosity,' said Mrs Encombe. 'I must say, it's more what you'd expect from a Frenchman than from an English gentlewoman.'

'Oh, but I understand she isn't really English. I've always heard her real name is Mademoiselle de la Ramée.'

It was then that Mr Galloway mentioned Edward Driffield.

'You know we have an author living here,' he said.

'We're not very proud of him,' said the major. 'He's the son of old Miss Wolfe's bailiff, and he married a barmaid.'

'Can he write?' asked Mrs Encombe.

'You can tell at once that he's not a gentleman,' said the curate, 'but when you consider the disadvantages he's had to struggle against it's rather remarkable that he should write as well as he does.'

'He's a friend of Willie's,' said my uncle.

Everyone looked at me, and I felt very uncomfortable.

'They bicycled together last summer, and after Willie had gone back to school I got one of his books from the library to see what it was like. I read the first volume and then I sent it back. I wrote a pretty stiff letter to the librarian and I was glad to hear that he'd withdrawn it from circulation. If it had been my own property I should have put it promptly in the kitchen stove.'

'I looked through one of his books myself,' said the doctor. 'It interested me because it was set in this neighbourhood, and I recognized some of the people. But I can't say I liked it; I thought it unnecessarily coarse.'

'I mentioned that to him,' said Mr Galloway, 'and he said the men in the colliers that run up to Newcastle and the fishermen and farm hands don't behave like ladies and gentlemen, and don't talk like them.'

'But why write about people of that character?' said my uncle.

'That's what I say,' said Mrs Hayforth. 'We all know that there are coarse and wicked and vicious people in the world, but I don't see what good it does to write about them.'

'I'm not defending him,' said Mr Galloway. 'I'm only telling you what explanation he gives himself. And then of course he brought up Dickens.'

'Dickens is quite different,' said my uncle. 'I don't see how anyone can object to the *Pickwick Papers*.'

'I suppose it's a matter of taste,' said my aunt. 'I always found Dickens very coarse. I don't want to read about people who drop their aitches. I must say I'm very glad the weather's so bad now and Willie can't take any more rides with Mr Driffield. I don't think he's quite the sort of person he ought to associate with.'

Both Mr Galloway and I looked down our noses.

chapter nine

As often as the mild Christmas gaieties of Blackstable allowed me I went to the Driffields' little house next door to the Congregational Chapel. I always found Lord George and often Mr Galloway. Our conspiracy of silence had made us friends, and when we met at the vicarage or in the vestry after church we looked at one another archly. We did not talk about our secret, but we enjoyed it; I think it gave us both a good deal of satisfaction to know that we were making a fool of my uncle. But once it occurred to me that George Kemp, meeting my uncle in the street, might remark casually that he had been seeing a lot of me at the Driffields'.

'What about Lord George?' I said to Mr Galloway.

'Oh, I made that all right.'

We chuckled. I began to like Lord George. At first I was very cold with him and scrupulously polite, but he seemed so unconscious of the social difference between us that I was forced to conclude that my haughty courtesy failed to put him in his place. He was always cordial, breezy, even boisterous; he chaffed me in his common way and I answered him back with schoolboy wit; we made the others laugh and this disposed me kindly toward him. He was for ever bragging about the great schemes he had in mind, but he took in good part my jokes at the expense of his grandiose imaginations. It amused me to hear him tell stories about the swells of Blackstable that made them look foolish and when he mimicked their oddities I roared with laughter. He was blatant and vulgar and the way he dressed was always a shock to me (I had never been to Newmarket nor seen a trainer, but that was my idea of how a Newmarket trainer dressed), and his table manners were offensive, but I found myself less and less affronted by him. He gave me the *Pink 'Un* every week and I took it home, carefully tucked away in my greatcoat pocket, and read it in my bedroom.

I never went to the Driffields' till after tea at the vicarage, but I always managed to make a second tea when I got there. Afterward Ted Driffield sang comic songs, accompanying himself sometimes on the banjo and sometimes on the piano. He would sing, peering at the music with his rather shortsighted eyes, for an hour at a time; there was a smile on his lips and he liked us all to join in the chorus. We played whist. I had learned the game when I was a child and my uncle and aunt and I used to play at the vicarage during the long winter evenings. My uncle always took dummy, and though of course we played for love, when my aunt and I lost I used to retire under the dining-room table and cry. Ted Driffield did not play cards, he said he had no head for them, and when we started a game he would sit down by the fire and, pencil in hand, read one of the books that had been sent down to him from London to review. I had never played with three people before and of course I did not play well, but Mrs Driffield had a natural card sense. Her movements as a rule were rather deliberate, but when it came to playing cards she was quick and alert. She played the rest of us right off our heads. Ordinarily she did not speak very much and then slowly, but when, after a hand was played, she took the trouble good-humouredly to point out to me my mistakes, she was not only lucid but voluble. Lord George chaffed her as he chaffed everybody; she would smile at his banter, for she very seldom laughed, and sometimes make a neat retort. They did not behave like lovers, but like familiar friends, and I should have quite forgotten what I had heard about them and what I had seen but that now and then she gave him a look that embarrassed me. Her

81

eyes rested on him quietly, as though he were not a man but a chair or a table, and in them was a mischievous, childlike smile. Then I would notice that his face seemed suddenly to swell and he moved uneasily in his chair. I looked quickly at the curate, afraid that he would notice something, but he was intent on the cards or else was lighting his pipe.

The hour or two I spent nearly every day in that hot, poky, smoke-laden room passed like lightning, and as the holidays drew nearer to their end I was seized with dismay at the thought that I must spend the next three months dully at school.

'I don't know what we shall do without you,' said Mrs Driffield. 'We shall have to play dummy.'

I was glad that my going would break up the game. While I was doing prep I did not want to think that they were sitting in that little room and enjoying themselves just as if I did not exist.

'How long do you get at Easter?' asked Mr Galloway.

'About three weeks.'

'We'll have a lovely time, then,' said Mrs Driffield. 'The weather ought to be all right. We can ride in the mornings and then after tea we'll play whist. You've improved a lot. If we play three or four times a week during your Easter holidays you won't need to be afraid to play with anybody.'

chapter ten

But the term came to an end at last. I was in high spirits when once more I got out of the train at Blackstable. I had grown a little and I had had a new suit made at Tercanbury, blue serge and very smart, and I had bought a new tie. I meant to go and see the Driffields immediately I had swallowed my tea, and I was full of hope that the carrier would have brought my box in time for me to put the new suit on. It made me look quite grown up. I had already begun putting vaseline on my upper lip every night to make my moustache grow. On my way through the town I looked down the street in which the Driffields lived, in the hope of seeing them. I should have liked to go in and say how-do-you-do, but I knew that Driffield wrote in the morning and Mrs Driffield was not 'presentable'. I had all sorts of exciting things to tell them. I had won a heat in the hundred-yard race in the sports, and I had been second in the hurdles. I meant to have a shot for the history prize in the summer, and I was going to swot up my English history during the holidays. Though there was an east wind blowing, the sky was blue and there was a feeling of spring in the air. The High Street, with its colours washed clean by the wind and its lines sharp as though drawn with a new pen, looked like a picture by Samuel Scott, quiet and naïve and cosy: now, looking back; then it looked like nothing but High Street, Blackstable. When I came to the railway bridge I noticed that two or three houses were being built.

'By Jove,' I said. 'Lord George *is* going it.'

In the fields beyond little white lambs were frisking. The elm trees were just beginning to turn green. I let myself in by the side door. My uncle was sitting in his arm-chair by the fire reading *The Times*. I shouted to my aunt and she came downstairs, a pink spot from the excitement of seeing me on each of her withered cheeks, and threw her thin old arms round my neck. She said all the right things.

'How you've grown' and 'Good gracious me, you'll be getting a moustache soon!'

I kissed my uncle on his bald forehead, and I stood in front of the fire, with my legs well apart and my back to it, and was extremely grown up and rather condescending. Then I went upstairs to say how-do-you-do to Emily, and into the kitchen to shake hands with Mary-Ann, and out into the garden to see the gardener.

When I sat down hungrily to dinner and my uncle carved the leg of mutton I asked my aunt:

'Well, what's happened at Blackstable since I was here?'

'Nothing very much. Mrs Greencourt went down to Mentone for six weeks, but she came back a few days ago. The major had an attack of gout.'

'And your friends the Driffields have bolted,' added my uncle.

'They've done what?' I cried.

'Bolted. They took their luggage away one night and just went up to London. They've left bills all over the place. They hadn't paid their rent and they hadn't paid for their furniture. They owed Harris the butcher the best part of thirty pounds.'

'How awful,' I said.

'That's bad enough,' said my aunt, 'but it appears they hadn't even paid the wages of the maid they had for three months.'

I was flabbergasted. I thought I felt a little sick.

'I think in future,' said my uncle, 'you would be wiser not to consort with people whom your aunt and I don't think proper associates for you.'

'One can't help feeling sorry for all those tradesmen they cheated,' said my aunt.

'It serves them right,' said my uncle. 'Fancy giving credit to people like that! I should have thought anyone could see they were nothing but adventurers.'

'I always wonder why they came down here at all.'

'They just wanted to show off, and I suppose they thought as people knew who they were here it would be easier to get things on credit.'

I did not think this quite logical, but was too much crushed to argue.

As soon as I had the chance I asked Mary-Ann what she knew of the incident. To my surprise she did not take it at all in the same way as my uncle and aunt. She giggled.

'They let everyone in proper,' she said. 'They were as free as you like with their money and everyone thought they 'ad plenty. It was always the best end of the neck for them at the butcher's and when they wanted a steak nothing would do but the undercut. Asparagus and grapes and I don't know what all. They ran up bills in every shop in town. I don't know 'ow people can be such fools.'

But it was evidently of the tradesmen she was speaking and not of the Driffields.

'But how did they manage to bunk without anyone knowing?' I asked.

'Well, that's what everybody's askin'. They do say it was Lord George 'elped them. How did they get their boxes to the station, I ask you, if 'e didn't take them in that there trap of 'is?'

'What does he say about it?'

'He says 'e knows no more about it than the man in the moon. There was a rare to-do all over the town when they found out the Driffields had shot the moon. It made me laugh. Lord George says 'e never knew they was broke, and 'e makes out 'e was as surprised as anybody. But I for one don't believe a word of it. We all know about 'im and Rosie before she was married, and between you and me and the gatepost I don't know that it ended there. They do say they was seen walkin' about the fields together last summer and 'e was in and out of the 'ouse pretty near every day.'

'How did people find out?'

'Well, it's like this. They 'ad a girl there and they told 'er she could go 'ome and spend the night with her mother, but she wasn't to be back later than eight o'clock in the morning. Well, when she come back she couldn't get in. She knocked and she rung but nobody answered, and so she went in next door and asked the lady there what she'd better do, and the lady said she'd better go to the police station. The sergeant come back with 'er and 'e knocked and 'e rung, but 'e couldn't get no answer. Then he asked the girl 'ad they paid 'er 'er wages, and she said no, not for three months, and then 'e said, you take my word for it, they've shot the moon, that's what they've done. An' when they come to get inside they found they'd took all their clothes, an' their books – they say as Ted Driffield 'ad a rare lot of books – an' every blessed thing that belonged to them.'

'And has nothing been heard of them since?'

'Well, not exactly, but when they'd been gone about a week the girl got a letter from London, and when she opened it there was no letter or anything, but just a postal order for 'er wages. An' if you ask me, I call that very 'andsome not to do a poor girl out of her wages.'

I was much more shocked than Mary-Ann. I was a very respectable youth. The reader cannot have failed to observe that I accepted the conventions of my class as if they were the laws of Nature, and though debts on the grand scale in books had seemed to me romantic, and duns and money-lenders were familiar figures to my fancy, I could not but think it mean and paltry not to pay the tradesmen's books. I listened with confusion when people talked in my presence of the Driffields, and, when they spoke of them as my friends, I said: 'Hang it all, I just knew them'; and when they asked: 'Weren't they fearfully common?' I said: 'Well, they didn't exactly suggest the Vere de Veres, you know.' Poor Mr Galloway was dreadfully upset.

'Of course I didn't think they were wealthy,' he told me, 'but I thought they had enough to get along. The house was very nicely furnished and the piano was new. It never struck me that they hadn't paid for a single thing. They never stinted themselves. What hurts me is the deceit. I used to see quite a lot of them and I thought they liked me. They always made one welcome. You'd hardly believe it but, the last time I saw them, when they shook hands with me Mrs Driffield asked me to come next day and Driffield said: "Muffins for tea tomorrow." And all the time they had everything packed upstairs and that very night they took the last train to London.'

'What does Lord George say about it?'

'To tell you the truth I haven't gone out of my way to see him lately. It's been a lesson to me. There's a little proverb about evil communications that I've thought well to bear in mind.'

I felt very much the same about Lord George, and I was a little nervous too. If he took it into his head to tell people that at Christmas I had been going to see the Driffields almost every day, and it came to my uncle's ears, I foresaw an unpleasant fuss. My uncle would accuse me of deceit and prevarication and disobedience and of not behaving like a gentleman, and I did not at the moment see what answer I could make. I knew him well enough to be aware that he would not let the matter drop, and that I should be reminded of my transgression for years. I was just as glad not to see Lord George. But one day I ran into him face to face in the High Street.

'Hallo, youngster!' he cried, addressing me in a way I particularly resented. 'Back for the holidays, I suppose.'

'You suppose quite correctly,' I answered with what I thought withering sarcasm.

Unfortunately he only bellowed with laughter.

'You're so sharp you'll cut yourself if you don't look out,' he answered heartily. 'Well, it looks as if there was no more whist for you and me just yet. Now you see what comes of living beyond your means. What I always say to my boys is, if you've got a pound and you spend nineteen and six you're a rich man, but if you spend twenty shillings and sixpence you're a pauper. Look after the pence, young fellow, and the pounds'll look after themselves.'

But though he spoke after this fashion there was in his voice no note of disapproval, but a bubble of laughter as though in his heart he were tittering at these admirable maxims.

'They say you helped them to bunk,' I remarked.

'Me?' His face assumed a look of extreme surprise, but his eyes glittered with sly mirth. 'Why, when they came and told me the Driffields had shot the moon you could have knocked me down with a feather. They owed me four pounds seventeen and six for coal. We've all been let in, even poor old Galloway, who never got his muffins for tea.'

I had never thought Lord George more blatant. I should have liked to say something final and crushing, but as I could not think of anything I just said that I must be getting along and with a curt nod left him.

chapter eleven

Musing thus over the past, while I waited for Alroy Kear, I chuckled when I considered this shabby incident of Edward Driffield's obscurity in the light of the immense respectability of his later years. I wondered whether it was because in my boyhood he was as a writer held in such small esteem by the people about me that I had never been able to see in him the astonishing merit that the best critical opinion eventually ascribed to him. He was for long thought to write very bad English, and indeed he gave you the impression of writing with the stub of a blunt pencil; his style was laboured, an uneasy mixture of the classical and the slangy, and his dialogue was such as could never have issued from the mouth of a human being. Toward the end of his career, when he dictated his books, his style, acquiring a conversational ease, became flowing and limpid; and then the critics, going back to the novels of his maturity, found that their English had a nervous, racy vigour that eminently suited the matter. His prime belonged to a period when the purple patch was in vogue, and there are descriptive passages in his works that have found their way into all the anthologies of English prose. His pieces on the sea, and spring in the Kentish woods, and sunset on the lower reaches of the Thames are famous. It should be a mortification to me that I cannot read them without discomfort.

When I was a young man, though his books sold but little, and one or two were banned by the libraries, it was very much a mark of culture to admire him. He was thought boldly realistic. He was a very good stick to beat the Philistines with. Somebody's lucky inspiration discovered that his sailors and peasants were Shakespearian, and when the advanced got together they uttered shrill cries of ecstasy over the dry and spicy humour of his yokels. This was a commodity that Edward Driffield had no difficulty in supplying. My own heart sank when he led me into the forecastle of a sailing ship or the tap-room of a public-house, and I knew I was in for half a dozen pages in dialect of facetious comment on life, ethics, and immortality. But, I admit, I have always thought the Shakespearian clowns tedious, and their innumerable progeny insupportable.

Driffield's strength lay evidently in his depiction of the class he knew best, farmers and farm labourers, shopkeepers and bartenders, skippers of sailing ships, mates, cooks, and ableseamen. When he introduces characters belonging to a higher station in life even his warmest admirers, one would have thought, must experience a certain malaise; his fine gentlemen are so incredibly fine, his high-born ladies are so good, so pure, so noble that you are not surprised that they can only express themselves with polysyllabic dignity. His women hardly come to life. But here again I must add that this is only my own opinion; the world at large and the most eminent critics have agreed that they are very winsome types of English womanhood, spirited, gallant, high-souled, and they have been often compared with the heroines of Shakespeare. We know of course that women are habitually constipated, but to represent them in fiction as being altogether devoid of a back passage seems to me really an excess of chivalry. I am surprised that they care to see themselves thus limned.

The critics can force the world to pay attention to a very indifferent writer, and the world may lose its head over one who has no merit at all, but the result in neither case is lasting; and I cannot help thinking that no writer can hold the public for as long as Edward Driffield without considerable gifts. The elect sneer at popularity; they are inclined even to assert that it is a proof of mediocrity; but they forget that posterity makes its choice not from among the unknown writers of a period, but from among the known. It may be that some great masterpiece which deserves immortality has fallen stillborn from the press, but posterity will never hear of it; it may be that posterity will scrap all the best-sellers of our day, but it is among them that it must choose. At all events Edward Driffield is in the running. His novels happen to bore me; I find them long; the melodramatic incidents with which he sought to stir the sluggish reader's interest leave me cold; but he certainly had sincerity. There is in his best books the stir of life, and in none of them can you fail to be aware of the author's enigmatic personality. In his earlier days he was praised or blamed for his realism; according to the idiosyncrasy of his critics he was extolled for his truth or censured for his coarseness. But realism has ceased to excite remark, and the library reader will take in his stride obstacles at which a generation back he would have violently shied. The cultured reader of these pages will remember the leading article in the *Literary Supplement* of *The Times* which appeared at the moment of Driffield's death. Taking the novels of Edward Driffield as his text, the author wrote what was very well described as a hymn to beauty. No one who read it could fail to be impressed by those swelling periods, which reminded one of the noble prose of Jeremy Taylor, by that reverence and piety, by all those high sentiments, in short, expressed in a style that was ornate without excess and dulcet without effeminacy. It was itself a thing of beauty. If some suggested that Edward Driffield was by way of being a humorist and that a jest would here and there have lightened this eulogious article, it must be replied that after all it was a funeral oration. And it is well known that Beauty does not look with good grace on the timid advances of Humour. Roy Kear, when he was talking to me of Driffield, claimed that, whatever his faults, they were redeemed by the beauty that suffused his pages. Now I come to look back on our conversation, I think it was this remark that had most exasperated me.

Thirty years ago in literary circles God was all the fashion. It was good form to believe and journalists used Him to adorn a phrase or balance a sentence; then God went out (oddly enough with cricket and beer) and Pan came in. In a hundred novels his cloven hoof left its imprint on the sward; poets saw him lurking in the twilight on London commons, and literary ladies in Surrey, nymphs of an industrial age, mysteriously surrendered their virginity to his rough embrace. Spiritually they were never the same again. But Pan went out and now beauty has taken his place. People find it in a phrase, or a turbot, a dog, a day, a picture, an action, a dress. Young women in cohorts, each of whom has written so promising and competent a novel, prattle of it in every manner from allusive to arch, from intense to charming; and the young men, more or less recently down from Oxford, but still trailing its clouds of glory, who tell us in the weekly papers what we should think of art, life, and the universe, fling the word with a pretty negligence about their close-packed pages. It is sadly frayed. Gosh, they have worked it hard! The ideal has many names and beauty is but one of them. I wonder if this clamour is anything more than the cry of distress of those who cannot make themselves at home in our heroic world of machines, and I wonder if their passion for beauty, the Little Nell of this shamefaced day, is anything more than sentimentality. It may be that another generation, accommodating itself more adequately to the stress of life, will look for inspiration not in a flight from reality, but in an eager acceptance of it.

I do not know if others are like myself, but I am conscious that I cannot contemplate beauty long. For me no poet made a falser statement than Keats when he wrote the first line of *Endymion*. When the thing of beauty has given me the magic of its sensation my mind quickly wanders; I listen with incredulity to the persons who tell me that they can look with rapture for hours at a view or a picture. Beauty is an ecstasy; it is as simple as hunger. There is really nothing to be said about it. It is like the perfume of a rose: you can smell it and that is all: that is why the criticism of art, except in so far as it is unconcerned with beauty and therefore with art, is tiresome. All the critic can tell you with regard to Titian's 'Entombment of Christ', perhaps of all the pictures in the world that which has most pure beauty, is to go and look at it. What else he has to say is history, or biography, or what not. But people add other qualities to beauty – sublimity, human interest, tenderness, love – because beauty does not long content them. Beauty is perfect, and perfection (such is human nature) holds our attention but for a little while. The mathematician who after seeing *Phèdre* asked: '*Qu'est-ce que ça prouve?*' was not such a fool as he has been generally made out. No one has ever been able to explain why the Doric temple of Paestum is more beautiful than a glass of cold beer except by bringing in considerations that have nothing to do with beauty. Beauty is a blind alley. It is a mountain peak which once reached leads nowhere. That is why in the end we find more to entrance us in El Greco than in Titian, in the incomplete achievement of Shakespeare than in the consummate success of Racine. Too much has been written about beauty. That is why I have written a little more. Beauty is that which satisfies the aesthetic instinct. But who wants to be satisfied? It is only to the dullard that enough is as good as a feast. Let us face it: beauty is a bit of a bore.

But of course what the critics wrote about Edward Driffield was eyewash. His outstanding merit was not the realism that gave vigour to his work, nor the beauty that informed it, nor his graphic portraits of seafaring men, nor his poetic descriptions of salty marshes, of storm and calm, and of nestling hamlets; it was his longevity. Reverence for old age is one of the most admirable traits of the human race, and I think it may safely be stated that in no other country than ours is this trait more marked. The awe and love with which other nations regard old age is often platonic; but ours is practical. Who but the English would fill Covent Garden to listen to an aged *prima donna* without a voice? Who but the English would pay to see dancers so decrepit that they can hardly put one foot before the other and say to one another admiringly in the intervals: 'By George, sir, d'you know he's a long way past sixty?' But compared with politicians and writers these are but striplings, and I often think that a *jeune premier* must be of a singularly amiable disposition if it does not make him bitter to consider that when at the age of seventy he must end his career the public man and the author are only at their prime. A man who is a politician at forty is a statesman at three score and ten. It is at this age, when he would be too old to be a clerk or a gardener or a police-court magistrate, that he is ripe to govern a country. This is not so strange when you reflect that from the earlier times the old have rubbed it into the young that they are wiser than they, and before the young discovered what nonsense this was they were old too, and it profited them to carry on the imposture; and besides, no one can have moved in the society of politicians without discovering that (if one may judge by results) it requires little mental ability to rule a nation. But why writers should be more esteemed the older they grow, has long perplexed me. At one time I thought that the praise accorded to them when they had ceased for twenty years to write anything of interest was largely due to the fact that the younger men, having no longer to fear their competition, felt it safe to extol their merit; and it is well known that to praise someone whose rivalry you do not dread is often a very good way of putting a spoke in the wheel of someone whose rivalry you do. But this is to take a low view of human nature and I would not for the world lay myself open to a charge of cheap cynicism. After mature consideration I have come to the conclusion that the real reason for the universal applause that comforts the declining years of the author who exceeds the common span of man is that intelligent people after the age of thirty read nothing at all. As they grow older the books they read in their youth are lit with its glamour and with every year that passes they ascribe greater merit to the author that wrote them. Of course he must go on; he must keep in the public eye. It is no good his thinking that it is enough to write one or two masterpieces; he must provide a pedestal for them of forty or fifty works of no particular consequence. This needs time. His production must be such that if he cannot captivate a reader by his charm he can stun him by his weight.

If, as I think, longevity is genius, few in our time have enjoyed it in a more conspicuous degree than Edward Driffield. When he was a young fellow in the sixties (the cultured having had their way with him and passed him by) his position in the world of letters was only respectable; the best judges praised him, but with moderation; the younger men were inclined to be frivolous at his expense. It was agreed that he had talent, but it never occurred to anyone that he was one of the glories of English literature. He celebrated his seventieth birthday; an uneasiness passed over the world of letters, like a ruffling of the waters when on an Eastern sea a typhoon lurks in the distance, and it grew evident that there had lived among us all these years a great novelist and none of us had suspected it. There was a rush for Driffield's books in the various libraries and a hundred busy pens, in Bloomsbury, in Chelsea, and in other places where men of letters congregate, wrote appreciations, studies, essays, and works, short and chatty or long and intense, on his novels. These were reprinted, in complete editions, in select editions, at a shilling and three and six and five shillings and a guinea. His style was analysed, his philosophy was examined, his technique was dissected. At seventy-five everyone agreed that Edward Driffield had genius. At eighty he was the Grand Old Man of English Letters. This position he held till his death.

Now we look about and think sadly that there is no one to take his place. A few septuagenarians are sitting up and taking notice, and they evidently feel that they could comfortably fill the vacant niche. But it is obvious that they lack something.

Though these recollections have taken so long to narrate they took but a little while to pass through my head. They came to me higgledy-piggledy, an incident and then a scrap of conversation that belonged to a previous time, and I have set them down in order for the convenience of the reader and because I have a neat mind. One thing that surprised me was that even at that far distance I could remember distinctly what people looked like and even the gist of what they said but only with vagueness what they wore. I knew of course that the dress, especially of women, was quite different forty years ago from what it was now, but if I recalled it at all it was not from life but from pictures and photographs that I had seen much later.

I was still occupied with my idle fancies when I heard a taxi stop at the door, the bell ring, and in a moment Alroy Kear's booming voice telling the butler that he had an appointment with me. He came in, big, bluff, and hearty; his vitality shattered with a single gesture the frail construction I had been building out of the vanished past. He brought in with him, like a blustering wind in March, the aggressive and inescapable present.

'I was just asking myself,' I said, 'who could possibly succeed Edward Driffield as the Grand Old Man of English Letters, and you arrive to answer my question.'

He broke into a jovial laugh, but into his eyes came a quick look of suspicion.

'I don't think there's anybody,' he said.

'How about yourself?'

'Oh, my dear boy, I'm not fifty yet. Give me another twenty-five years.' He laughed, but his eyes held mine keenly. 'I never know when you're pulling my leg.' He looked down suddenly. 'Of course one can't help thinking about the future sometimes. All the people who are at the top of the tree now are anything from fifteen to twenty years older than me. They can't last for ever, and when they're gone who is there? Of course there's Aldous; he's a good deal younger than me, but he's not very strong and I don't believe he takes great care of himself. Barring accidents, by which I mean barring some genius who suddenly springs up and sweeps the board, I don't quite see how in another twenty or twenty-five years I can help having the field pretty well to myself. It's just a question of pegging away and living on longer than the others.'

Roy sank his virile bulk into one of my landlady's armchairs and I offered him a whisky and soda.

'No, I never drink spirits before six o'clock,' he said. He looked about him. 'Jolly, these digs are.'

'I know. What have you come to see me about?'

'I thought I'd better have a little chat with you about Mrs Driffield's invitation. It was rather difficult to explain over the telephone. The truth of the matter is that I've arranged to write Driffield's life.'

'Oh! Why didn't you tell me the other day?'

I felt friendly disposed toward Roy. I was happy to think that I had not misjudged him when I suspected that it was not merely for the pleasure of my company that he had asked me to luncheon.

'I hadn't entirely made up my mind. Mrs Driffield is very keen on my doing it. She's going to help me in every way she can. She's giving me all the material she has. She's been col-

95

lecting it for a good many years. It's not an easy thing to do, and of course I can't afford not to do it well. But if I can make a pretty good job of it, it can't fail to do me a lot of good. People have so much more respect for a novelist if he writes something serious now and then. Those critical works of mine were an awful sweat, and they sold nothing, but I don't regret them for a moment. They've given me a position I could never have got without them.'

'I think it's a very good plan. You've known Driffield more intimately than most people for the last twenty years.'

'I think I have. But of course he was over sixty when I first made his acquaintance. I wrote and told him how much I admired his books, and he asked me to go and see him. But I know nothing about the early part of his life. Mrs Driffield used to try to get him to talk about those days, and she made very copious notes of all he said, and then there are diaries that he kept now and then, and of course a lot of the stuff in the novels is obviously autobiographical. But there are immense lacunae. I'll tell you the sort of book I want to write: a sort of intimate life, with a lot of those little details that make people feel warm inside, you know, and then woven in with this a really exhaustive criticism of his literary work, not ponderous, of course, but although sympathetic, searching and . . . subtle. Naturally it wants some doing, but Mrs Driffield seems to think I can do it.'

'I'm sure you can,' I put in.

'I don't see why not,' said Roy. 'I am a critic, and I'm a novelist. It's obvious that I have certain literary qualifications. But I can't do anything unless everyone who can is willing to help me.'

I began to see where I came in. I tried to make my face look quite blank. Roy leaned forward.

'I asked you the other day if you were going to write any-thing about Driffield yourself and you said you weren't. Can I take that as definite?'

'Certainly.'

'Then have you got any objection to giving me your material?'

'My dear boy, I haven't got any.'

'Oh, that's nonsense,' said Roy good-humouredly, with the tone of a doctor who is trying to persuade a child to have its throat examined. 'When he was living at Blackstable you must have seen a lot of him.'

'I was only a boy then.'

'But you must have been conscious of the unusual experience. After all, no one could be for half an hour in Edward Driffield's society without being impressed by his extraordinary personality. It must have been obvious even to a boy of sixteen, and you were probably more observant and sensitive than the average boy of that age.'

'I wonder if his personality would have seemed extraordinary without the reputation to back it up. Do you imagine that if you went down to a spa in the west of England as Mr Atkins, a chartered accountant taking the waters for his liver, you would impress the people you met there as a man of character?'

'I imagine they'd soon realize that I was not quite the common or garden chartered accountant,' said Roy, with a smile that took from his remark any appearance of self-esteem.

'Well, all I can tell you is that what chiefly bothered me about Driffield in those days was that the knickerbocker suit he wore was dreadfully loud. We used to bicycle a lot together, and it always made me feel a trifle uncomfortable to be seen with him.'

'It sounds comic now. What did he talk about?'

'I don't know; nothing very much. He was rather keen on architecture, and he talked about farming, and if a pub looked nice he generally suggested stopping for five minutes and having a glass of bitter, and then he would talk to the landlord about the crops and the price of coal and things like that.'

I rambled on, though I could see by the look of Roy's face that he was disappointed with me; he listened, but he was a trifle bored, and it struck me that when he was bored he looked peevish. But though I couldn't remember that Driffield had ever said anything significant during those long rides of ours, I had a very acute recollection of the *feel* of them. Blackstable was peculiar in this, that though it was on the sea, with a long shingly beach and marshland at the back, you had only to go about half a mile inland to come into the most rural country in Kent. Winding roads that ran between the great fat green fields and clumps of huge elms, substantial and with a homely stateliness like good old Kentish farmers' wives, high-coloured and robust, who had grown portly on good butter and home-made bread and cream and fresh eggs. And sometimes the road was only a lane, with thick hawthorn hedges, and the green elms overhung it on either side so that when you looked up there was only a strip of blue sky between. And as you rode along in the warm, keen air, you had a sensation that the world was standing still and life would last for ever. Although you were pedalling with such energy you had a delicious feeling of laziness. You were quite happy when no one spoke, and if one of the party from sheer high spirits suddenly put on speed and shot ahead it was a joke that everyone laughed at and for a few minutes you pedalled as hard as you could. And we chaffed one another innocently and giggled at our own humour. Now and then one would pass cottages with little gardens in front of them, and in the gardens were hollyhocks and tiger lilies; and a little way from the road were farmhouses, with their spacious barns and oasthouses; and one would pass through hop-fields with the ripening hops hanging in garlands. The public-houses were friendly and informal, hardly more important than cottages, and on the porches often honeysuckle would be growing. The names they bore were usual and familiar: The Jolly Sailor, The Merry Ploughman, The Crown and Anchor, The Red Lion.

But of course all that could matter nothing to Roy, and he interrupted me.

'Did he never talk of literature?' he asked.

'I don't think so. He wasn't that sort of writer. I suppose he thought about his writing, but he never mentioned it. He used to lend the curate books. In the winter, one Christmas holiday, I used to have tea at his house nearly every day, and some-times the curate and he would talk about books, but we used to shut them up.'

'Don't you remember anything he said?'

'Only one thing. I remember it because I hadn't ever read the things he was talking about, and what he said made me do so. He said that when Shakespeare retired to Stratford-on-Avon and became respectable, if he ever thought of his plays at all, probably the two that he remembered with most interest were *Measure for Measure* and *Troilus and Cressida*.'

'I don't think that's very illuminating. Didn't he say anything about anyone more modern than Shakespeare?'

'Well, not then, that I can remember; but when I was lunching with the Driffields a few years ago I overheard him saying that Henry James had turned his back on one of the great events of the world's history, the rise of the United States, in order to report tittle-tattle at tea parties in English country houses. Driffield called it *il gran rifiuto*. I was surprised at hearing the old man use an Italian phrase, and amused because a great big bouncing duchess who was there was the only person who knew what the devil he was talking about. He said: "Poor Henry, he's spending eternity wandering round and round a stately park and the fence is just too high for him to peep over, and they're having tea just too far away for him to hear what the countess is saying." '

Roy listened to my little anecdote with attention. He shook his head reflectively.

'I don't think I could use that. I'd have the Henry James gang down on me like a thousand of bricks. . . . But what used you to do during those evenings?'

'Well, we played whist while Driffield read books for review, and he used to sing.'

'That's interesting,' said Roy, leaning forward eagerly. 'Do you remember what he sang?'

'Perfectly. *All through stickin' to a Soljer* and *Come where the Booze is cheaper* were his favourites.'

'Oh!'

I could see that Roy was disappointed.

'Did you expect him to sing Schumann?' I asked.

'I don't know why not. It would have been rather a good point. But I think I should have expected him to sing sea chanties or old English country airs, you know, the sort of thing they used to sing at fairings – blind fiddlers and the village swains dancing with the girls on the threshing-floor and all that sort of thing. I might have made something rather beautiful out of that, but I can't *see* Edward Driffield's singing music-hall songs. After all, when you're drawing a man's portrait you must get the values right; you only confuse the impression if you put in stuff that's all out of tone.'

'You know that shortly after this he shot the moon. He let everybody in.'

Roy was silent for fully a minute, and he looked down at the carpet reflectively.

'Yes, I knew there'd been some unpleasantness. Mrs Driffield mentioned it. I understand everything was paid up later before he finally bought Ferne Court and settled down in the district. I don't think it's necessary to dwell on an incident that is not really of any importance in the history of his development. After all, it happened nearly forty years ago. You know, there were some very curious sides to the old man. One would have thought that after a rather sordid little scandal like that the neighbourhood of Blackstable would be the last place he'd choose to spend the rest of his life in when he'd become celebrated, especially when it was the scene of his rather humble origins; but he didn't seem to mind a bit. He seemed to think the whole thing rather a good joke. He was quite capable of telling people who came to lunch about it and it was very embarrassing for Mrs Driffield. I should like you to know Amy better. She's a very remarkable woman. Of course the old man had written all his great books before he ever set eyes on her, but I don't think anyone can deny that it was she who created the rather imposing and dignified figure that the world saw for the last twenty-five years of his life. She's been very frank with me. She didn't have such an easy job of it. Old Driffield had some very queer ways and she had to use a good deal of tact to get him to behave decently. He was very obstinate in some things, and I think a woman of less character would have been discouraged. For instance, he had a habit that poor Amy had a lot of trouble to break him of: after he'd finished his meat and vegetables he'd take a piece of bread and wipe the plate clean with it and eat it.'

'Do you know what that means?' I said. 'It means that for long he had so little to eat that he couldn't afford to waste any food he could get.'

'Well, that may be, but it's not a very pretty habit for a distinguished man of letters. And then, he didn't exactly tipple, but he was rather fond of going down to the Bear and Key at Blackstable and having a few beers in the public bar. Of course there was no harm in it, but it did make him rather conspicuous, especially in summer when the place was full of trippers. He didn't mind who he talked to. He didn't seem able to realize that he had a position to keep up. You can't deny it was rather awkward after they'd been having a lot of interesting people to lunch – people like Edmund Gosse, for instance, and Lord Curzon – that he should go down to a public-house and tell the plumber and the baker and the sanitary inspector what he thought about them. But of course that could be explained away. One could say that he was after local colour and was interested in types. But he had some habits that really were rather difficult to cope with. Do you know that it was with the greatest difficulty that Amy Driffield could ever get him to take a bath?'

'He was born at a time when people thought it unhealthy to take too many baths. I don't suppose he ever lived in a house that had a bathroom till he was fifty.'

'Well, he said he never had had a bath more than once a week and he didn't see why he should change his habits at his time of life. Then Amy said that he must change his under-linen every day, but he objected to that too. He said he'd always been used to wearing his vest and drawers for a week and it was nonsense, it only wore them out to have them washed so often. Mrs Driffield did everything she could to tempt him to have a bath every day, with bath salts and perfumes, you know, but nothing would induce him to, and as he grew older he wouldn't even have one once a week. She tells me that for the last three years of his life he never had a bath at all. Of course all this is between ourselves; I'm merely telling it to show you that in writing his life I shall have to use a good deal of tact. I don't see how one can deny that he was just a wee bit unscrupulous in money matters, and he had a kink in him that made him take a strange pleasure in the society of his inferiors and some of his personal habits were rather disagreeable, but I don't think that side of him was the most significant. I don't want to say anything that's untrue, but I do think there's a certain amount that's better left unsaid.'

'Don't you think it would be more interesting if you went the whole hog and drew him warts and all?'

'Oh, I couldn't. Amy Driffield would never speak to me again. She only asked me to do the life because she felt she could trust my discretion. I must behave like a gentleman.'

'It's very hard to be a gentleman and a writer.'

'I don't see why. And besides, you know what the critics are. If you tell the truth they only say you're cynical and it does an author no good to get a reputation for cynicism. Of course I don't deny that if I were thoroughly unscrupulous I could make a sensation. It would be rather amusing to show the man with his passion for beauty and his careless treatment of his obligations, his fine style and his personal hatred for soap and water, his idealism and his tippling in disreputable pubs; but honestly, would it pay? They'd only say I was imitating Lytton Strachey. No. I think I shall do much better to be allusive and charming and rather subtle, you know the sort of thing, and tender. I think one ought always to *see* a book before one starts it. Well, I see this rather like a portrait by Van Dyck, with a good deal of atmosphere, you know, and a certain gravity, and with a sort of aristocratic distinction. Do you know what I mean? About eighty thousand words.'

He was absorbed for a moment in the ecstasy of aesthetic contemplation. In his mind's eye he saw a book, in royal octavo, slim and light in the hand, printed with large margins on handsome paper in a type that was both clear and comely, and I think he saw a binding in smooth black cloth with a decoration in gold and gilt lettering. But being human, Alroy

Kear could not, as I suggested a few pages back, hold the ecstasy that beauty yields for more than a little while. He gave me a candid smile.

'But how the devil am I to get over the first Mrs Driffield?'

'The skeleton in the cupboard,' I murmured.

'She is damned awkward to deal with. She was married to Driffield for a good many years. Amy has very decided views on the subject, but I don't see how I can possibly meet them. You see, her attitude is that Rose Driffield exerted a most pernicious influence on her husband, and that she did everything possible to ruin him morally, physically, and financially; she was beneath him in every way, at least intellectually and spiritually, and it was only because he was a man of immense force and vitality that he survived. It was of course a very unfortunate marriage. It's true that she's been dead for ages and it seems a pity to rake up old scandals and wash a lot of dirty linen in public; but the fact remains that all Driffield's greatest books were written when he was living with her. Much as I admire the later books, and no one is more conscious of their genuine beauty than I am, and they have a restraint and a sort of classical sobriety which are admirable, I must admit that they haven't the tang and the vigour and the smell and bustle of life of the early ones. It does seem to me that you can't altogether ignore the influence his first wife had on his work.'

'What are you going to do about it?' I asked.

'Well, I can't see why all that part of his life shouldn't be treated with the greatest possible reserve and delicacy, so as not to offend the most exacting susceptibility, and yet with a sort of manly frankness, if you understand what I mean, that would be rather moving.'

'It sounds a very tall order.'

'As I see it, there's no need to dot the i's or to cross the t's. It can only be a question of getting just the right touch. I wouldn't state more than I could help, but I would suggest what was essential for the reader to realize. You know, however gross a subject is you can soften its unpleasantness if you treat it with dignity. But I can do nothing unless I am in complete possession of the facts.'

'Obviously you can't cook them unless you have them.'

Roy had been speaking with a fluent ease that revealed the successful lecturer. I wished (a) that I could express myself with so much force and aptness, never at a loss for a word, rolling off the sentences without a moment's hesitation; and (b) that I did not feel so miserably incompetent with my one small insignificant person to represent the large and appreciative audience that Roy was instinctively addressing. But now he paused. A genial look came over his face, which his enthusiasm had reddened and the heat of the day caused to perspire, and the eyes that had held me with a dominating brilliance softened and smiled.

'This is where you come in, old boy,' he said pleasantly.

I have always found it a very good plan in life to say nothing when I had nothing to say and when I do not know how to answer a remark to hold my tongue. I remained silent and looked back at Roy amiably.

'You know more about his life at Blackstable than anybody else.'

'I don't know about that. There must be a number of people at Blackstable who saw as much of him in the old days as I did.'

'That may be, but after all they're presumably not people of any importance, and I don't think they matter very much.'

'Oh, I see. You mean that I'm the only person who might blow the gaff.'

'Roughly, that is what I do mean, if you feel that you must put it in a facetious way.'

I saw that Roy was not inclined to be amused. I did not mind, for I am quite used to people not being amused at my jokes. I often think that the purest type of the artist is the humorist who laughs alone at his own jests.

'And you saw a good deal of him later on in London, I believe.'

'Yes.'

'That is when he had an apartment somewhere in Lower Belgravia.'

'Well, lodgings in Pimlico.'

Roy smiled dryly.

'We won't quarrel about the exact designation of the quarter of London in which he lived. You were very intimate with him then.'

'Fairly.'

'How long did that last?'

'About a couple of years.'

'How old were you then?'

'Twenty.'

'Now look here, I want you to do me a great favour. It won't take you very long and it will be of quite inestimable value to me. I want you to jot down as fully as you can all your recollections of Driffield, and all you remember about his wife and his relations with her and so on, both at Blackstable and in London.'

'Oh, my dear fellow, that's asking a great deal. I've got a lot of work to do just now.'

'It needn't take you very long. You can write it quite roughly, I mean. You needn't bother about style, you know, or anything like that. I'll put the style in. All I want are the facts. After all, you know them and nobody else does. I don't want to be pompous or anything like that, but Driffield was a great man and you owe it to his memory and to English literature to tell everything you know. I shouldn't have asked you, but you told me the other day that you weren't going to write anything about him yourself. It would be rather like a dog in a manger to keep to yourself a whole lot of material that you have no intention of using.'

Thus Roy appealed at once to my sense of duty, my indolence, my generosity, and my rectitude.

'But why does Mrs Driffield want me to go down and stay at Ferne Court?' I asked.

'Well, we talked it over. It's a very jolly house to stay in. She does one very well, and it ought to be divine in the country just now. She thought it would be very nice and quiet for you if you felt inclined to write your recollections there; of course, I said I couldn't promise that, but naturally being so near Blackstable would remind you of all sorts of things that you might otherwise forget. And then, living in his house, among his books and things, it would make the past seem much more real. We could all talk about him, and you know how in the heat of conversation things come back. Amy's very quick and clever. She's been in the habit of making notes of Driffield's talk for years, and after all it's quite likely that you'll say things on the spur of the moment that you wouldn't think of writing and she can just jot them down afterward. And we can play tennis and bathe.'

'I'm not very fond of staying with people,' I said. 'I hate getting up for a nine o'clock breakfast to eat things I have no mind to. I don't like going for walks, and I'm not interested in other people's chickens.'

'She's a lonely woman now. It would be a kindness to her and it would be a kindness to me too.'

I reflected.

'I'll tell you what I'll do: I'll go down to Blackstable, but I'll go down on my own. I'll put up at the Bear and Key and I'll come over and see Mrs Driffield while you're there. You can both talk your heads off about Edward Driffield, but I shall be able to get away when I'm fed up with you.'

Roy laughed good-naturedly.

'All right. That'll do. And will you jot down anything you can remember that you think will be useful to me?'

'I'll try.'

'When will you come? I'm going down on Friday.'

'I'll come with you if you'll promise not to talk to me in the train.'

'All right. The five-ten's the best one. Shall I come and fetch you?'

'I'm capable of getting to Victoria by myself. I'll meet you on the platform.'

I don't know if Roy was afraid of me changing my mind, but he got up at once, shook my hand heartily, and left. He begged me on no account to forget my tennis racquet and bathing suit.

chapter twelve

My promise to Roy sent my thoughts back to my first years in London. Having nothing much to do that afternoon, it occurred to me to stroll along and have a cup of tea with my old landlady. Mrs Hudson's name had been given to me by the secretary of the medical school at St Luke's when, a callow youth just arrived in town, I was looking for lodgings. She had a house in Vincent Square. I lived there for five years, in two rooms on the ground floor, and over me on the drawing-room floor lived a master at Westminster School. I paid a pound a week for my rooms and he paid twenty-five shillings. Mrs Hudson was a little, active, bustling woman, with a sallow face, a large aquiline nose, and the brightest, the most vivacious black eyes that I ever saw. She had a great deal of very dark hair, in the afternoons and all day on Sunday arranged in a fringe on the forehead with a bun at the nape of the neck as you may see in old photographs of the Jersey Lily. She had a heart of gold (though I did not know it then, for when you are young you take the kindness people show you as your right) and she was an excellent cook. No one could make a better *omelette soufflée* than she. Every morning she was up betimes to get the fire lit in her gentlemen's sitting-rooms so that 'they needn't eat their breakfasts simply perishin' with the cold, my word it's bitter this morning'; and if she didn't hear you having your bath, a flat tin bath that slipped under the bed, the water put in the night before to take the chill off, she'd say: 'There now, there's my dining-room floor not up yet, 'e'll be late for his lecture again,' and she would come tripping upstairs and thump on the door, and you would hear her shrill voice: 'If you don't get up at once you won't 'ave time to 'ave breakfast, an' I've got a lovely 'addick for you.' She worked all day long and she sang at her work, and she was gay and happy and smiling. Her husband was much older than she. He had been a butler in very good families, and wore side-whiskers and a perfect manner; he was verger at a neighbouring church, highly respected, and he waited at table and cleaned the boots and helped with the washing-up. Mrs Hudson's only relaxation was to come up after she had served the dinners (I had mine at half past six and the schoolmaster at seven) and have a little chat with her gentlemen. I wish to goodness I had had the sense (like Amy Driffield with her celebrated husband) to take notes of her conversation, for Mrs Hudson was a mistress of Cockney humour. She had a gift of repartee that never failed her, she had a racy style and an apt and vivid vocabulary, she was never at a loss for the comic metaphor or the vivid phrase. She was a pattern of propriety, and she would never have women in her house, you never knew what they were up to ('It's men, men, men all the time with them, and afternoon tea and thin bread and butter, and openin' the door and ringin' for 'ot water and I don't know what all'); but in conversation she did not hesitate to use what was called in those days the blue bag. One could have said of her what she said of Marie Lloyd: 'What I like about 'er is that she gives you a good laugh. She goes pretty near the knuckle some- times, but she never jumps over the fence.' Mrs Hudson en- joyed her own humour and I think she talked more willingly to her lodgers because her husband was a serious man ('It's as it should be,' she said, ' 'im bein' a verger and attendin' weddings and funerals and what all') and wasn't much of a one for a joke. 'Wot I says to 'Udson is, laugh while you've got the chance, you won't laugh when you're dead and buried.'

Mrs Hudson's humour was cumulative, and the story of her feud with Miss Butcher who let lodgings at number fourteen was a great comic saga that went on year in and year out.

'She's a disagreeable old cat, but I give you my word I'd miss 'er if the Lord took 'er one fine day. Though what 'E'd do with 'er when 'E got 'er I can't think. Many's the good laugh she's given me in 'er time.'

Mrs Hudson had very bad teeth, and the question whether she should have them taken out and have false ones was discussed by her for two or three years with an unimaginable variety of comic invention.

'But as I said to 'Udson on'y last night, when he said: "Oh, come on, 'ave 'em out and 'ave done with it," I shouldn't 'ave anythin' to talk about.'

I had not seen Mrs Hudson for two or three years. My last visit had been in answer to a little letter in which she asked me to come and drink a nice strong cup of tea with her and announced: 'Hudson died three months ago next Saturday, aged seventy-nine, and George and Hester send their respectful compliments.' George was the issue of her marriage with Hudson. He was now a man approaching middle age who worked at Woolwich Arsenal, and his mother had been repeating for twenty years that George would be bringing a wife home one of these days. Hester was the maid-of-all-work she had engaged toward the end of my stay with her, and Mrs Hudson still spoke of her as 'that dratted girl of mine'. Though Mrs Hudson must have been well over thirty when I first took her rooms, and that was five and thirty years ago, I had no feelings as I walked leisurely through the Green Park that I should not find her alive. She was as definitely part of the recollections of my youth as the pelicans that stood at the edge of my ornamental water.

I walked down the area steps and the door was opened to me by Hester, a woman getting on for fifty now, and stoutish, but still bearing on her shyly grinning face the irresponsibility of the dratted girl. Mrs Hudson was darning George's socks when I was shown into the front room of the basement, and she took off her spectacles to look at me.

'Well, if that isn't Mr Ashenden! Whoever thought of seeing you? Is the water boiling, 'Ester? You will 'ave a nice cup of tea, won't you?'

Mrs Hudson was a little heavier than when I first knew her, and her movements were more deliberate, but there was scarcely a white hair on her head, and her eyes, as black and shining as buttons, sparkled with fun. I sat down in a shabby little arm-chair covered with maroon leather.

'How are you getting on, Mrs Hudson?' I asked.

'Oh, I've got nothin' much to complain of except that I'm not so young as I used to was,' she answered. 'I can't do so much as I could when you was 'ere. I don't give my gentlemen dinner now, only breakfast.'

'Are all your rooms let?'

'Yes, I'm thankful to say.'

Owing to the rise of prices Mrs Hudson was able to get more for her rooms than in my day, and I think in her modest way she was quite well off. But of course people wanted a lot nowadays.

'You wouldn't believe it, first I 'ad to put in a bathroom, and then I 'ad to put in the electric light, and then nothin' would satisfy them but I must 'ave a telephone. What they'll want next I can't think.'

'Mr George says it's pretty near time Mrs 'Udson thought of retiring,' said Hester, who was laying the tea.

'You mind your own business, my girl,' said Mrs Hudson tartly. 'When I retire it'll be to the cemetery. Fancy me livin' all alone with George and 'Ester without nobody to talk to.'

'Mr George says she ought to take a little 'ouse in the country an' take care of 'erself,' said Hester, unperturbed by the reproof.

'Don't talk to me about the country. The doctor said I was to go there for six weeks last summer. It nearly killed me, I give you my word. The noise of it. All them birds singin' all the time, and the cocks crowin' and the cows mooin'. I couldn't stick it. When you've lived all the years I 'ave in peace and quietness you can't get used to all that racket goin' on all the time.'

A few doors away was the Vauxhall Bridge Road and down it trams were clanging, ringing their bells as they went, motor buses were lumbering along, taxis were tooting their horns. If Mrs Hudson heard it, it was London she heard, and it soothed her as a mother's crooning soothes a restless child.

I looked round the cosy, shabby, homely little parlour in which Mrs Hudson had lived so long. I wondered if there was anything I could do for her. I noticed that she had a gramophone. It was the only thing I could think of.

'Is there anything you want, Mrs Hudson?' I asked.

She fixed her beady eyes on me reflectively.

'I don't know as there is, now you come to speak of it, except me 'ealth and strength for another twenty years so as I can go on workin'.'

I do not think I am a sentimentalist, but her reply, unexpected but so characteristic, made a sudden lump come to my throat.

When it was time for me to go I asked if I could see the rooms I had lived in for five years.

'Run upstairs, 'Ester, and see if Mr Graham's in. If he ain't, I'm sure 'e wouldn't mind you 'avin' a look at them.'

Hester scurried up, and in a moment, slightly breathless, came down again to say that Mr Graham was out. Mrs Hudson came with me. The bed was the same narrow iron bed that I had slept in and dreamed in and there was the same chest of drawers and the same washing-stand. But the sitting-room had the grim heartiness of the athlete; on the walls were photographs of cricket elevens and rowing men in shorts; golf clubs stood in the corner and pipes and tobacco jars, ornamented with the arms of a college, were littered on the chimney-piece. In my days we believed in art for art's sake and this I exemplified by draping the chimney-piece with a Moorish rug, putting up curtains of art serge and a bilious green, and hanging on the walls autotypes of pictures by Perugino, Van Dyck, and Hobbema.

'Very artistic you was, wasn't you?' Mrs Hudson remarked, not without irony.

'Very,' I murmured.

I could not help feeling a pang as I thought of all the years that had passed since I inhabited that room, and of all that had happened to me. It was at that same table that I had eaten my hearty breakfast and my frugal dinner, read my medical books and written my first novel. It was in that same arm-chair that I had read for the first time Wordsworth and Stendhal, the Elizabethan dramatists and the Russian novelists, Gibbon, Boswell, Voltaire, and Rousseau. I wondered who had used them since. Medical students, articled clerks, young fellows making their way in the City and elderly men retired from the colonies or thrown unexpectedly upon the world by the

111

break-up of an old home. The room made me, as Mrs Hudson would have put it, go queer all over. All the hopes that had been cherished there, the bright visions of the future, the flaming passion of youth; the regrets, the disillusion, the weariness, the resignation; so much had been felt in that room, by so many, the whole gamut of human emotion, that it seemed strangely to have acquired a troubling and enigmatic personality of its own. I have no notion why, but it made me think of a woman at a cross-road with a finger on her lips, looking back, and with her other hand beckoning. What I obscurely (and rather shamefacedly) felt, communicated itself to Mrs Hudson, for she gave a laugh, and with a characteristic gesture rubbed her prominent nose.

'My word, people are funny,' she said. 'When I think of all the gentlemen I've 'ad here, I give you my word you wouldn't believe it if I told you some of the things I know about them. One of them's funnier than the other. Sometimes I lie abed thinkin' of them, and *laugh*. Well, it would be a bad world if you didn't get a good laugh now and then, but, lor', lodgers really are the limit.'

chapter thirteen

I lived with Mrs Hudson for nearly two years before I met the Driffields again. My life was very regular. I spent all day at the hospital, and about six walked back to Vincent Square. I bought the *Star* at Lambeth Bridge, and read it till my dinner was served. Then I read seriously for an hour or two, works to improve my mind, for I was a strenuous, earnest, and industrious youth, and after that wrote novels and plays till bedtime. I do not know for what reason it was that one day toward the end of June, happening to leave the hospital early, I thought I would walk down the Vauxhall Bridge Road. I liked it for its noisy bustle. It had a sordid vivacity that was pleasantly exciting, and you felt that at any moment an adventure might there befall you. I strolled along in a daydream and was surprised suddenly to hear my name. I stopped and looked, and there to my astonishment stood Mrs Driffield. She was smiling at me.

'Don't you know me?' she cried.

'Yes. Mrs Driffield.'

And though I was grown up I was conscious that I was blushing as furiously as when I was sixteen. I was embarrassed. With my lamentably Victorian notions of honesty I had been much shocked by the Driffields' behaviour in running away from Blackstable without paying their bills. It seemed to me very shabby. I felt deeply the shame I thought they must feel, and I was astounded that Mrs Driffield should speak to someone who knew of the discreditable incident. If I had seen her coming I should have looked away, my delicacy presuming that she would wish to avoid the mortification of being seen by me; but she held out her hand and shook mine with obvious pleasure.

'I am glad to see a Blackstable face,' she said. 'You know we left there in a hurry.'

She laughed and I laughed too; but her laugh was mirthful and childlike, while mine, I felt, was strained.

'I hear there *was* a to-do when they found out we'd skipped. I thought Ted would never stop laughing when he heard about it. What did your uncle say?'

I was quick to get the right tone. I wasn't going to let her think that I couldn't see a joke as well as anyone.

'Oh, you know what he is. He's very old-fashioned.'

'Yes, that's what's wrong with Blackstable. They want waking up.' She gave me a friendly look. 'You've grown a lot since I saw you last. Why, you're growing a moustache.'

'Yes,' I said, giving it as much of a twirl as its size allowed me. 'I've had that for ages.'

'How time does fly, doesn't it? You were just a boy four years ago, and now you're a man.'

'I ought to be,' I replied somewhat haughtily. 'I'm nearly twenty-one.'

I was looking at Mrs Driffield. She wore a very small hat with feathers in it, and a pale grey dress with large leg-of-mutton sleeves and a long train. I thought she looked very smart. I had always thought that she had a nice face, but I noticed now, for the first time, that she was pretty. Her eyes were bluer than I remembered and her skin was like ivory.

'You know we live just round the corner,' she said.

'So do I.'

'We live in Limpus Road. We've been there almost ever since we left Blackstable.'

'Well, I've been in Vincent Square for nearly two years.'

'I knew you were in London. George Kemp told me so, and I often wondered where you were. Why don't you walk back with me now? Ted will be so pleased to see you.'

'I don't mind,' I said.

As we walked along she told me that Driffield was now literary editor of a weekly paper; his last book had done much better than any of his others, and he was expecting to get quite a bit as an advance on royalties for the next one. She seemed to know most of the Blackstable news, and I remembered how it had been suspected that Lord George had helped the Driffields in their flight. I guessed that he wrote to them now and then. I noticed as we walked along that sometimes the men who passed us stared at Mrs Driffield. It occurred to me presently that they must think her pretty too. I began to walk with a certain swagger.

Limpus Road was a long, wide, straight street that ran parallel with the Vauxhall Bridge Road. The houses were all alike, of stucco, dingily painted, solid, and with substantial porticoes. I suppose they had been built to be inhabited by men of standing in the city of London, but the street had gone down in the world or had never attracted the right sort of tenant; and its decayed respectability had an air at once furtive and shabbily dissipated, that made you think of persons who had seen better days and now, genteelly fuddled, talked of the social distinction of their youth. The Driffields lived in a house painted a dull red, and Mrs Driffield, letting me into a narrow dark hall, opened a door and said:

'Go in. I'll tell Ted you're here.'

She walked down the hall and I entered the sitting-room. The Driffields had the basement and the ground floor of the house, which they rented from the lady who lived in the upper part. The room into which I went looked as if it had been furnished with the scourings of auction sales. There were heavy velvet curtains with great fringes, all loops and festoons, and a gilt suite, upholstered in yellow damask, heavily buttoned; and there was a great pouffe in the middle of the room. There were gilt cabinets in which were masses of little articles, pieces of china, ivory figures, wood-carvings, bits of Indian brass; and on the walls hung large oil-paintings of Highland glens and stags and gillies. In a moment Mrs Driffield brought her husband, and he greeted me warmly. He wore a shabby alpaca coat and grey trousers; he had shaved his beard, and wore now a moustache and a small imperial. I noticed for the first time how short he was; but he looked more distinguished than he used to. There was something a trifle foreign in his appearance, and I thought this was much more what I should expect an author to look like.

'Well, what do you think of our new abode?' he asked. 'It looks rich, doesn't it? I think it inspires confidence.'

He looked round him with satisfaction.

'And Ted's got his den at the back where he can write, and we've got a dining-room in the basement,' said Mrs Driffield. 'Miss Cowley was companion for many years to a lady of title, and when she died she left her all her furniture. You can see everything's good, can't you? You can see it came out of a gentleman's house.'

'Rosie fell in love with the place the moment we saw it,' said Driffield.

'You did too, Ted.'

'We've lived in sordid circumstances so long; it's a change to be surrounded by luxury. Madame de Pompadour and all that sort of thing.'

When I left them it was with a very cordial invitation to

115

come again. It appeared that they were at home every Saturday afternoon, and all sorts of people whom I would like to meet were in the habit of dropping in.

chapter fourteen

I went. I enjoyed myself. I went again. When the autumn came and I returned to London for the winter session at St Luke's I got into the habit of going every Saturday. It was my introduction into the world of art and letters; I kept it a profound secret that in the privacy of my lodgings I was busily writing; I was excited to meet people who were writing also, and I listened entranced to their conversation. All sorts of persons came to these parties: at that time weekends were rare, golf was still a subject for ridicule and few had much to do on Saturday afternoons. I do not think anyone came who was of any great importance; at all events, of all the painters, writers, and musicians I met at the Driffields' I cannot remember one whose reputation has endured; but the effect was cultured and animated. You found young actors who were looking for parts and middle-aged singers who deplored the fact that the English were not a musical race, composers who played their compositions on the Driffields' cottage piano and complained in a whispered aside that they sounded nothing except on a concert grand, poets who on pressure consented to read a little thing that they had just written, and painters who were looking for commissions. Now and then a person of title added a certain glamour; seldom, however, for in those days the aristocracy had not yet become Bohemian, and if a person of quality cultivated the society of artists it was generally because a notorious divorce or a little difficulty over cards had made life in his own station (or hers) a bit awkward. We have changed all that. One of the greatest benefits that compulsory education has conferred upon the world is the wide diffusion among the nobility and gentry of the practice of writing. Horace Walpole once wrote a *Catalogue of Royal and Noble Authors*; such a work now would have the dimensions of an encyclopedia. A title, even a courtesy one, can make a well-known author of almost anyone, and it may be safely asserted that there is no better passport to the world of letters than rank.

I have indeed sometimes thought that now that the House of Lords must inevitably in a short while be abolished, it would be a very good plan if the profession of literature were by law confined to its members and their wives and children. It would be a graceful compensation that the British people might offer the peers in return for the surrender of their hereditary privileges. It would be a means of support for those (too many) whom devotion to the public cause in keeping chorus girls and race-horses and playing *chemin de fer* has impoverished, and a pleasant occupation for the rest who by the process of natural selection have in the course of time become unfit to do anything but govern the British Empire. But this is an age of specialization, and if my plan is adopted it is obvious that it cannot but be to the greater glory of English literature that its various provinces should be apportioned among the various ranks of the nobility. I would suggest, therefore, that the humbler branches of literature should be practised by the lower orders of the peerage and that the barons and viscounts should devote themselves exclusively to journalism and the drama. Fiction might be the privileged demesne of the earls. They have already shown their aptitude for this difficult art and their numbers are so great that they would very competently supply the demand. To the marquises might safely be left the production of that part of literature which is known (I have never quite seen why) as *belles lettres*. It is perhaps not very profitable from a pecuniary standpoint, but it has a distinction that very well suits the holders of this romantic title.

The crown of literature is poetry. It is its end and aim. It is the sublimest activity of the human mind. It is the achievement of beauty. The writer of prose can only step aside when the poet passes; he makes the best of us look like a piece of

117

cheese. It is evident then that the writing of poetry should be left to the dukes, and I should like to see their rights protected by the most severe pains and penalties, for it is intolerable that the noblest of arts should be practised by any but the noblest of men. And since here, too, specialization must prevail, I foresee that the dukes (like the successors of Alexander) will divide the realm of poetry between them, each confining himself to that aspect with which hereditary influence and natural bent have rendered him competent to deal: thus I see the dukes of Manchester writing poems of a didactic and moral character, the dukes of Westminster composing stirring odes on Duty and the Responsibilities of Empire; whereas I imagine that the dukes of Devonshire would be more likely to write love lyrics and elegies in the Propertian manner, while it is almost inevitable that the dukes of Marlborough should pipe in an idyllic strain on such subjects as domestic bliss, conscription, and content with modest station.

But if you say that this is somewhat formidable and remind me that the muse does not only stalk with majestic tread, but on occasion trips on a light fantastic toe; if, recalling the wise person who said that he did not care who made a nation's laws so long as he wrote its songs, you ask me (thinking rightly that it would ill become the dukes to do so) who shall twang those measures on the lyre that the diverse and inconstant soul of man occasionally hankers after – I answer (obviously enough, I should have thought) the duchesses. I recognize that the day is past when the amorous peasants of the Romagna sang to their sweethearts the verses of Torquato Tasso and Mrs Humphry Ward crooned over young Arnold's cradle the choruses of Oedipus in Colonus. The age demands something more up to date. I suggest, therefore, that the more domestic duchesses should write our hymns and our nursery rhymes; while the skittish ones, those who incline to mingle vine leaves with the strawberry, should write the lyrics for musical comedies, humorous verse for the comic papers, and mottoes for Christmas cards and crackers. Thus would they retain in the hearts of the British public that place which they have held hitherto only on account of their exalted station.

It was at these parties on Saturday afternoon that I discovered very much to my surprise that Edward Driffield was a distinguished person. He had written something like twenty books, and though he had never made more than a pittance out of them his reputation was considerable. The best judges admired them and the friends who came to his house were agreed that one of these days he would be recognized. They upbraided the public because it would not see that here was a great writer, and since the easiest way to exalt one man is to kick another in the pants, they reviled freely all the novelists whose contemporary fame obscured his. If, indeed, I had known as much of literary circles as I learned later I should have guessed by the not infrequent visits of Mrs Barton Trafford that the time was approaching when Edward Driffield, like a runner in a long-distance race breaking away suddenly from the little knot of plodding athletes, must forge ahead. I admit that when first I was introduced to this lady her name meant nothing to me. Driffield presented me as a young neighbour of his in the country and told her that I was a medical student. She gave me a mellifluous smile, murmured in a soft voice something about Bob Sawyer, and, accepting the bread and butter I offered her, went on talking with her host. But I noticed that her arrival had made an impression, and the conversation, which had been noisy and hilarious, was hushed. When in an undertone I asked who she was, I found that my ignorance was amazing; I was told that she had 'made' So-and-so and So-and-so. After half an hour she rose, shook hands very graciously with such of the people as she was acquainted with, and with a sort of lithe sweetness sidled out of the room. Driffield accompanied her to the door and put her in a hansom.

Mrs Barton Trafford was then a woman of about fifty; she was small and slight, but with rather large features, which made her head look a little too big for her body; she had crisp, white hair which she wore like the Venus of Milo, and she was supposed in her youth to have been very comely. She dressed discreetly in black silk, and wore round her neck jangling chains of beads and shells. She was said to have been unhappily

119

married in early life, but now for many years had been congenially united to Barton Trafford, a clerk in the Home Office and a well-known authority on prehistoric man. She gave you the curious impression of having no bones in her body, and you felt that if you pinched her shin (which, of course, my respect for her sex as well as something of quiet dignity in her appearance would have never allowed me to do) your fingers would meet. When you took her hand it was like taking a fillet of sole. Her face, notwithstanding its large features, had something fluid about it. When she sat it was as though she had no backbone and were stuffed, like an expensive cushion, with swansdown.

Everything was soft about her, her voice, her smile, her laugh; her eyes, which were small and pale, had the softness of flowers; her manner was as soft as the summer rain. It was this extraordinary and charming characteristic that made her the wonderful friend she was. It was this that had gained her the celebrity that she now enjoyed. The whole world was aware of her friendship with the great novelist whose death a few years back had come as such a shock to the English-speaking peoples. Everyone had read the innumerable letters which he had written to her and which she was induced to publish shortly after his demise. Every page revealed his admiration for her beauty and his respect for her judgement; he could never say often enough how much he owed to her encouragement, her ready sympathy, her tact, her taste; and if certain of his expressions of passion were such as some persons might think would not be read by Mr Barton Trafford with unmixed feelings, that only added to the human interest of the work. But Mr Barton Trafford was above the prejudices of vulgar men (his misfortune, if such it was, was one that the greatest personages in history have endured with philosophy) and, abandoning his studies of aurignacian flints and neolithic axe-heads, he consented to write a Life of the deceased novelist in which he showed quite definitely how great a part of the writer's genius was due to his wife's influence.

But Mrs Barton Trafford's interest in literature, her passion for art, were not dead because the friend for whom she had done so much had become part, with her far from negligible assistance, of posterity. She was a great reader. Little that was noteworthy escaped her attention, and she was quick to establish personal relations with any young writer who showed promise. Her fame, especially since the Life, was now such that she was sure that no one would hesitate to accept the sympathy she was prepared to offer. It was inevitable that Mrs Barton Trafford's genius for friendship should in due course find an outlet. When she read something that struck her, Mr Barton Trafford, himself no mean critic, wrote a warm letter of appreciation to the author and asked him to luncheon. After luncheon, having to get back to the Home Office, he left him to have a chat with Mrs Barton Trafford. Many were called. They all had *something*, but that was not enough. Mrs Barton Trafford had a *flair*, and she trusted her *flair*; her *flair* bade her wait.

She was so cautious indeed that with Jasper Gibbons she almost missed the bus. The records of the past tell us of writers who grew famous in a night, but in our more prudent day this is unheard of. The critics want to see which way the cat will jump, and the public has been sold a pup too often to take unnecessary chances. But in the case of Jasper Gibbons it is almost the exact truth that he did thus jump into celebrity. Now that he is so completely forgotten and the critics who praised him would willingly eat their words if they were not carefully guarded in the files of innumerable newspaper offices, the sensation he made with his first volume of poems is almost unbelievable. The most important papers gave to reviews of it as much space as they would have to the report of a prize-fight, the most influential critics fell over one another in their eagerness to welcome him. They likened him to Milton (for the sonority of his blank verse), to Keats (for the opulence of his sensuous imagery), and to Shelley (for his airy fantasy); and, using him as a stick to beat idols of whom they were weary, they gave in his name many a resounding whack on the emaciated buttocks of Lord Tennyson and a few good husky smacks on the bald pate of Robert Browning. The public fell like the walls of Jericho. Edition after edition was sold, and you saw Jasper Gibbons's handsome volume in the boudoirs of countesses in Mayfair, in vicarage drawing-rooms from Land's End to John o' Groats, and in the parlours of many an honest but cultured merchant in Glasgow, Aberdeen, and Belfast. When it became known that Queen Victoria had accepted a specially bound copy of the book from the hands of the loyal publisher, and had given him (not the poet, the publisher) a copy of *Leaves from a Journal in the Highlands* in exchange, the national enthusiasm knew no bounds.

And all this happened, as it were, in the twinkling of an eye. Seven cities in Greece disputed the honour of having given birth to Homer, and though Jasper Gibbons's birthplace (Walsall) was well known, twice seven critics claimed the honour of having discovered him; eminent judges of literature who, for twenty years, had written eulogies of one another's works in the weekly papers quarrelled so bitterly over this matter that one cut the other dead in the Athenaeum. Nor was the great world remiss in giving him its recognition. Jasper Gibbons was asked to luncheon and invited to tea by dowager duchesses, the wives of cabinet ministers, and the widows of bishops. It is said that Harrison Ainsworth was the first English man of letters to move in English society on terms of equality (and I have sometimes wondered that an enterprising publisher on this account has not thought of bringing out a complete edition of his works); but I believe that Jasper Gibbons was the first poet to have his name engraved at the bottom of an At Home card as a draw as enticing as an opera singer or a ventriloquist.

It was out of the question then for Mrs Barton Trafford to get in on the ground floor. She could only buy in the open market. I do not know what prodigious strategy she employed, what miracles of tact, what tenderness, what exquisite sympathy, what demure blandishments; I can only surmise and admire; she nobbled Jasper Gibbons. In a little while he was eating out of her soft hand. She was admirable. She had him to lunch to meet the right people; she gave At Homes where he recited his poems before the most distinguished persons in England; she introduced him to eminent actors who gave him commissions to write plays; she saw that his poems should only appear in the proper places; she dealt with the publishers and made contracts for him that would have staggered even a Cabinet minister; she took care that he should accept only the invitations of which she approved; she even went so far as to separate him from his wife, with whom he had lived happily for ten years, since she felt that a poet to be true to himself and his art must not be encumbered with domestic ties. When the crash came Mrs Barton Trafford, had she chosen, might have said that she had done everything for him that it was humanly possible to do.

For there was a crash. Jasper Gibbons brought out another volume of poetry; it was neither better nor worse than the first; it was very much like the first; it was treated with respect, but the critics made reservations; some of them even carped. The book was a disappointment. Its sale also. And unfortunately Jasper Gibbons was inclined to tipple. He had never been accustomed to having money to spend, he was quite unused to the lavish entertainments that were offered him, perhaps he missed his homely, common little wife; once or twice he came to dinner at Mrs Barton Trafford's in a condition that anyone less unworldly, less simple-minded than she, would have described as blind to the world. She told her guests gently that the bard was not quite himself that evening. His third book was a failure. The critics tore him limb from limb, they knocked him down and stamped on him, and, to quote one of Edward Driffield's favourite songs, then they lugged him round the room and then they jumped upon his face; they were quite naturally annoyed that they had mistaken a fluent versifier for a deathless poet, and were determined that he should suffer for their error. Then Jasper Gibbons was arrested for being drunk and disorderly in Piccadilly and Mr Barton Trafford had to go to Vine Street at midnight to bail him out.

Mrs Barton Trafford at this juncture was perfect. She did not repine. No harsh word escaped her lips. She might have been excused if she had felt a certain bitterness because this man for whom she had done so much had let her down. She remained tender, gentle, and sympathetic. She was the woman who understood. She dropped him, but not like a hot brick, or a hot potato. She dropped him with infinite gentleness, as softly as the tear that she doubtless shed when she made up her mind to do something so repugnant to her nature; she dropped him with so much tact, with such sensibility, that Jasper Gibbons perhaps hardly knew he was dropped. But there was no doubt about it. She would say nothing against him, indeed she would not discuss him at all, and when mention was made of him she merely smiled, a little sadly, and sighed. But her smile was the *coup de grâce*, and her sigh buried him deep.

Mrs Barton Trafford had a passion for literature too sincere to allow a setback of this character long to discourage her; and however great her disappointment she was a woman of too disinterested a nature to let the gifts of tact, sympathy, and understanding with which she was blessed by nature lie fallow. She continued to move in literary circles, going to tea parties here and there, to soirées, and to At Homes, charming always and gentle, listening intelligently, but watchful, critical, and determined (if I may put it crudely) next time to back a winner. It was then that she met Edward Driffield, and formed a favourable opinion of his gifts. It is true that he was not young, but then he was unlikely like Jasper Gibbons to go to pieces. She offered him her friendship. He could not fail to be moved when, in that gentle way of hers, she told him that it was a scandal that his exquisite work remained known only in the narrow circle. He was pleased and flattered. It is always pleasant to be assured that you are a genius. She told him that Barton Trafford was reflecting on the possibility of writing an important article on him for the *Quarterly Review*. She asked him to luncheon to meet people who might be useful to him. She wanted him to know his intellectual equals. Sometimes she took him for a walk on the Chelsea Embankment, and they talked of poets dead and gone, and love and friendship, and had tea in an ABC shop. When Mrs Barton Trafford came to Limpus Street on Saturday afternoon she had the air of the queen bee preparing herself for the nuptial flight.

Her manner with Mrs Driffield was perfect. It was affable, but not condescending. She always thanked her very prettily for having allowed her to come and see her and complimented her on her appearance. If she praised Edward Driffield to her, telling her with a little envy in her tone what a privilege it was to enjoy the companionship of such a great man, it was certainly from pure kindness, and not because she knew that there is nothing that exasperates the wife of a literary man more than to have another woman tell her flattering things about him. She talked to Mrs Driffield of the simple things her simple nature might be supposed to be interested in, of cooking and servants and Edward's health, and how careful she must be with him. Mrs Barton Trafford treated her exactly as you would expect a woman of very good Scotch family, which she was, to treat an ex-barmaid with whom a distinguished man of letters had made an unfortunate marriage. She was cordial, playful, and gently determined to put her at her ease.

It was strange that Rosie could not bear her; indeed, Mrs Barton Trafford was the only person that I ever knew her dislike. In those days even barmaids did not habitually use the 'bitches' and 'bloodys' that are part and parcel of the current vocabulary of the best-brought-up young ladies and I never heard Rosie use a word that would have shocked my Aunt Sophie. When anyone told a story that was a little near the knuckle she would blush to the roots of her hair. But she referred to Mrs Barton Trafford as 'that damned old cat'. It needed the most urgent persuasions of her more intimate friends to induce her to be civil to her.

'Don't be a fool, Rosie,' they said. They all called her Rosie, and presently I, though very shyly, got in the habit of doing so too. 'If she wants to she can make him. He must play up to her. She can work the trick if anyone can.'

Though most of the Driffields' visitors were occasional, appearing every other Saturday, say, or every third, there was a little band that, like myself, came almost every week. We were the stand-bys; we arrived early and stayed late. Of these the most faithful were Quentin Forde, Harry Retford, and Lionel Hillier.

Quentin Forde was a stocky little man with a fine head of the type that was afterward for a time much admired in the moving pictures, a straight nose and handsome eyes, neatly cropped grey hair and a black moustache; if he had been four or five inches taller he would have been the perfect type of the villain of melodrama. He was known to be very 'well connected', and he was affluent; his only occupation was to cultivate the arts. He went to all the first nights and all the private views. He had the amateur's severity, and cherished for the productions of his contemporaries a polite but sweeping contempt. I discovered that he did not come to the Driffields' because Edward was a genius, but because Rosie was beautiful.

Now that I look back I cannot get over my surprise that I should have had to be told what was surely so obvious. When I first knew her it never occurred to me to ask myself whether she was pretty or plain, and when, seeing her again after five years, I noticed for the first time that she was very pretty, I was interested but did not trouble to think much about it. I took it as part of the natural order of things, just as I took the sun setting over the North Sea or the towers of Tercanbury Cathedral. I was quite startled when I heard people speak of Rosie's beauty, and when they complimented Edward on her looks and his eyes rested on her for a moment, mine followed his. Lionel Hillier was a painter, and he asked her to sit for him. When he talked of the picture he wanted to paint and told me what he saw in her, I listened to him stupidly. I was puzzled and confused. Harry Retford knew one of the fashionable photographers of the period and, arranging special terms, he took Rosie to be photographed. A Saturday or two later the proofs were there, and we all looked at them. I had never seen Rosie in evening dress. She was wearing a dress in white satin, with a low train and puffy sleeves, and it was cut low; her hair was more elaborately done than usual. She looked very different from the strapping young woman I had first met in Joy Lane in a boater and a starched shirt. But Lionel Hillier tossed the photographs aside impatiently.

'Rotten,' he said. 'What can a photographer give of Rosie? The thing about her is her colour.' He turned to her. 'Rosie, don't you know that your colour is *the* great miracle of the age?'

She looked at him without answering, but her full red lips broke into their childlike, mischievous smile.

'If I can only get a suggestion of it I'm made for life,' he said. 'All the rich stockbrokers' wives will come on their bended knees and beg me to paint them like you.'

Presently I learned that Rosie was sitting to him, but when, never having been in a painter's studio and looking upon it as the gateway of romance, I asked if I might not come one day and see how the picture was getting on, Hillier said that he did not want anyone to see it yet. He was a man of five and thirty and of a flamboyant appearance. He looked like a portrait of Van Dyck in which the distinction had been replaced by good humour. He was slightly above the middle height, slim; and he had a fine mane of black hair and flowing moustaches and a pointed beard. He favoured broad-brimmed sombreros and Spanish capes. He had lived a long time in Paris, and talked admiringly of painters, Monet, Sisley, Renoir, of whom we had never heard, and with contempt of Sir Frederick Leighton and Mr Alma-Tadema and Mr G. F. Watts, whom in our heart of hearts we very much admired. I have often wondered what became of him. He spent a few years in London trying to make his way, failed, I suppose, and then drifted to Florence. I was told that he had a drawing school there, but when, years later, chancing to be in that city, I asked about him, I could find no one who had ever heard of him. I think he must have had some talent, for I have even now a very vivid recollection of the portrait he painted of Rosie Driffield. I wonder what has happened to it. Has it been destroyed, or is it hidden away, its face to the wall, in the attic of a junk shop in Chelsea? I should like to think that it has at least found a place on the walls of some provincial gallery.

When I was at last allowed to come and see it, I put my foot in it fine and proper. Hillier's studio was in the Fulham Road, one of a group at the back of a row of shops, and you went in through a dark and smelly passage. It was a Sunday afternoon in March, a fine blue day, and I walked from Vincent Square through deserted streets. Hillier lived in his studio; there was a large divan on which he slept, and a tiny little room at the back where he cooked his breakfast, washed his brushes and, I suppose, himself.

When I arrived Rosie still wore the dress in which she had been sitting, and they were having a cup of tea. Hillier opened the door for me, and, still holding my hand, led me up to the large canvas.

'There she is,' he said.

He had painted Rosie full length, just a little less than life-size, in an evening dress of white silk. It was not at all like the academy portraits I was accustomed to. I did not know what to say, so I said the first thing that came into my head.

'When will it be finished?'

'It is finished,' he answered.

I blushed furiously. I felt a perfect fool. I had not then acquired the technique that I flatter myself now enables me to deal competently with the works of modern artists. If this were the place I could write a very neat little guide to enable the amateur of pictures to deal to the satisfaction of their painters with the most diverse manifestations of the creative instinct. There is the intense 'By God!' that acknowledges the power of the ruthless realist, the 'It's so awfully sincere' that covers your embarrassment when you are shown the coloured photograph of an alderman's widow, the low whistle that exhibits your admiration for the post-impressionist, the 'Terribly amusing' that expresses what you feel about the cubist, the 'Oh!' of one who is overcome, the 'Ah!' of him whose breath is taken away.

'It's awfully like,' was all that then I could lamely say.

'It's not chocolate-boxy enough for you,' said Hillier.

'I think it's awfully good,' I answered quickly, defending myself. 'Are you going to send it to the Academy?'

'Good God, no! I might send it to the Grosvenor.'

I looked from the painting to Rosie and from Rosie to the painting.

'Get into the pose, Rosie,' said Hillier, 'and let him see you.'

She got up on to the model stand. I stared at her and I stared at the picture. I had such a funny little feeling in my heart. It was as though someone softly plunged a sharp knife into it, but it was not an unpleasant sensation at all, painful but strangely agreeable; and then suddenly I felt quite weak at the knees. But now I do not know if I remember Rosie in the flesh or in the picture. For when I think of her it is not in the shirt and boater that I first saw her in, nor in any of the other dresses I saw her in then or later, but in the white silk that Hillier painted, with a black velvet bow in her hair, and in the pose he had made her take.

I never exactly knew Rosie's age, but reckoning the years out as well as I can, I think she must have been then thirty-five. She did not look anything like it. Her face was quite un-lined and her skin as smooth as a child's. I do not think she had very good features. They certainly had none of the aristo-cratic distinction of the great ladies whose photographs were at that time sold in all the shops; they were rather blunt. Her short nose was a little thick, her eyes were smallish, her mouth was large; but her eyes had the blue of cornflowers, and they smiled with her lips, very red and sensual, and her smile was the gayest, the most friendly, the sweetest thing I ever saw. She had by nature a heavy, sullen look, but when she smiled this sullenness became on a sudden infinitely attractive. She had no colour in her face; it was of a very pale brown except under the eyes where it was faintly blue. Her hair was pale gold and it was done in the fashion of the day, high on the head with an elaborate fringe.

'She's the very devil to paint,' said Hillier, looking at her and at his picture. 'You see, she's all gold, her face and her hair, and yet she doesn't give you a golden effect, she gives you a silvery effect.'

I knew what he meant. She glowed, but palely, like the moon rather than the sun, or if it was like the sun it was like the sun in the white mist of dawn. Hillier had placed her in the middle of his canvas and she stood, with her arms by her sides, the palms of her hands toward you and her head a little thrown back, in an attitude that gave value to the pearly beauty of her neck and bosom. She stood like an actress taking a call, confused by unexpected applause, but there was something so virginal about her, so exquisitely springlike, that the comparison was absurd. This artless creature had never known grease paint or footlights. She stood like a maiden apt for love offering herself guiltlessly, because she was fulfilling the purposes of Nature, to the embraces of a lover. She belonged to a generation that did not fear a certain opulence of line; she was slender, but her breasts were ample and her hips well marked. When, later, Mrs Barton Trafford saw the picture she said it reminded her of a sacrificial heifer.

chapter fifteen

Edward Driffield worked at night, and Rosie, having nothing to do, was glad to go out with one or other of her friends. She liked luxury and Quentin Forde was well-to-do. He would fetch her in a cab and take her to dine at Kettner's or the Savoy, and she would put on her grandest clothes for him; and Harry Retford, though he never had a bob, behaved as if he had, and took her about in hansoms, too, and gave her dinner at Romano's or in one or other of the little restaurants that were becoming modish in Soho. He was an actor and a clever one, but he was difficult to suit and so was often out of work. He was about thirty, a man with a pleasantly ugly face and a clipped way of speaking that made what he said sound funny. Rosie liked his devil-may-care attitude toward life, the swagger with which he wore clothes made by the best tailor in London and unpaid for, the recklessness with which he would put a fiver he hadn't got on a horse, and the generosity with which he flung his money about when a lucky win put him in funds. He was gay, charming, vain, boastful, and unscrupulous. Rosie told me that once he had pawned his watch to take her out to dinner and then borrowed a couple of pounds from the actor-manager who had given them seats for the play, in order to take him out to supper with them afterward.

But she was just as well pleased to go with Lionel Hillier to his studio and eat a chop that he and she cooked between them and spend the evening talking, and it was only very rarely that she would dine with me at all. I used to fetch her after I had had my dinner in Vincent Square and she hers with Driffield, and we would get on a bus and go to a music-hall. We went here and there, to the Pavilion or the Tivoli, sometimes to the Metropolitan if there was a particular turn we wanted to see; but our favourite was the Canterbury. It was cheap and the show was good. We ordered a couple of beers and I smoked my pipe. Rosie looked round with delight at the great dark smoky house, crowded to the ceiling with the inhabitants of South London.

'I like the Canterbury,' she said. 'It's so homy.'

I discovered that she was a great reader. She liked history, but only history of a certain kind, the lives of queens and of mistresses of royal personages; and she would tell me with a childlike wonder of the strange things she read. She had a wide acquaintance with the six consorts of King Henry VIII and there was little she did not know about Mrs Fitzherbert and Lady Hamilton. Her appetite was prodigious and she ranged from Lucrezia Borgia to the wives of Philip of Spain; then there was the long list of the royal mistresses of France. She knew them all, and all about them, from Agnes Sorel down to Madame du Barry.

'I like to read about real things,' she said. 'I don't much care for novels.'

She liked to gossip about Blackstable, and I thought it was on account of my connexion with it that she liked to come out with me. She seemed to know all that was going on there.

'I go down every other week or so to see my mother,' she said. 'Just for the night, you know.'

'To Blackstable?'

I was surprised.

'No, not to Blackstable,' Rosie smiled. 'I don't know that

131

I'd care to go there just yet. To Haversham. Mother comes over to meet me. I stay at the hotel where I used to work.'

She was never a great talker. Often when, the night being fine, we decided to walk back from the music-hall at which we had been spending the evening, she never opened her mouth. But her silence was intimate and comfortable. It did not exclude you; it included you in a pervasive well-being.

I was talking about her once to Lionel Hillier and I said to him that I could not understand how she had turned from the fresh, pleasant-looking young woman I had first known at Blackstable into the lovely creature whose beauty now practically everyone acknowledged. (There were people who made reservations. 'Of course she has a very good figure,' they said, 'but it's not the sort of face I very much admire personally.' And others said: 'Oh, yes, a very pretty woman; but it's a pity she hasn't a little more distinction.')

'I can explain that to you in half a jiffy,' said Lionel Hillier. 'She was only a fresh buxom wench when you first met her. *I* made her beauty.'

I forget what my answer was, but I know it was ribald.

'All right. That just shows you don't know anything about beauty. No one ever thought very much of Rosie till I saw her like the sun shining silver. It wasn't till I painted it that anyone knew that her hair was the most lovely thing in the world.'

'Did you make her neck and her breasts and her carriage and her bones?' I asked.

'Yes, damn you, that's just what I did do.'

When Hillier talked of Rosie in front of her she listened to him with a smiling gravity. A little flush came into her pale cheeks. I think that first when he spoke to her of her beauty she believed he was just making game of her; but when she found out that he wasn't, when he painted her silvery gold, it had no particular effect on her. She was a trifle amused, pleased, of course, and a little surprised, but it did not turn her head. She thought him a little mad. I often wondered whether there was anything between them. I could not forget all I had heard of Rosie at Blackstable and what I had seen in the vicarage garden; I wondered about Quentin Forde, too, and Harry

132

Retford. I used to watch them with her. She was not exactly familiar with them, comradely rather; she used to make her appointments with them quite openly in anybody's hearing; and when she looked at them it was with that mischievous, childlike smile which I had now discovered held such a mysterious beauty. Sometimes when we were sitting side by side in a music-hall I looked at her face; I do not think I was in love with her, I merely enjoyed the sensation of sitting quietly beside her and looking at the pale gold of her hair and the pale gold of her skin. Of course Lionel Hillier was right; the strange thing was that this gold did give one a strange moonlight feeling. She had the serenity of a summer evening when the light fades slowly from the unclouded sky. There was nothing dull in her immense placidity; it was as living as the sea when under the August sun it lay calm and shining along the Kentish coast. She reminded me of a sonatina by an old Italian composer with its wistfulness in which there is yet an urbane flippancy and its light rippling gaiety in which echoes still the trembling of a sigh. Sometimes, feeling my eyes on her, she would turn round and for a moment or two look me full in the face. She did not speak. I did not know of what she was thinking.

Once, I remember, I fetched her at Limpus Road, and the maid, telling me she was not ready, asked me to wait in the parlour. She came in. She was in black velvet, with a picture hat covered with ostrich feathers (we were going to the Pavilion and she had dressed up for it), and she looked so lovely that it took my breath away. I was staggered. The clothes of that day gave a woman dignity, and there was something amazingly attractive in the way her virginal beauty (sometimes she looked like the exquisite statue of Psyche in the museum at Naples) contrasted with the stateliness of her gown. She had a trait that I think must be very rare: the skin under her eyes, faintly blue, was all dewy. Sometimes I could not persuade myself that it was natural, and once I asked her if she had rubbed vaseline under her eyes. That was just the effect it gave. She smiled, took a handkerchief, and handed it to me.

'Rub them and see,' she said.

Then one night when we had walked home from the Canterbury, and I was leaving her at her door, when I held out my hand she laughed a little, a low chuckle it was, and leaned forward.

'You old silly,' she said.

She kissed me on the mouth. It was not a hurried peck, nor was it a kiss of passion. Her lips, those very full red lips of hers, rested on mine long enough for me to be conscious of their shape and their warmth and their softness. Then she withdrew them, but without hurry, in silence pushed open the door, skipped inside and left me. I was so startled that I had not been able to say anything. I accepted her kiss stupidly. I remained inert. I turned away and walked back to my lodgings. I seemed to hear still in my ears Rosie's laughter. It was not contemptuous or wounding, but frank and affectionate; it was as though she laughed because she was fond of me.

chapter sixteen

I did not go out with Rosie again for more than a week. She was going down to Haversham to spend a night with her mother. I had various engagements in London. Then she asked me if I would go to the Haymarket Theatre with her. The play was a success and free seats were not to be had, so we made up our minds to go in the pit. We had a steak and a glass of beer at the Café Monico and then stood with the crowd. In those days there was no orderly queue and when the doors were opened there was a mad rush and scramble to get in. We were hot and breathless and somewhat battered when at last we pushed our way into our seats.

We walked back through St James's Park. The night was so lovely that we sat down on a bench. In the starlight Rosie's face and her fair hair glowed softly. She was suffused, as it were (I express it awkwardly, but I do not know how to describe the emotion she gave me), with a friendliness at once candid and tender. She was like a silvery flower of the night that only gave its perfume to the moonbeams. I slipped my arm round her waist and she turned her face to mine. This time it was I who kissed. She did not move; her soft red lips submitted to the pressure of mine with a calm, intensive passivity as the water of a lake accepts the light of the moon. I don't know how long we stayed there.

'I'm awfully hungry,' she said suddenly.

'So am I,' I laughed.

'Couldn't we go and have some fish and chips somewhere?'

'Rather.'

In those days I knew my way very well about Westminster, not yet a fashionable quarter for parliamentary and otherwise cultured persons, but slummy and down-at-heel; and after we had come out of the park, crossing Victoria Street, I led Rosie to a fried-fish shop in Horseferry Row. It was late and the only other person there was the driver of a four-wheeler waiting outside. We ordered our fish and chips and a bottle of beer. A poor woman came in and bought two penn'orth of mixed and took it away with her in a piece of paper. We ate with appetite.

Our way back to Rosie's led through Vincent Square and as we passed my house I asked her:

'Won't you come in for a minute? You've never seen my rooms.'

'What about your landlady? I don't want to get you into trouble.'

'Oh, she sleeps like a rock.'

'I'll come in for a little.'

I slipped my key into the lock and, because the passage was dark, took Rosie's hand to lead her in. I lit the gas in my sitting-room. She took off her hat and vigorously scratched her head. Then she looked for a glass, but I was very artistic and had taken down the mirror that was over the chimney-piece and there was no means in the room for anyone to see what he looked like.

'Come into my bedroom,' I said. 'There's a glass there.'

I opened the door and lit the candle. Rosie followed me in and I held it up so that she should be able to see herself. I looked at her in the glass as she arranged her hair. She took two or three pins out, which she put in her mouth, and taking one of my brushes, brushed her hair up from the nape of her neck. She twisted it, patted it, and put back the pins, and as she was intent on this her eyes caught mine in the glass and she smiled at me. When she had replaced the last pin she turned and faced me; she did not say anything; she looked at me tranquilly still with that little friendly smile in her blue eyes. I put down the candle. The room was very small and the dressing-table was by the bed. She raised her hand and softly stroked my cheek.

I wish now that I had not started to write this book in the first person singular. It is all very well when you can show yourself in an amiable or touching light, and nothing can be more effective than the modest heroic or pathetic humorous which in this mode is much cultivated; it is charming to write about yourself when you see on the reader's eyelash the glittering tear and on his lips the tender smile; but it is not so nice when you have to exhibit yourself as a plain damned fool.

A little while ago I read in the *Evening Standard* an article by Mr Evelyn Waugh in the course of which he remarked that to write novels in the first person was a contemptible practice. I wish he had explained why, but he merely threw out the statement with just the same take-it-or-leave-it casualness as Euclid used when he made his celebrated observation about parallel straight lines. I was much concerned, and forthwith asked Alroy Kear (who reads everything, even the books he writes prefaces for) to recommend to me some works on the art of fiction. On his advice I read *The Craft of Fiction* by Mr Percy Lubbock, from which I learned that the only way to write novels was like Henry James; after that I read *Aspects of the Novel* by Mr E. M. Forster, from which I learned that the only way to write novels was like Mr E. M. Forster; then I read *The Structure of the Novel* by Mr Edwin Muir, from which I learned nothing at all. In none of them could I discover anything to the point at issue. All the same I can find one reason why certain novelists, such as Defoe, Sterne, Thackeray, Dickens, Emily Brontë, and Proust, well known in their day but now doubtless forgotten, have used the method that Mr Evelyn Waugh reprehends. As we grow older we become more conscious of the complexity, incoherence, and unreasonableness of human beings; this indeed is the only excuse that offers for the middle-aged or elderly writer whose thoughts should more properly be turned to graver matters, occupying himself with the trivial concerns of imaginary people. For if the proper study of mankind is man it is evidently more sensible to occupy yourself with the coherent, substantial, and significant creatures of fiction than with the irrational and shadowy figures of real life. Sometimes the novelist feels himself like God and is prepared to tell you everything about his characters; sometimes, however, he does not; and then he tells you not everything that is to be known about them but the little he knows himself; and since as we grow older we feel ourselves less and less like God I should not be surprised to learn that with advancing years the novelist grows less and less inclined to describe more than his own experience has given him. The first person singular is a very useful device for this limited purpose.

Rosie raised her hand and softly stroked my face. I do not know why I should have behaved as I then did; it was not at all how I had seen myself behaving on such an occasion. A sob broke from my tight throat. I do not know whether it was because I was shy and lonely (not lonely in the body, for I spent all day at the hospital with all kinds of people, but lonely in the spirit) or because my desire was so great, but I began to cry. I felt terribly ashamed of myself; I tried to control myself, I couldn't; the tears welled up in my eyes and poured down my cheeks. Rosie saw them and gave a little gasp.

'Oh, honey, what is it? What's the matter? Don't. Don't!'

She put her arms round my neck and began to cry too, and she kissed my lips and my eyes and my wet cheeks. She undid her bodice and lowered my head till it rested on her bosom. She stroked my smooth face. She rocked me back and forth as though I were a child in her arms. I kissed her breasts and I kissed the white column of her neck; and she slipped out of her bodice and out of her skirt and her petticoats and I held her for a moment by her corseted waist; then she undid it, holding her breath for an instant to enable her to do so, and stood before me in her shift. When I put my hands on her sides I could feel the ribbing of the skin from the pressure of the corsets.

'Blow out the candle,' she whispered.

It was she who awoke me when the dawn peering through the curtains revealed the shape of the bed and of the wardrobe against the darkness of the lingering night. She woke me by kissing me on the mouth and her hair falling over my face tickled me.

'I must get up,' she said. 'I don't want your landlady to see me.'

'There's plenty of time.'

Her breasts when she leaned over me were heavy on my chest. In a little while she got out of bed. I lit the candle. She turned to the glass and tied up her hair and then she looked for a moment at her naked body. Her waist was naturally small; though so well developed she was very slender; her breasts were straight and firm and they stood out from the chest as though carved in marble. It was a body made for the act of love. In the light of the candle, struggling now with the increasing day, it was all silvery gold: and the only colour was the rosy pink of the hard nipples.

We dressed in silence. She did not put on her corsets again, but rolled them up and I wrapped them in a piece of newspaper. We tiptoed along the passage and when I opened the door and we stepped out into the street the dawn ran to meet us like a cat leaping up the steps. The square was empty; already the sun was shining on the eastern windows. I felt as young as the day We walked arm in arm till we came to the corner of Limpus Road.

'Leave me here,' said Rosie. 'One never knows.'

I kissed her and I watched her walk away. She walked rather slowly, with the firm tread of the country woman who likes to feel the good earth under her feet, and held herself erect. I could not go back to bed. I strolled on till I came to the

Embankment. The river had the bright hues of the early morning. A brown barge came down stream and passed under Vauxhall Bridge. In a dinghy two men were rowing close to the side. I was hungry.

chapter seventeen

After that for more than a year whenever Rosie came out with me she used on the way home to drop into my rooms, sometimes for an hour, sometimes till the breaking day warned us that the slaveys would soon be scrubbing the doorsteps. I have a recollection of warm sunny mornings when the tired air of London had a welcome freshness, and of our footfalls that seemed so noisy in the empty streets, and then of scurrying along huddled under an umbrella, silent but gay, when the winter brought cold and rain. The policeman on point duty gave us a stare as we passed, sometimes of suspicion; but sometimes also there was a twinkle of comprehension in his eyes. Now and then we would see a homeless creature huddled up asleep in a portico and Rosie gave my arm a friendly little pressure when (chiefly for show and because I wanted to make a good impression on her, for my shillings were scarce) I placed a piece of silver on a shapeless lap or in a skinny fist. Rosie made me very happy. I had a great affection for her. She was easy and comfortable. She had a placidity of temper that communicated itself to the people she was with; you shared her pleasure in the passing moment.

Before I became her lover I had often asked myself if she was the mistress of the others, Forde, Harry Retford, and Hillier, and afterward I questioned her. She kissed me.

'Don't be so silly. I like them, you know that. I like to go out with them, but that's all.'

I wanted to ask her if she had been the mistress of George

Kemp, but I did not like to. Though I had never seen her in a temper, I had a notion that she had one, and I vaguely felt that this was a question that might anger her. I did not want to give her the opportunity of saying things so wounding that I could not forgive her. I was young, only just over one and twenty, Quentin Forde and the others seemed old to me; it did not seem unnatural to me that to Rosie they were only friends. It gave me a little thrill of pride to think that I was her lover. When I used to look at her chatting and laughing with all and sundry at tea on Saturday afternoons, I glowed with self-satisfaction. I thought of the nights we passed together, and I was inclined to laugh at the people who were so ignorant of my great secret. But sometimes I thought that Lionel Hillier looked at me in a quizzical way, as if he were enjoying a good joke at my expense, and I asked myself uneasily if Rosie had told him that she was having an affair with me. I wondered if there was anything in my manner that betrayed me. I told Rosie that I was afraid Hillier suspected something; she looked at me with those blue eyes of hers that always seemed ready to smile.

'Don't bother about it,' she said. 'He's got a nasty mind.'

I had never been intimate with Quentin Forde. He looked upon me as a dull and insignificant young man (which of course I was) and though he had always been civil he had never taken any notice of me. I thought it could only be my fancy that now he began to be a little more frigid with me than before. But one day Harry Retford to my surprise asked me to dine with him and go to the play. I told Rosie.

'Oh, of course you must go. He'll give you an awfully good time. Good old Harry, he always makes me laugh.'

So I dined with him. He made himself very pleasant, and I was impressed to hear him talk of actors and actresses. He had a sarcastic humour, and was very funny at the expense of Quentin Forde, whom he did not like; I tried to get him to talk of Rosie, but he had nothing to say of her. He seemed to be a gay dog. With leers and laughing innuendoes he gave me to understand that he was a devil with the girls. I could not but ask myself if he was standing me this dinner because he knew

I was Rosie's lover and so felt friendly disposed toward me. But if he knew, of course the others knew too. I hope I did not show it, but in my heart I certainly felt somewhat patronizing toward them.

Then in winter, toward the end of January, someone new appeared at Limpus Road. This was a Dutch Jew named Jack Kuyper, a diamond merchant from Amsterdam, who was spending a few weeks in London on business. I do not know how he had come to know the Driffields, and whether it was esteem for the author that brought him to the house, but it was certainly not that which caused him to come again. He was a tall, stout, dark man, with a bald head and a big hooked nose, a man of fifty, but of a powerful appearance, sensual, determined, and jovial. He made no secret of his admiration for Rosie. He was rich apparently, for he sent her roses every day; she chid him for his extravagance, but was flattered. I could not bear him. He was blatant and loud. I hated his fluent conversation in perfect but foreign English; I hated the extravagant compliments he paid Rosie; I hated the heartiness with which he treated her friends. I found that Quentin Forde liked him as little as I; we almost became cordial with one another.

'Mercifully he's not staying long.' Quentin Forde pursed his lips and raised his black eyebrows; with his white hair and long sallow face he looked incredibly gentlemanly. 'Women are always the same; they adore a bounder.'

'He's so frightfully vulgar,' I complained.

'That is his charm,' said Quentin Forde.

For the next two or three weeks I saw next to nothing of Rosie. Jack Kuyper took her out night after night, to this smart restaurant and that, to one play after another. I was vexed and hurt.

'He doesn't know anyone in London,' said Rosie, trying to soothe my ruffled feelings. 'He wants to see everything he can while he's here. It wouldn't be very nice for him to go alone all the time. He's only here for a fortnight more.'

I did not see the object of this self-sacrifice on her part.

'But don't you think he's awful?' I said.

'No. I think he's fun. He makes me laugh.'

'Don't you know that he's absolutely gone on you?'

'Well, it pleases him, and it doesn't do me any harm.'

'He's old and fat and horrible. It gives me the creeps to look at him.'

'I don't think he's so bad,' said Rosie.

'You shouldn't have anything to do with him,' I protested. 'I mean, he's such an awful cad.'

Rosie scratched her head. It was an unpleasant habit of hers.

'It's funny how different foreigners are from English people,' she said.

I was thankful when Jack Kuyper went back to Amsterdam. Rosie had promised to dine with me the day after, and as a treat we arranged to dine in Soho. She fetched me in a hansom and we drove on.

'Has your horrible old man gone?' I asked.

'Yes,' she laughed.

I put my arm round her waist. (I have elsewhere remarked how much more convenient the hansom was for this pleasant and indeed almost essential act in human intercourse than the taxi of the present day, so unwillingly refrain from labouring the point.) I put my arm round her waist and kissed her. Her lips were like spring flowers. We arrived. I hung my hat and my coat (it was very long and tight at the waist, with a velvet collar and velvet cuffs; very smart) on a peg, and asked Rosie to give me her cape.

'I'm going to keep it on,' she said.

'You'll be awfully hot. You'll only catch cold when we go out.'

'I don't care. It's the first time I've worn it. Don't you think it's lovely? And look: the muff matches.'

I gave the cape a glance. It was of fur. I did not know it was sable.

'It looks awfully rich. How did you get that?'

'Jack Kuyper gave it to me. We went and bought it yesterday just before he went away.' She stroked the smooth fur; she was as happy with it as a child with a toy. 'How much d'you think it cost?'

142

'I haven't an idea.'

'Two hundred and sixty pounds. Do you know I've never had anything that cost so much in my life? I told him it was far too much, but he wouldn't listen. He made me have it.'

Rosie chuckled with glee and her eyes shone. But I felt my face go stiff and a shiver run down my spine.

'Won't Driffield think it's rather funny, Kuyper giving you a fur cape that costs all that?' said I, trying to make my voice sound natural.

Rosie's eyes danced mischievously.

'You know what Ted is, he never notices anything; if he says anything about it I shall tell him I gave twenty pounds for it in a pawnshop. He won't know any better.' She rubbed her face against the collar. 'It's so soft. And everyone can see it cost money.'

I tried to eat and in order not to show the bitterness in my heart I did my best to keep the conversation going on one topic or another. Rosie did not much mind what I said. She could only think of her new cape, and every other minute her eyes returned to the muff that she insisted on holding on her lap. She looked at it with an affection in which there was something lazy, sensual, and self-complacent. I was angry with her. I thought her stupid and common.

'You look like a cat that's swallowed a canary,' I could not help snapping.

She only giggled.

'That's what I feel like.'

Two hundred and sixty pounds was an enormous sum to me. I did not know one *could* pay so much for a cape. I lived on fourteen pounds a month, and not at all badly either; and in case any reader is not a ready reckoner I will add that this is one hundred and sixty-eight pounds a year. I could not believe that anyone would make as expensive a present as that from pure friendship; what did it mean but that Jack Kuyper had been sleeping with Rosie, night after night, all the time he was in London, and now when he went away was paying her? How could she accept it? Didn't she see how it degraded her? Didn't she see how frightfully vulgar it was of him to give her a thing that cost so much? Apparently not, for she said to me:

'It was nice of him, wasn't it? But then Jews are always generous.'

'I suppose he could afford it,' I said.

'Oh, yes, he's got lots of money. He said he wanted to give me something before he went away and asked me what I wanted. Well, I said, I could do with a cape and a muff to match, but I never thought he'd buy me anything like this. When we went into the shop I asked them to show me something in astrakhan, but he said: No, sable, and the best money can buy. And when we saw this he absolutely insisted on my having it.'

I thought of her with her white body, her skin so milky, in the arms of that old fat gross man and his thick loose lips kissing hers. And then I knew that the suspicion that I had refused to believe was true; I knew that when she went out to dinner with Quentin Forde and Harry Retford and Lionel Hillier she went to bed with them just as she came to bed with me. I could not speak; I knew that if I did I should insult her. I do not think I was jealous so much as mortified. I felt that she had been making a damned fool of me. I used all my determination to prevent the bitter jibes from passing my lips.

We went on to the theatre. I could not listen to the play. I could only feel against my arm the smoothness of the sable cape; I could only see her fingers for ever stroking the muff. I could have borne the thought of the others; it was Jack Kuyper who horrified me. How could she? It was abominable to be poor. I longed to have enough money to tell her that if she would send the fellow back his beastly furs I would give her better ones instead. At last she noticed that I did not speak.

'You're very silent tonight.'

'Am I?'

'Aren't you well?'

'Perfectly.'

She gave me a sidelong look. I did not meet her eyes, but I knew they were smiling with that smile at once mischievous and childlike that I knew so well. She said nothing more. At the end of the play, since it was raining, we took a hansom, and I gave the driver her address in Limpus Road. She did not speak till we got to Victoria Street, then she said:

'Don't you want me to come home with you?'

'Just as you like.'

She lifted up the trap and gave the driver my address. She took my hand and held it, but I remained inert. I looked straight out of the window with angry dignity. When we reached Vincent Square I handed her out of the cab, and let her into the house without a word. I took off my hat and coat. She threw her cape and her muff on the sofa.

'Why are you so sulky?' she asked, coming up to me.

'I'm not sulky,' I answered, looking away.

She took my face in her two hands.

'How can you be so silly? Why should you be angry because Jack Kuyper gives me a fur cape? You can't afford to give me one, can you?'

'Of course I can't.'

'And Ted can't either. You can't expect me to refuse a fur cape that cost two hundred and sixty pounds. I've wanted a fur cape all my life. It means nothing to Jack.'

'You don't expect me to believe that he gave it you just out of friendship.'

'He might have. Anyhow, he's gone back to Amsterdam, and who knows when he'll come back?'

'He isn't the only one, either.'

I looked at Rosie now, with angry, hurt, resentful eyes; she smiled at me, and I wish I knew how to describe the sweet kindliness of her beautiful smile; her voice was exquisitely gentle.

'Oh, my dear, why d'you bother your head about any others? What harm does it do you? Don't I give you a good time! Aren't you happy when you're with me?'

'Awfully.'

'Well, then. It's so silly to be fussy and jealous. Why not be happy with what you can get? Enjoy yourself while you have the chance, I say; we shall all be dead in a hundred years, and what will anything matter then? Let's have a good time while we can.'

She put her arms round my neck and pressed her lips against mine. I forgot my wrath. I only thought of her beauty and her enveloping kindness.

'You must take me as I am, you know,' she whispered.

'All right,' I said.

chapter eighteen

During all this time I saw really very little of Driffield. His editorship occupied much of his day, and in the evening he wrote. He was, of course, there every Saturday afternoon, amiable and ironically amusing; he appeared glad to see me and chatted with me for a little while pleasantly of indifferent things; but naturally most of his attention was given to guests older and more important than I. But I had a feeling that he was growing more aloof; he was no longer the jolly, rather vulgar companion that I had known at Blackstable. Perhaps it was only my increasing sensibility that discerned as it were an invisible barrier that existed between him and the people he chaffed and joked with. It was as though he lived a life of the imagination that made the life of every day a little shadowy. He was asked to speak now and then at public dinners. He joined a literary club. He began to know a good many people outside the narrow circle into which his writing had drawn him, and he was increasingly asked to luncheon and tea by the ladies who like to gather about them distinguished authors. Rosie was asked too, but seldom went; she said she didn't care for parties, and after all they didn't want her, they only wanted Ted. I think she was shy and felt out of it. It may be that hostesses had more than once let her see how tiresome they thought it that she must be included; and after inviting her because it was polite, ignored her because to be polite irked them.

It was just about then that Edward Driffield published *The Cup of Life*. It is not my business to criticize his works, and of late as much has been written about them as must satisfy the appetite of any ordinary reader; but I will permit myself to say that *The Cup of Life*, though certainly not the most celebrated of his books, nor the most popular, is to my mind the most interesting. It has a cold ruthlessness that in all the sentimentality of English fiction strikes an original note. It is refreshing and astringent. It tastes of tart apples. It sets your teeth on edge, but it has a subtle, bitter-sweet savour that is very agreeable to the palate. Of all Driffield's books it is the only one I should like to have written. The scene of the child's death, terrible and heart-rending, but written without slop or sickliness, and the curious incident that follows it, cannot easily be forgotten by anyone who has read them.

It was this part of the book that caused the sudden storm that burst on the wretched Driffield's head. For a few days after publication it looked as though it would run its course like the rest of his novels, namely that it would have substantial reviews, laudatory on the whole, but with reservations, and that the sales would be respectable, but modest. Rosie told me that he expected to make three hundred pounds out of it, and was talking of renting a house on the river for the summer. The first two or three notices were non-committal; then in one of the morning papers appeared a violent attack. There was a column of it. The book was described as gratuitously offensive, obscene, and the publishers were rated for putting it before the public. Harrowing pictures were drawn of the devastating effect it must have on the youth of England. It was described as an insult to womanhood. The reviewer protested against the possibility of such a work falling into the hands of young boys and innocent maidens. Other papers followed suit. The more foolish demanded that the book should be suppressed and some asked themselves gravely if this was not a case where the public prosecutor might with fitness intervene. Condemnation was universal; if here and there a courageous writer, ac-

147

customed to the more realistic tone of continental fiction, asserted that Edward Driffield had never written anything better, he was ignored. His honest opinion was ascribed to a base desire to play to the gallery. The libraries barred the book and the lessors of the railway bookstalls refused to stock it.

All this was naturally very unpleasant for Edward Driffield, but he bore it with philosophic calm. He shrugged his shoulders.

'They say it isn't true,' he smiled. 'They can go to hell. It is true.'

He was supported in this trial by the fidelity of his friends. To admire *The Cup of Life* became a mark of aesthetic acumen: to be shocked by it was to confess yourself a philistine. Mrs Barton Trafford had no hesitation in saying that it was a masterpiece, and though this wasn't quite the moment for Barton's article in the *Quarterly*, her faith in Edward Driffield's future remained unshaken. It is strange (and instructive) to read now the book that created such a sensation; there is not a word that could bring a blush to the cheek of the most guileless, not an episode that could cause the novel-reader of the present day to turn a hair.

chapter nineteen

About six months later, when the excitement over *The Cup of Life* had subsided and Driffield had already begun the novel which he published under the name of *By Their Fruits*, I, being then an in-patient dresser and in my fourth year, in the course of my duties went one day into the main hall of the hospital to await the surgeon whom I was accompanying on his round of the wards. I glanced at the rack in which letters were placed, for sometimes people, not knowing my address in Vincent

Square, wrote to me at the hospital. I was surprised to find a telegram for me. It ran as follows:

Please come and see me at five o'clock this afternoon without fail. Important.
Isabel Trafford

I wondered what she wanted me for. I had met her perhaps a dozen times during the last two years, but she had never taken any notice of me, and I had never been to her house. I knew that men were scarce at teatime, and a hostess, short of them at the last moment, might think that a young medical student was better than nothing; but the wording of the telegram hardly suggested a party.

The surgeon for whom I dressed was prosy and verbose. It was not till past five that I was free and then it took me a good twenty minutes to get down to Chelsea. Mrs Barton Trafford lived in a block of flats on the Embankment. It was nearly six when I rang at her door and asked if she was at home. But when I was ushered into her drawing-room and began to explain why I was late she cut me short.

'We supposed you couldn't get away. It doesn't matter.'

Her husband was there.

'I expect he'd like a cup of tea,' he said.

'Oh, I think it's rather late for tea, isn't it?' She looked at me gently, her mild, rather fine eyes full of kindness. 'You don't want any tea, do you?'

I was thirsty and hungry, for my lunch had consisted of a scone and butter and a cup of coffee, but I did not like to say so. I refused tea.

'Do you know Allgood Newton?' asked Mrs Barton Trafford, with a gesture toward a man who had been sitting in a big arm-chair when I was shown in, and now got up. 'I expect you've met him at Edward's.'

I had. He did not come often, but his name was familiar to me and I remembered him. He made me very nervous and I do not think I had ever spoken to him. Though now completely forgotten, in those days he was the best-known critic in England. He was a large, fat, blond man, with a fleshy white

149

face, pale blue eyes, and greying fair hair. He generally wore a pale blue tie to bring out the colour of his eyes. He was very amiable to the authors he met at Driffield's, and said charming and flattering things to them, but when they were gone he was very amusing at their expense. He spoke in a low, even voice, with an apt choice of words: no one could with more point tell a malicious story about a friend.

Allgood Newton shook hands with me and Mrs Barton Trafford, with her ready sympathy, anxious to put me at my ease, took me by the hand and made me sit on the sofa beside her. The tea was still on the table and she took a jam sandwich and delicately nibbled it.

'Have you seen the Driffields lately?' she asked me, as though making conversation.

'I was there last Saturday.'

'You haven't seen either of them since?'

'No.'

Mrs Barton Trafford looked from Allgood Newton to her husband and back again as though mutely demanding their help.

'Nothing will be gained by circumlocution, Isabel,' said Newton, a faintly malicious twinkle in his eye, in his fat, precise way.

Mrs Barton Trafford turned to me.

'Then you don't know that Mrs Driffield has run away from her husband.'

'What!'

I was flabbergasted. I could not believe my ears.

'Perhaps it would be better if you told him the facts, Allgood,' said Mrs Trafford.

The critic leaned back in his chair and placed the tips of the fingers of one hand against the tips of the fingers of the other. He spoke with unction.

'I had to see Edward Driffield last night about a literary article that I am doing for him, and after dinner, since the night was fine, I thought I would walk round to his house. He was expecting me; and I knew besides that he never went out at night except for some function as important as the Lord

Mayor's banquet or the Academy dinner. Imagine my surprise then, nay, my utter and complete bewilderment, when as I approached I saw the door of his house open and Edward in person emerge. You know, of course, that Immanuel Kant was in the habit of taking his daily walk at a certain hour with such punctuality that the inhabitants of Königsberg were accustomed to set their watches by the event, and when once he came out of his house an hour earlier than usual they turned pale, for they knew that this could only mean that some terrible thing had happened. They were right; Immanuel Kant had just received intelligence of the fall of the Bastille.'

Allgood Newton paused for a moment to mark the effect of his anecdote. Mrs Barton Trafford gave him her understanding smile.

'I did not envisage so world-shaking a catastrophe as this when I saw Edward hurrying toward me, but it immediately occurred to me that something untoward was afoot. He carried neither cane nor gloves. He wore his working coat, a venerable garment in black alpaca, and a wide-awake hat. There was something wild in his mien and distraught in his bearing. I asked myself, knowing the vicissitudes of the conjugal state, whether a matrimonial difference had driven him headlong from the house or whether he was hastening to a letter-box in order to post a letter. He sped like Hector flying the noblest of the Greeks. He did not seem to see me and the suspicion flashed across my mind that he did not want to. I stopped him. "Edward," I said. He looked startled. For a moment I could have sworn he did not know who I was. "What avenging furies urge you with such hot haste through the rakish purlieus of Pimlico?" I asked. "Oh, it's you," he said. "Where are you going?" I asked. "Nowhere," he replied.'

At this rate I thought Allgood Newton would never finish his story, and Mrs Hudson would be vexed with me for turning up to dinner half an hour late.

'I told him on what errand I had come, and proposed that we should return to his house where we could more conveniently discuss the question that perturbed me. "I'm too restless to go home," he said; "let's walk. You can talk to me as we go along." Assenting, I turned round and we began to walk; but his pace was so rapid that I had to beg him to moderate it. Even Dr Johnson could not have carried on a conversation when he was walking down Fleet Street at the speed of an express train. Edward's appearance was so peculiar and his manner so agitated that I thought it wise to lead him through the less frequented streets. I talked to him of my article. The subject that occupied me was more copious than had at first sight appeared, and I was doubtful whether after all I could do justice to it in the columns of a weekly journal. I put the matter before him fully and fairly and asked him his opinion. "Rosie has left me," he answered. For a moment I did not know what he was talking about, but in a trice it occurred to me that he was speaking of the buxom and not unprepossessing female from whose hands I had on occasion accepted a cup of tea. From his tone I divined that he expected condolence from me rather than felicitation.'

Allgood Newton paused again and his blue eyes twinkled.

'You're wonderful, Allgood,' said Mrs Barton Trafford.

'Priceless,' said her husband.

'Realizing that the occasion demanded sympathy, I said: "My dear fellow." He interrupted me. "I had a letter by the last post," he said. "She's run away with Lord George Kemp."'

I gasped, but said nothing. Mrs Trafford gave me a quick look.

' "Who is Lord George Kemp?" "He's a Blackstable man," he replied. I had little time to think. I determined to be frank. "You're well rid of her," I said. "Allgood!" he cried. I stopped and put my hand on his arm. "You must know that she was deceiving you with all your friends. Her behaviour was a public scandal. My dear Edward, let us face the fact: your wife was nothing but a common strumpet." He snatched his arm away from me and gave a sort of low roar, like an orang-utan in the forests of Borneo forcibly deprived of a coconut, and before I could stop him he broke away and fled. I was so startled that I could do nothing but listen to his cries and his hurrying footsteps.'

'You shouldn't have let him go,' said Mrs Barton Trafford. 'In the state he was he might have thrown himself in the Thames.'

'The thought occurred to me, but I noticed that he did not run in the direction of the river, but plunged into the meaner streets of the neighbourhood in which we had been walking. And I reflected also that there is no example in literary history of an author committing suicide while engaged on the composition of a literary work. Whatever his tribulations, he is unwilling to leave to posterity an uncompleted opus.'

I was astounded at what I heard and shocked and dismayed; but I was worried too because I could not make out why Mrs Trafford had sent for me. She knew me much too little to think that the story could be of any particular interest to me; nor would she have troubled to let me hear it as a piece of news.

'Poor Edward,' she said. 'Of course no one can deny that it is a blessing in disguise, but I'm afraid he'll take it very much to heart. Fortunately he's done nothing rash.' She turned to me. 'As soon as Mr Newton told us about it I went round to Limpus Road. Edward was out, but the maid said he'd only just left; that means that he must have gone home between the time he ran away from Allgood and this morning. You'll wonder why I asked you to come and see me.'

I did not answer. I waited for her to go on.

'It was at Blackstable you first knew the Driffields, wasn't it? You can tell us who is this Lord George Kemp. Edward said he was a Blackstable man.'

'He's middle-aged. He's got a wife and two sons. They're as old as I am.'

'But I don't understand who he can be. I can't find him in Debrett.'

I almost laughed.

'Oh, he's not really a lord. He's the local coal merchant. They call him Lord George at Blackstable because he's so grand. It's just a joke.'

'The quiddity of bucolic humour is often a trifle obscure to the uninitiated,' said Allgood Newton.

'We must all help dear Edward in every way we can,' said Mrs Barton Trafford. Her eyes rested on me thoughtfully. 'If Kemp has run away with Rosie Driffield he must have left his wife.'

'I suppose so,' I replied.

'Will you do something very kind?'

'If I can.'

'Will you go down to Blackstable and find out exactly what has happened? I think we ought to get in touch with the wife.'

I have never been fond of interfering in other people's affairs.

'I don't know how I could do that,' I answered.

'Couldn't you see her?'

'No, I couldn't.'

If Mrs Barton Trafford thought my reply blunt she did not show it. She smiled a little.

'At all events that can be left over. The urgent thing is to go down and find out about Kemp. I shall try to see Edward this evening. I can't bear the thought of his staying on in that odious house by himself. Barton and I have made up our minds to bring him here. We have a spare room and I'll arrange it so that he can work there. Don't you agree that that would be the best thing for him, Allgood?'

'Absolutely.'

'There's no reason why he shouldn't stay here indefinitely, at all events for a few weeks, and then he can come away with us in the summer. We're going to Brittany. I'm sure he'd like that. It would be a thorough change for him.'

'The immediate question,' said Barton Trafford, fixing on me an eye nearly as kindly as his wife's, 'is whether this young sawbones will go to Blackstable and find out what he can. We must know where we are. That is essential.'

Barton Trafford excused his interest in archaeology by a hearty manner and a jocose, even slangy way of speech.

'He couldn't refuse,' said his wife, giving me a soft, appealing glance. 'You won't refuse, will you? It's so important and you're the only person who can help us.'

Of course she did not know that I was as anxious to find out what had happened as she; she could not tell what a bitter, jealous pain stabbed my heart.

'I couldn't possibly get away from the hospital before Saturday,' I said.

'That'll do. It's very good of you. All Edward's friends will be grateful to you. When shall you return?'

'I have to be back in London early on Monday morning.'

'Then come and have tea with me in the afternoon. I shall await you with impatience. Thank God, that's settled. Now I must try and get hold of Edward.'

I understood that I was dismissed. Allgood Newton took his leave and came downstairs with me.

'Our Isabel has *un petit air* of Catherine of Aragon today that I find vastly becoming,' he murmured, when the door was closed behind us. 'This is a golden opportunity and I think we may safely trust our friend not to miss it. A charming woman with a heart of gold. *Vénus toute entière à sa proie attachée.*'

I did not understand what he meant, for what I have already told the reader about Mrs Barton Trafford I only learned much later, but I realized that he was saying something vaguely malicious about her, and probably amusing, so I sniggered.

'I suppose your youth inclines you to what my good Dizzy named in an unlucky moment the gondola of London.'

'I'm going to take a bus,' I answered.

'Oh? Had you proposed to go by hansom I was going to ask you to be good enough to drop me on your way, but if you are going to use the homely conveyance which I, in my old-fashioned manner, still prefer to call an omnibus, I shall hoist my unwieldy carcass into a four-wheeler.'

He signalled to one and gave me two flabby fingers to shake.

'I shall come on Monday to hear the result of what dear Henry would call your so exquisitely delicate mission.'

chapter twenty

But it was years before I saw Allgood Newton again, for when I got to Blackstable I found a letter from Mrs Barton Trafford (who had taken the precaution to note my address) asking me, for reasons that she would explain when she saw me, not to come to her flat but to meet her at six o'clock in the first-class waiting-room at Victoria Station. As soon then as I could get away from the hospital on Monday I made my way there, and after waiting for a while saw her come in. She came toward me with little tripping steps.

'Well, have you anything to tell me? Let us find a quiet corner and sit down.'

We sought a place and found it.

'I must explain why I asked you to come here,' she said. 'Edward is staying with me. At first he did not want to come, but I persuaded him. But he's nervous and ill and irritable. I did not want to run the risk of his seeing you.'

I told Mrs Trafford the bare facts of my story and she listened attentively. Now and then she nodded her head. But I could not hope to make her understand the commotion I had found at Blackstable. The town was beside itself with excitement. Nothing so thrilling had happened there for years, and no one could talk of anything else. Humpty-dumpty had had a great fall. Lord George Kemp had absconded. About a week before he had announced that he had to go up to London on business, and two days later a petition in bankruptcy was filed against him. It appeared that his building operations had not been successful, his attempt to make Blackstable into a frequented seaside resort meeting with no response, and he had been forced to raise money in every way he could. All kinds of rumours ran through the little town. Quite a number of small people who had entrusted their savings to him were faced with the loss of all they had. The details were vague, for neither my uncle nor my aunt knew anything of business matters, nor had I the knowledge to make what they told me comprehensible. But there was a mortgage on George Kemp's house and a bill of sale on his furniture. His wife was left without a penny. His two sons, lads of twenty and twenty-one, were in the coal business, but that too was involved in the general ruin. George Kemp had gone off with all the cash he could lay hands on, something like fifteen hundred pounds, they said, though how they knew I cannot imagine; and it was reported that a warrant had been issued for his arrest. It was supposed that he had left the country; some said he had gone to Australia and some to Canada.

'I hope they catch him,' said my uncle. 'He ought to get penal servitude for life.'

The indignation was universal. They could not forgive him because he had always been so noisy and boisterous, because he had chaffed them and stood them drinks and given them garden parties, because he had driven such a smart trap and worn his brown billycock hat at such a rakish angle. But it was on Sunday night after church in the vestry that the church-warden told my uncle the worst. For the last two years he had been meeting Rosie Driffield at Haversham almost every week and they had been spending the night together at a public-house. The licensee of this had put money into one of Lord George's wildcat schemes, and on discovering that he had lost it blurted out the whole story. He could have borne it if Lord George had defrauded others, but that he should defraud him who had done him a good turn and whom he looked upon as a chum, that was the limit.

'I expect they've run away together,' said my uncle.

'I shouldn't be surprised,' said the churchwarden.

After supper, while the housemaid was clearing away, I went into the kitchen to talk to Mary-Ann. She had been at church and had heard the story too. I cannot believe that the congregation had listened very attentively to my uncle's sermon.

'The vicar says they've run away together,' I said. I had not breathed a word of what I knew.

'Why, of course they 'ave,' said Mary-Ann. 'He was the only man she ever really fancied. He only 'ad to lift 'is little finger and she'd leave anyone, no matter who it was.'

I lowered my eyes. I was suffering from bitter mortification; and I was angry with Rosie: I thought she had behaved very badly to me.

'I suppose we shall never see her again,' I said.

It gave me a pang to utter the words.

'I don't suppose we shall,' said Mary-Ann cheerfully.

When I had told Mrs Barton Trafford as much of this story as I thought she need know, she sighed, but whether from satisfaction or distress I had no notion.

'Well, that's the end of Rosie at all events,' she said. She got up and held out her hand. 'Why will these literary men make these unfortunate marriages? It's all very sad, very sad. Thank you so much for what you've done. We know where we are now. The great thing is that it shouldn't interfere with Edward's work.'

Her remarks seemed a trifle disconnected to me. The fact was, I have no doubt, that she was giving me not the smallest thought. I led her out of Victoria Station and put her into a bus that went down the King's Road, Chelsea; then I walked back to my lodgings.

chapter twenty-one

I lost touch with Driffield. I was too shy to seek him out; I was busy with my examinations, and when I had passed them I went abroad. I remember vaguely to have seen in the paper that he had divorced Rosie. Nothing more was heard of her. Small sums reached her mother occasionally, ten or twenty pounds, and they came in a registered letter with a New York postmark; but no address was given, no message enclosed, and they were presumed to come from Rosie only because no one else could possibly send Mrs Gann money. Then in the fullness of years Rosie's mother died, and it may be supposed that in some way the news reached her, for the letters ceased to come.

chapter twenty-two

Alroy Kear and I, as arranged, met on Friday at Victoria Station to catch the five-ten to Blackstable. We made ourselves comfortable in opposite corners of a smoking compartment. From him I now learned roughly what had happened to Driffield after his wife ran away from him. Roy had in due course become very intimate with Mrs Barton Trafford. Knowing him and remembering her, I realized that this was inevitable. I was not surprised to hear that he had travelled with her and Barton on the Continent, sharing with them to the full their passion for Wagner, post-impressionist painting, and baroque architecture. He had lunched assiduously at the flat in Chelsea, and when advancing years and failing health had imprisoned Mrs Trafford to her drawing-room, notwithstanding the many claims on his time he had gone regularly once a week to sit with her. He had a good heart. After her death he wrote an article about her in which with admirable emotion he did justice to her great gifts of sympathy and discrimination.

It pleased me to think that his kindliness should receive its due and unexpected reward, for Mrs Barton Trafford had told him much about Edward Driffield that could not fail to be of service to him in the work of love on which he was now engaged. Mrs Barton Trafford, exercising a gentle violence, not only took Edward Driffield into her house when the flight of his faithless wife left him what Roy could only describe by the French word *désemparé*, but persuaded him to stay for nearly a year. She gave him the loving care, the unfailing kindness, and the intelligent understanding of a woman who combined feminine tact with masculine vigour, a heart of gold with an unerring eye for the main chance. It was in her flat that he finished *By Their Fruits*. She was justified in looking upon it as her book and the dedication to her is a proof that Driffield was not unmindful of his debt. She took him to Italy (with Barton of course, for Mrs Trafford knew too well how malicious people were, to give occasion for scandal) and with

159

a volume of Ruskin in her hand revealed to Edward Driffield the immortal beauties of that country. Then she found him rooms in the Temple, and arranged little luncheons there, she acting very prettily the part of hostess, where he could receive the persons whom his increasing reputation attracted.

It must be admitted that this increasing reputation was very largely due to her. His great celebrity came only during his last years when he had long ceased to write, but the foundations of it were undoubtedly laid by Mrs Trafford's untiring efforts. Not only did she inspire (and perhaps write not a little, for she had a dexterous pen) the article that Barton at last contributed to the *Quarterly* in which the claim was first made that Driffield must be ranked with the masters of British fiction, but as each book came out she organized its reception. She went here and there, seeing editors and, more important still, proprietors of influential organs; she gave soirées to which everyone was invited who could be of use. She persuaded Edward Driffield to give readings at the houses of the very great for charitable purposes; she saw to it that his photograph should appear in the illustrated weeklies; she revised personally any interview he gave. For ten years she was an indefatigable press agent. She kept him steadily before the public.

Mrs Barton Trafford had a grand time, but she did not get above herself. It was useless indeed to ask him to a party without her; he refused. And when she and Barton and Driffield were invited anywhere to dinner they came together and went together. She never let him out of her sight. Hostesses might rave; they could take it or leave it. As a rule they took it. If Mrs Barton Trafford happened to be a little out of temper it was through him she showed it, for while she remained charming, Edward Driffield would be uncommonly gruff. But she knew exactly how to draw him out and when the company was distinguished could make him brilliant. She was perfect with him. She never concealed from him her conviction that he was the greatest writer of his day; she not only referred to him invariably as the master, but, perhaps a little playfully and yet how flatteringly, addressed him always as such. To the end she retained something kittenish.

Then a terrible thing happened. Driffield caught pneumonia and was extremely ill; for some time his life was despaired of. Mrs Barton Trafford did everything that such a woman could do, and would willingly have nursed him herself, but she was frail, she was indeed over sixty, and he had to have professional nurses. When at last he pulled through, the doctors said that he must go into the country, and since he was still extremely weak insisted that a nurse should go with him. Mrs Trafford wanted him to go to Bournemouth so that she could run down for weekends and see that everything was well with him, but Driffield had a fancy for Cornwall, and the doctors agreed that the mild airs of Penzance would suit him. One would have thought that a woman of Isabel Trafford's delicate intuition would have had some foreboding of ill. No. She let him go. She impressed on the nurse that she entrusted her with a grave responsibility; she placed in her hands, if not the future of English literature, at least the life and welfare of its most distinguished living representative. It was a priceless charge.

Three weeks later Edward Driffield wrote and told her that he had married his nurse by special licence.

I imagine that never did Mrs Barton Trafford exhibit more pre-eminently her greatness of soul than in the manner in which she met this situation. Did she cry, Judas, Judas? Did she tear her hair and fall on the floor and kick her heels in an attack of hysterics? Did she turn on the mild and learned Barton and call him a blithering old fool? Did she inveigh against the faithlessness of men and the wantonness of women or did she relieve her wounded feelings by shouting at the top of her voice a string of those obscenities with which the alienists tell us the chastest females are surprisingly acquainted? Not at all. She wrote a charming letter of congratulation to Driffield and she wrote to his bride telling her that she was glad to think that now she would have two loving friends instead of one. She begged them both to come and stay with her on their return to London. She told everyone she met that the marriage had made her very, very happy, for Edward Driffield would soon be an old man, and must have someone to take care of him; who could do this better than a hospital nurse? She never had anything but praise for the new Mrs Driffield; she was not exactly pretty, she said, but she had a very nice face; of course she wasn't quite, quite a lady, but Edward would only have been uncomfortable with anyone too grand. She was just the sort of wife for him. I think it may be not unjustly said that Mrs Barton Trafford fairly ran over with the milk of human kindness, but all the same I have an inkling that if ever the milk of human kindness was charged with vitriol, here was a case in point.

chapter twenty-three

When we arrived at Blackstable, Roy and I, a car, neither ostentatiously grand nor obviously cheap, was waiting for him, and the chauffeur had a note for me asking me to lunch with Mrs Driffield next day. I got into a taxi and went to the Bear and Key. I had learned from Roy that there was a new Marine Hotel on the front, but I did not propose for the luxuries of civilization to abandon a resort of my youth. Change met me at the railway station, which was not in its old place, but up a new road, and of course it was strange to be driven down the High Street in a car. But the Bear and Key was unaltered. It received me with its old churlish indifference: there was no one at the entrance, the driver put my bag down and drove away; I called, no one answered; I went into the bar and found a young lady with shingled hair reading a book by Mr Compton Mackenzie. I asked her if I could have a room. She gave me a slightly offended look, and said she thought so, but as that seemed to exhaust her interest in the matter I asked politely whether there was anyone who could show it to me. She got up and, opening a door, in a shrill voice called: 'Katie.'

'What is it?' I heard.

'There's a gent wants a room.'

In a little while appeared an ancient and haggard female in a very dirty print dress, with an untidy mop of grey hair, and showed me, two flights up, a very small grubby room.

'Can't you do something better than that for me?' I asked.

'It's the room commercials generally 'ave,' she answered with a sniff.

'Haven't you got any others?'

'Not single.'

'Then give me a double room.'

'I'll go and ask Mrs Brentford.'

I accompanied her down to the first floor and she knocked at a door. She was told to come in, and when she opened it I caught sight of a stout woman with grey hair elaborately marcelled. She was reading a book. Apparently everyone at the Bear and Key was interested in literature. She gave me an indifferent look when Katie said I wasn't satisfied with number seven.

'Show him number five,' she said.

I began to feel that I had been a trifle rash in declining so haughtily Mrs Driffield's invitation to stay with her and then putting aside in my sentimental way Roy's wise suggestion that I should stay at the Marine Hotel. Katie took me upstairs again and ushered me into a largish room looking on the High Street. Most of its space was occupied by a double bed. The windows had certainly not been opened for a month.

I said that would do and asked about dinner.

'You can 'ave what you like,' said Katie. 'We 'aven't got nothing in, but I'll run round and get it.'

Knowing English inns, I ordered a fried sole and a grilled chop. Then I went for a stroll. I walked down to the beach and found that they had built an esplanade, and there was a row of bungalows and villas where I remembered only wind-swept fields. But they were seedy and bedraggled, and I guessed that even after all these years Lord George's dream of turning Blackstable into a popular seaside resort had not come true. A retired military man, a pair of elderly ladies walked along the crumbling asphalt. It was incredibly dreary. A chill wind was blowing and a light drizzle swept over from the sea.

I went back into the town and here, in the space between the Bear and Key and the Duke of Kent, were little knots of men standing about notwithstanding the inclement weather; and their eyes had the same pale blue, their high cheekbones the same ruddy colour as that of their fathers before them. It was strange to see that some of the sailors in blue jerseys still wore little gold rings in their ears; and not only old ones but boys scarcely out of their teens. I sauntered down the street, and there was the bank refronted, but the stationery shop where I had bought paper and wax to make rubbings with an obscure writer whom I had met by chance was unchanged; there were two or three cinemas, and their garish posters suddenly gave the prim street a dissipated air so that it looked like a respectable elderly woman who had taken a drop too much.

It was cold and cheerless in the commercial room where I ate my dinner alone at a large table laid for six. I was served by the slatternly Katie. I asked if I could have a fire.

'Not in June,' she said. 'We don't 'ave fires after April.'

'I'll pay for it,' I protested.

'Not in June. In October, yes, but not in June.'

When I had finished I went into the bar to have a glass of port.

'Very quiet,' I said to the shingled barmaid.

'Yes, it is quiet,' she answered.

'I should have thought on a Friday night you'd have quite a lot of people in here.'

'Well, one would think that, wouldn't one?'

Then a stout, red-faced man with a close-cropped head of grey hair came in from the back and I guessed that this was my host.

'Are you Mr Brentford?' I asked him.

'Yes, that's me.'

'I knew your father. Will you have a glass of port?'

I told him my name, in the days of his boyhood better known than any other at Blackstable, but somewhat to my mortification I saw that it aroused no echo in his memory. He consented, however, to let me stand him a glass of port.

'Down here on business?' he asked me. 'We get quite a few

commercial gents at one time and another. We always like to do what we can for them.'

I told him that I had come down to see Mrs Driffield, and left him to guess on what errand.

'I used to see a lot of the old man,' said Mr Brentford. 'He used to be very partial to dropping in here and having his glass of bitter. Mind you, I don't say he ever got tiddly, but he used to like to sit in the bar and talk. My word, he'd talk by the hour, and he never cared who he talked to. Mrs Driffield didn't half like his coming here. He'd slip away, out of the house, without saying a word to anybody, and come toddling down. You know it's a bit of a walk for a man of that age. Of course when they missed him Mrs Driffield knew where he was, and she used to telephone and ask if he was here. Then she'd drive over in the car and go in and see my wife. "You go in and fetch him, Mrs Brentford," she'd say; "I don't like to go in the bar meself, not with all those men hanging about"; so Mrs Brentford would come in and she'd say, "Now, Mr Driffield, Mrs Driffield's come for you in the car, so you'd better finish your beer and let her take you home." He used to ask Mrs Brentford not to say he was here when Mrs Driffield rang up, but of course we couldn't do that. He was an old man and all that, and we didn't want to take the responsibility. He was born in the parish, you know, and his first wife, she was a Blackstable girl. She's been dead these many years. I never knew her. He was a funny old fellow. No side, you know; they tell me they thought a rare lot of him in London, and when he died the papers were full of him; but you'd never have known it to talk to him. He might have been just nobody, like you and me. Of course we always tried to make him comfortable; we tried to get him to sit in one of them easy-chairs, but no, he must sit up at the bar; he said he liked to feel his feet on a rail. My belief is he was happier here than anywhere. He always said he liked a bar. He said you saw life there, and he said he'd always loved life. Quite a character he was. Reminded me of my father except that my old governor never read a book in his life and he drank a bottle of French brandy a day and he was seventy-eight when he died and his last illness was his first. I quite missed old Driffield when he popped off. I was only saying to Mrs Brentford the other day, I'd like to read one of his books some time. They tell me he wrote several about these parts.'

chapter twenty-four

Next morning it was cold and raw, but it was not raining, and I walked down the High Street toward the vicarage. I recognized the names over the shops, the Kentish names that have been borne for centuries – the Ganns, the Kemps, the Cobbs, the Igguldens – but I saw no one that I knew. I felt like a ghost walking down that street where I had once known nearly everyone, if not to speak to, at least by sight. Suddenly a very shabby little car passed me, stopped, and backed, and I saw someone looking at me curiously. A tall, heavy, elderly man got out and came toward me.

'Aren't you Willie Ashenden?' he asked.

Then I recognized him. He was the doctor's son, and I had been at school with him; we had passed from form to form together, and I knew that he had succeeded his father in his practice.

'Hallo, how are you?' he asked. 'I've just been along to the vicarage to see my grandson. It's a preparatory school now, you know, and I put him there at the beginning of this term.'

He was shabbily dressed and unkempt, but he had a fine head, and I saw that in youth he must have had unusual beauty. It was funny that I had never noticed it.

'Are you a grandfather?' I asked.

'Three times over,' he laughed.

It gave me a shock. He had drawn breath, walked the earth, and presently grown to man's estate, married, had children, and they in turn had had children; I judged from the look of him that he had lived, with incessant toil in penury. He had

166

the peculiar manner of the country doctor, bluff, hearty, and unctuous. His life was over. I had plans in my head for books and plays, I was full of schemes for the future; I felt that a long stretch of activity and fun still lay before me; and yet, I supposed, to others I must seem the elderly man that he seemed to me. I was so shaken that I had not the presence of mind to ask about his brothers, whom as a child I had played with, or about the old friends who had been my companions; after a few foolish remarks I left him. I walked on to the vicarage, a roomy, rambling house, too far out of the way for the modern incumbent who took his duties more seriously than did my uncle, and too large for the present cost of living. It stood in a big garden and was surrounded by green fields. There was a great square notice-board that announced that it was a preparatory school for the sons of gentlemen, and gave the name and the degrees of the head master. I looked over the paling; the garden was squalid and untidy, and the pond in which I used to fish for roach was choked up. The glebe fields had been cut up into building lots. There were rows of little brick houses with bumpy ill-made roads. I walked along Joy Lane, and there were houses here too, bungalows facing the sea; and the old turnpike house was a trim tea shop.

I wandered about here and there. There seemed innumerable streets of little houses of yellow brick, but I do not know who lived in them, for I saw no one about. I went down to the harbour. It was deserted. There was but one tramp lying a little way out from the pier. Two or three sailormen were sitting outside a warehouse, and they stared at me as I passed. The bottom had fallen out of the coal trade and colliers came to Blackstable no longer.

Then it was time for me to go to Ferne Court, and I went back to the Bear and Key. The landlord had told me that he had a Daimler for hire, and I had arranged that it should take me to my luncheon. It stood at the door when I came up, a brougham, but the oldest, most dilapidated car of its make that I had ever seen; it panted along with squeaks and thumps and rattlings, with sudden angry jerks, so that I wondered if I should ever reach my destination. But the extraordinary, the amazing thing about it was that it smelled exactly like the old landau which my uncle used to hire every Sunday morning to go to church in. This was a rank odour of stables and of stale straw that lay at the bottom of the carriage; and I wondered in vain why, after all these years, the motor-car should have it too. But nothing can bring back the past like a perfume or a stench, and, oblivious to the country I was trundling through, I saw myself once more a little boy on the front seat with the communion plate beside me and, facing me, my aunt, smelling slightly of clean linen and eau-de-Cologne, in her black silk cloak and her little bonnet with a feather, and my uncle in his cassock, a broad band of ribbed silk round his ample waist, and a gold cross hanging over his stomach from the gold chain round his neck.

'Now, Willie, mind you behave nicely today. You're not to turn round, and sit up properly in your seat. The Lord's House isn't the place to loll in and you must remember that you should set an example to other little boys who haven't had your advantages.'

When I arrived at Ferne Court, Mrs Driffield and Roy were walking round the garden, and they came up to me as I got out of the car.

'I was showing Roy my flowers,' said Mrs Driffield, as she shook hands with me. And then with a sigh: 'They're all I have now.'

She looked no older than when I last saw her six years before. She wore her weeds with quiet distinction. At her neck was a collar of white crêpe and at her wrists cuffs of the same. Roy, I noticed, wore with his neat blue suit a black tie; I supposed it was a sign of respect for the illustrious dead.

'I'll just show you my herbaceous borders,' said Mrs Driffield, 'and then we'll go in to lunch.'

We walked round, and Roy was very knowledgeable. He knew what all the flowers were called, and the Latin names tripped off his tongue like cigarettes out of a cigarette-making machine. He told Mrs Driffield where she ought to get certain varieties that she absolutely must have, and how perfectly lovely were certain others.

'Shall we go in through Edward's study?' suggested Mrs Driffield. 'I keep it exactly as it was when he was here. I haven't changed a thing. You'd be surprised how many people come over to see the house, and of course above all they want to see the room he worked in.'

We went in through an open window. There was a bowl of roses on the desk, and on a little round table by the side of the arm-chair a copy of the *Spectator*. In the ash trays were the master's pipes and there was ink in the inkstand. The scene was perfectly set. I do not know why the room seemed so strangely dead; it had already the mustiness of a museum. Mrs Driffield went to the bookshelves and with a little smile, half playful, half sad, passed a rapid hand across the back of half a dozen volumes bound in blue.

'You know that Edward admired your work so much,' said Mrs Driffield. 'He re-read your books quite often.'

'I'm very glad to think that,' I said politely.

I knew very well that they had not been there on my last visit, and in a casual way I took one of them out and ran my fingers along the top to see whether there was dust on it. There was not. Then I took another book down, one of Charlotte Brontë's, and making a little plausible conversation tried the same experiment. No, there was no dust there either. All I learned was that Mrs Driffield was an excellent housekeeper and had a conscientious maid.

We went in to luncheon, a hearty British meal of roast beef and Yorkshire pudding, and we talked of the work on which Roy was engaged.

'I want to spare dear Roy all the labour I can,' said Mrs Driffield, 'and I've been gathering together as much of the material as I could myself. Of course it's been rather painful, but it's been very interesting too. I came across a lot of old photographs that I must show you.'

After luncheon we went into the drawing-room, and I noticed again with what perfect taste Mrs Driffield had arranged it. It suited the widow of a distinguished man of letters almost more than it had suited the wife. Those chintzes, those bowls of potpourri, those Dresden China figures – there was about them a faint air of regret; they seemed to reflect pensively upon a past of distinction. I could have wished on this chilly day that there was a fire in the grate, but the English are a hardy as well as a conservative race, and it is not difficult for them to maintain their principles at the cost of the discomfort of others. I doubted whether Mrs Driffield would have conceived the possibility of lighting a fire before the first of October. She asked me whether I had lately seen the lady who had brought me to lunch with the Driffields, and I surmised from her faint acerbity that since the death of her eminent husband the great and fashionable had shown a distinct tendency to take no further notice of her. We were just settling down to talk about the defunct; Roy and Mrs Driffield were putting artful questions to incite me to disclose my recollections, and I was gathering my wits about me so that I should not in an unguarded moment let slip anything that I had made up my mind to keep to myself; when suddenly the trim parlourmaid brought in two cards on a small salver.

'Two gentlemen in a car, mum, and they say, could they look at the house and garden?'

'What a bore!' cried Mrs Driffield, but with astonishing alacrity. 'Isn't it funny I should have been speaking just now about the people who want to see the house? I never have a moment's peace.'

'Well, why don't you say you're sorry you can't see them?' said Roy, with what I thought a certain cattiness.

'Oh, I couldn't do that. Edward wouldn't have liked me to.' She looked at the cards. 'I haven't got my glasses on me.'

She handed them to me, and on one I read: 'Henry Beard MacDougal, University of Virginia'; and in pencil was written: 'Assistant professor in English Literature.' The other was 'Jean-Paul Underhill,' and there was at the bottom an address in New York.

'Americans,' said Mrs Driffield. 'Say I shall be very pleased if they'll come in.'

Presently the maid ushered the strangers in. They were both tall young men and broad-shouldered, with heavy, clean-shaven, swarthy faces and handsome eyes; they both wore horn-rimmed spectacles, and they both had thick black hair combed straight back from their foreheads. They both wore English suits that were evidently brand new; they were both slightly embarrassed, but verbose and extremely civil. They explained that they were making a literary tour of England and, being admirers of Edward Driffield, had taken the liberty of stopping off on their way to Rye to visit Henry James's house in the hope that they would be permitted to see a spot sanctified by so many associations. The reference to Rye did not go down very well with Mrs Driffield.

'I believe they have some very good links there,' she said.

She introduced the Americans to Roy and me. I was filled with admiration for the way in which Roy rose to the occasion. It appeared that he had lectured before the University of Virginia and had stayed with a distinguished member of the faculty. It had been an unforgettable experience. He did not know whether he had been more impressed by the lavish hospitality with which those charming Virginians had entertained him or by their intelligent interest in art and literature. He asked how So-and-so was, and So-and-so; he had made lifelong friends there, and it looked as though everyone he had met was good and kind and clever. Soon the young professor was telling Roy how much he liked his books, and Roy was modestly telling him what in this one and the other his aim had been and how conscious he was that he had come far short of achieving it. Mrs Driffield listened with smiling sympathy, but I had a feeling that her smile was growing a trifle strained. It may be that Roy had too, for he suddenly broke off.

'But you don't want me to bore you with my stuff,' he said in his loud, hearty way. 'I'm only here because Mrs Driffield has entrusted to me the great honour of writing Edward Driffield's life.'

This, of course, interested the visitors very much.

'It's some job, believe me,' said Roy, playfully American. 'Fortunately I have the assistance of Mrs Driffield, who was not only a perfect wife, but an admirable amanuensis and secretary; the materials she has placed at my disposal are so amazingly full that really little remains for me to do but take

171

advantage of her industry and her – her affectionate zeal.'

Mrs Driffield looked down demurely at the carpet and the two young Americans turned on her their large dark eyes in which you could read their sympathy, their interest, and their respect. After a little more conversation – partly literary, but also about golf, for the visitors admitted that they hoped to get a round or two at Rye, and here again Roy was on the spot, for he told them to look out for such and such a bunker, and when they came to London hoped they would play with him at Sunningdale; after this, I say, Mrs Driffield got up and offered to show them Edward's study and bedroom, and of course the garden. Roy rose to his feet, evidently bent on accompanying them, but Mrs Driffield gave him a little smile; it was pleasant but firm.

'Don't you bother to come, Roy,' she said. 'I'll take them round. You stay here and talk to Mr Ashenden.'

'Oh, all right. Of course.'

The strangers bade us farewell, and Roy and I settled down again in the chintz arm-chairs.

'Jolly room this is,' said Roy.

'Very.'

'Amy had to work hard to get it. You know the old man bought this house two or three years before they were married. She tried to make him sell it, but he wouldn't. He was very obstinate in some ways. You see it belonged to a certain Miss Wolfe, whose bailiff his father was, and he said that when he was a little boy his one idea was to own it himself, and now he'd got it he was going to keep it. One would have thought the last thing he'd want to do was to live in a place where everyone knew all about his origins and everything. Once poor Amy very nearly engaged a housemaid before she discovered she was Edward's great-niece. When Amy came here the house was furnished from attic to cellar in the best Tottenham Court Road manner; you know the sort of thing, Turkey carpets and mahogany sideboards, and a plush-covered suite in the drawing-room, and modern marquetry. It was his idea of how a gentleman's house should be furnished. Amy says it was simply awful. He wouldn't let her change a thing, and she had to go to work with the greatest care; she says she simply couldn't have lived in it, and she was determined to have things right, so she had to change things one by one so that he didn't pay any attention. She told me the hardest job she had was with his writing-desk. I don't know whether you've noticed the one there is in his study now. It's a very good period piece; I wouldn't mind having it myself. Well, he had a horrible American roll-top desk. He'd had it for years, and he'd written a dozen books on it, and he simply wouldn't part with it, he had no feeling for things like that; he just happened to be attached to it because he'd had it so long. You must get Amy to tell you the story how she managed to get rid of it in the end. It's really priceless. She's a remarkable woman, you know; she generally gets her own way.'

'I've noticed it,' I said.

It had not taken her long to dispose of Roy when he showed signs of wishing to go over the house with the visitors. He gave me a quick look and laughed. Roy was not stupid.

'You don't know America as well as I do,' he said. 'They always prefer a live mouse to a dead lion. That's one of the reasons why I like America.'

chapter twenty-five

When Mrs Driffield, having sent the pilgrims on their way, came back she bore under her arm a portfolio.

'What very nice young men!' she said. 'I wish young men in England took such a keen interest in literature. I gave them that photo of Edward when he was dead, and they asked me for one of mine, and I signed it for them.' Then very graciously: 'You made a great impression on them, Roy. They said it was a real privilege to meet you.'

'I've lectured in America so much,' said Roy, with modesty.

'Oh, but they've read your books. They say that what they like about them is that they're so virile.'

The portfolio contained a number of old photographs, groups of schoolboys among whom I recognized an urchin with untidy hair as Driffield only because his widow pointed him out, Rugby fifteens with Driffield a little older, and then one of a young sailor in a jersey and a reefer jacket, Driffield when he ran away to sea.

'Here's one taken when he was first married,' said Mrs Driffield.

He wore a beard and black-and-white check trousers; in his button-hole was a large white rose backed by maidenhair, and on the table beside him was a chimney-pot hat.

'And here is the bride,' said Mrs Driffield, trying not to smile.

Poor Rosie, seen by a country photographer over forty years ago, was grotesque. She was standing very stiffly against a background of baronial hall, holding a large bouquet; her dress was elaborately draped, pinched at the waist, and she wore a bustle. Her fringe came down to her eyes. On her head was a wreath of orange blossoms, perched high on a mass of hair, and from it was thrown back a long veil. Only I knew how lovely she must have looked.

'She looks fearfully common,' said Roy.

'She was,' murmured Mrs Driffield.

We looked at more photographs of Edward, photographs that had been taken of him when he began to be known, photographs when he wore only a moustache, and others, all the later ones, when he was clean-shaven. You saw his face grown thinner and more lined. The stubborn commonplace of the early portraits melted gradually into a weary refinement. You saw the change in him wrought by experience, thought, and achieved ambition. I looked again at the photograph of the young sailorman, and fancied that I saw in it already a trace of that aloofness that seemed to me so marked in the older ones and that I had had years before the vague sensation of in the man himself. The face you saw was a mask and the actions he performed were without significance. I had an impression that the real man, to his death unknown and lonely, was a wraith that went a silent way unseen between the writer of his books and the man who led his life, and smiled with ironical detachment at the two puppets that the world took for Edward Driffield. I am conscious that in what I have written of him I have not presented a living man, standing on his feet, rounded with comprehensible motives and logical activities; I have not tried to: I am glad to leave that to the abler pen of Alroy Kear.

I came across the photographs that Harry Retford, the actor, had had taken of Rosie, and then a photograph of the picture that Lionel Hillier had painted of her. It gave me a pang. That was how I best remembered her. Notwithstanding the old-fashioned gown, she was alive there, and tremulous with the passion that filled her. She seemed to offer herself to the assault of love.

'She gives you the impression of a hefty wench,' said Roy.

'If you like the milkmaid type,' answered Mrs Driffield. 'I've always thought she looked rather like a white nigger.'

That was what Mrs Barton Trafford had been fond of calling her, and with Rosie's thick lips and broad nose there was indeed a hateful truth in the description. But they did not know how silvery golden her hair was, nor how golden silver her skin; they did not know her enchanting smile.

'She wasn't a bit like a white nigger,' I said. 'She was virginal like the dawn. She was like Hebe. She was like a tea rose.'

Mrs Driffield smiled and exchanged a meaning glance with Roy.

'Mrs Barton Trafford told me a great deal about her. I don't wish to seem spiteful, but I'm afraid I don't think that she can have been a very nice woman.'

'That's where you make a mistake,' I replied. 'She was a very nice woman. I never saw her in a bad temper. You only had to say you wanted something for her to give it to you. I never heard her say a disagreeable thing about anyone. She had a heart of gold.'

'She was a terrible slattern. Her house was always in a mess;

you didn't like to sit down in a chair because it was so dusty, and you dared not look in the corners. And it was the same with her person. She could never put a skirt on straight, and you'd see about two inches of petticoat hanging down on one side.'

'She didn't bother about things like that. They didn't make her any the less beautiful. And she was as good as she was beautiful.'

Roy burst out laughing, and Mrs Driffield put up her hand to her mouth to hide her smile.

'Oh, come, Mr Ashenden, that's really going too far. After all, let's face it, she was a nymphomaniac.'

'I think that's a very silly word,' I said.

'Well, then, let me say that she can hardly have been a very good woman to treat poor Edward as she did. Of course it was a blessing in disguise. If she hadn't run away from him he might have had to bear that burden for the rest of his life, and with such a handicap he could never have reached the position he did. But the fact remains that she was notoriously unfaithful to him. From what I hear she was absolutely promiscuous.'

'You don't understand,' I said. 'She was a very simple woman. Her instincts were healthy and ingenuous. She loved to make people happy. She loved love.'

'Do you call that love?'

'Well, then, the act of love. She was naturally affectionate. When she liked anyone it was quite natural for her to go to bed with him. She never thought twice about it. It was not vice; it wasn't lasciviousness; it was her nature. She gave herself as naturally as the sun gives heat or the flowers their perfume. It was a pleasure to her and she liked to give pleasure to others. It had no effect on her character; she remained sincere, unspoiled, and artless.'

Mrs Driffield looked as though she had taken a dose of castor oil and had just been trying to get the taste of it out of her mouth by sucking a lemon.

'I don't understand,' she said. 'But then I'm bound to admit that I never understood what Edward saw in her.'

'Did he know that she was carrying on with all sorts of people?' asked Roy.

'I'm sure he didn't,' she replied quickly.

'You think him a bigger fool than I do, Mrs Driffield,' I said.

'Then why did he put up with it?'

'I think I can tell you. You see, she wasn't a woman who ever inspired love. Only affection. It was absurd to be jealous over her. She was like a clear, deep pool in a forest glade, into which it's heavenly to plunge, but it is neither less cool nor less crystalline because a tramp and a gipsy and a gamekeeper have plunged into it before you.'

Roy laughed again, and this time Mrs Driffield without concealment smiled thinly.

'It's comic to hear you so lyrical,' said Roy.

I stifled a sigh. I have noticed that when I am most serious people are apt to laugh at me, and indeed when after a lapse of time I have read passages that I wrote from the fullness of my heart I have been tempted to laugh at myself. It must be that there is something naturally absurd in a sincere emotion, though why there should be I cannot imagine, unless it is that man, the ephemeral inhabitant of an insignificant planet, with all his pain and all his striving is but a jest in an eternal mind.

I saw that Mrs Driffield wished to ask me something. It caused her a certain embarrassment.

'Do you think he'd have taken her back if she'd been willing to come?'

'You knew him better than I. I should say no. I think that when he had exhausted an emotion he took no further interest in the person who had aroused it. I should say that he had a peculiar combination of strong feeling and extreme callousness.'

'I don't know how you can say that,' cried Roy. 'He was the kindest man I ever met.'

Mrs Driffield looked at me steadily and then dropped her eyes.

'I wonder what happened to her when she went to America,' he asked.

'I believe she married Kemp,' said Mrs Driffield. 'I heard they had taken another name. Of course they couldn't show their faces over here again.'

'When did she die?'

'Oh, about ten years ago.'

'How did you hear?' I asked.

'From Harold Kemp, the son; he's in some sort of business at Maidstone. I never told Edward. She'd been dead to him for many years and I saw no reason to remind him of the past. It always helps you if you put yourself in other people's shoes, and I said to myself that if I were he I shouldn't want to be reminded of an unfortunate episode of my youth. Don't you think I was right?'

chapter twenty-six

Mrs Driffield very kindly offered to send me back to Black-stable in her car, but I preferred to walk. I promised to dine at Ferne Court next day, and meanwhile to write down what I could remember of the two periods during which I had been in the habit of seeing Edward Driffield. As I walked along the winding road, meeting no one by the way, I mused upon what I should say. Do they not tell us that style is the art of omission? If that is so I should certainly write a very pretty piece, and it seemed almost a pity that Roy should use it only as material. I chuckled when I reflected what a bombshell I could throw if I chose. There was one person who could tell them all they wanted to know about Edward Driffield and his first marriage, but this fact I proposed to keep to myself. They thought Rosie was dead; they erred; Rosie was very much alive.

Being in New York for the production of a play, and my arrival having been advertised to all and sundry by my manager's energetic press representative, I received one day a letter addressed in a handwriting I knew but could not place.

178

It was large and round, firm but uneducated. It was so familiar to me that I was exasperated not to remember whose it was. It would have been more sensible to open the letter at once, but instead I looked at the envelope and racked my brain. There are handwritings I cannot see without a little shiver of dismay, and some letters that look so tiresome that I cannot bring myself to open them for a week. When at last I tore open the envelope what I read gave me a strange feeling. It began abruptly:

I have just seen that you are in New York and would like to see you again. I am not living in New York any more, but Yonkers is quite close and if you have a car you can easily do it in half an hour. I expect you are very busy so leave it to you to make a date. Although it is many years since we last met I hope you have not forgotten your old friend
Rose Iggulden (formerly Driffield)

I looked at the address; it was the Albemarle, evidently an hotel or an apartment house, then there was the name of a street, and Yonkers. A shiver passed through me as though someone had walked over my grave. During the years that had passed I had sometimes thought of Rosie, but of late I had said to myself that she must surely be dead. I was puzzled for a moment by the name. Why Iggulden and not Kemp? Then it occurred to me that they had taken this name, a Kentish one too, when they fled from England. My first impulse was to make an excuse not to see her; I am always shy of seeing again people I have not seen for a long time; but then I was seized with curiosity. I wanted to see what she was like and to hear what had happened to her. I was going down to Dobb's Ferry for the weekend, to reach which I had to pass through Yonkers, and so answered that I would come at about four on the following Saturday.

The Albemarle was a huge block of apartments, comparatively new, and it looked as though it were inhabited by persons in easy circumstance. My name was telephoned up by a Negro porter in uniform, and I was taken up in the elevator by another. I felt uncommonly nervous. The door was opened for me by a coloured maid.

'Come right in,' she said. 'Mrs Iggulden's expecting you.'

I was ushered into a living-room that served also as dining-room, for at one end of it was a square table of heavily carved oak, a dresser, and four chairs of the kind that the manufacturers in Grand Rapids would certainly describe as Jacobean. But the other end was furnished with a Louis XV suite, gilt and upholstered in pale blue damask; there were a great many small tables, richly carved and gilt, on which stood Sèvres vases with ormolu decorations and nude bronze ladies with draperies flowing as though in a howling gale that artfully concealed those parts of their bodies that decency required; and each one held at the end of a playfully outstretched arm an electric lamp. The gramophone was the grandest thing I had ever seen out of a shop window, all gilt and shaped like a sedan chair, and painted with Watteau courtiers and their ladies.

After I had waited for about five minutes a door was opened and Rosie came briskly in. She gave me both her hands.

'Well, this is a surprise,' she said. 'I hate to think how many years it is since we met. Excuse me one moment.' She went to the door and called: 'Jessie, you can bring the tea in. Mind the water's boiling properly.' Then coming back: 'The trouble I've had to teach that girl to make tea properly, you'd never believe.'

Rosie was at least seventy. She was wearing a very smart sleeveless frock of green chiffon, heavily *diamanté*, cut square at the neck and very short; it fitted like a bursting glove. By her shape I gathered that she wore rubber corsets. Her nails were blood-coloured and her eyebrows plucked. She was stout, and she had a double chin; the skin of her bosom, although she had powdered it freely, was red, and her face was red too. But she looked well and healthy and full of beans. Her hair was still abundant, but it was quite white, shingled and permanently waved. As a young woman she had had soft, naturally waving hair, and these stiff undulations, as though she had just come out of a hairdresser's, seemed more than anything else to change her. The only thing that remained was her smile, which had still its old childlike and mischievous sweetness. Her teeth had never been very good, irregular, and of bad shape; but these now were replaced by a set of perfect evenness and snowy brilliance: they were obviously the best money could buy.

The coloured maid brought in an elaborate tea with *pâté* and wiches and cookies and candy and little knives and forks and tiny napkins. It was all very neat and smart.

'That's one thing I've never been able to do without – my tea,' said Rosie, helping herself to a hot buttered scone. 'It's my best meal, really, though I know I shouldn't eat it. My doctor keeps on saying to me: "Mrs Iggulden, you can't expect to get your weight down if you will eat half a dozen cookies at tea."' She gave me a smile, and I had a sudden inkling that, notwithstanding the marcelled hair and the powder and the fat, Rosie was the same as ever. 'But what I say is: A little of what you fancy does you good.'

I had always found her easy to talk to. Soon we were chatting away as though it were only a few weeks since we had last seen one another.

'Were you surprised to get my letter? I put Driffield so as you should know who it was from. We took the name of Iggulden when we came to America. George had a little unpleasantness when he left Blackstable, perhaps you heard about it, and he thought in a new country he'd better start with a new name, if you understand what I mean.'

I nodded vaguely.

'Poor George, he died ten years ago, you know.'

'I'm sorry to hear that.'

'Oh, well, he was getting on in years. He was past seventy, though you'd never have guessed it to look at him. It was a great blow to me. No woman could want a better husband than what he made me. Never a cross word from the day we married till the day he died. And I'm pleased to say he left me very well provided for.'

'I'm glad to know that.'

'Yes, he did very well over here. He went into the building trade, he always had a fancy for it, and he got in with Tammany. He always said the greatest mistake he ever made was not coming over here twenty years before. He liked the country from the first day he set foot in it. He had plenty of go, and that's what you want here. He was just the sort to get on.'

'Have you never been back to England?'

'No, I've never wanted to. George used to talk about it sometimes, just for a trip, you know, but we never got down to it, and now he's gone I haven't got the inclination. I expect London would seem very dead and alive to me after New York. We used to live in New York, you know. I only came here after his death.'

'What made you choose Yonkers?'

'Well, I always fancied it. I used to say to George, when we retire we'll go and live at Yonkers. It's like a little bit of England to me, you know. Maidstone or Guildford, or some place like that.'

I smiled, but I understood what she meant. Notwithstanding its trams and its tooting cars, its cinemas and electric signs, Yonkers, with its winding main street, has a faint air of an English market town gone jazz.

'Of course I sometimes wonder what's happened to all the folks at Blackstable. I suppose they're most of them dead by now, and I expect they think I am too.'

'I haven't been there for thirty years.'

I did not know then that the rumour of Rosie's death had reached Blackstable. I dare say that someone had brought back the news that George Kemp was dead, and thus a mistake had arisen.

'I suppose nobody knows here that you were Edward Driffield's first wife?'

'Oh, no; why, if they had I should have had the reporters buzzing around my apartment like a swarm of bees. You know sometimes I've hardly been able to help laughing when I've been out somewhere playing bridge and they've started talking about Ted's books. They like them no end in America. I never thought so much of them myself.'

'You never were a great novel-reader, were you?'

'I used to like history better, but I don't seem to have much time for reading now. Sunday's my great day. I think the Sunday papers over here are lovely. You don't have anything like them in England. Then, of course, I play a lot of bridge; I'm crazy about contract.'

I remembered that when as a young boy I had first met Rosie her uncanny skill at whist had impressed me. I felt that I knew the sort of bridge player she was, quick, bold, and accurate; a good partner and a dangerous opponent.

'You'd have been surprised at the fuss they made over here when Ted died. I knew they thought a lot of him, but I never knew he was such a big bug as all that. The papers were full of him, and they had pictures of him and Ferne Court; he always said he meant to live in that house some day. Whatever made him marry that hospital nurse? I always thought he'd marry Mrs Barton Trafford. They never had any children, did they?'

'No.'

'Ted would have liked to have some. It was a great blow to him that I couldn't have any more after the first.'

'I didn't know you'd ever had a child,' I said with surprise.

'Oh, yes. That's why Ted married me. But I had a very bad time when it came, and the doctors said I couldn't have another. If she'd lived, poor little thing, I don't suppose I'd ever have run away with George. She was six when she died. A dear little thing she was, and as pretty as a picture.'

'You never mentioned her.'

'No, I couldn't bear to speak about her. She got meningitis, and we took her to the hospital. They put her in a private room, and they let us stay with her. I shall never forget what she went through, screaming, screaming all the time, and nobody able to do anything.'

Rosie's voice broke.

'Was it that death Driffield described in *The Cup of Life*?'

'Yes, that's it. I always thought it so funny of Ted. He couldn't bear to speak of it, any more than I could, but he wrote it all down; he didn't leave out a thing; even little things I hadn't noticed at the time he put in, and then I remembered them. You'd think he was just heartless, but he wasn't, he was upset just as much as I was. When we used to go home at night he'd cry like a child. Funny chap, wasn't he?'

183

It was *The Cup of Life* that had raised such a storm of protest; and it was the child's death and the episode that followed it that had especially brought down on Driffield's head such virulent abuse. I remembered the description very well. It was harrowing. There was nothing sentimental in it; it did not excite the reader's tears, but his anger rather that such cruel suffering should be inflicted on a little child. You felt that God at the Judgement Day would have to account for such things as this. It was a very powerful piece of writing. But if this incident was taken from life, was the one that followed it also? It was this that had shocked the public of the nineties, and this that the critics had condemned as not only indecent, but incredible. In *The Cup of Life* the husband and wife (I forget their names now) had come back from the hospital after the child's death – they were poor people, and they lived from hand to mouth in lodgings – and had their tea. It was latish: about seven o'clock. They were exhausted by the strain of a week's ceaseless anxiety and shattered by their grief. They had nothing to say to one another. They sat in a miserable silence. The hours passed. Then on a sudden the wife got up and going into their bedroom put on her hat.

'I'm going out,' she said.

'All right.'

They lived near Victoria Station. She walked along the Buckingham Palace Road and through the park. She came into Piccadilly and went slowly toward the Circus. A man caught her eye, paused, and turned round.

'Good evening,' he said.

'Good evening.'

She stopped and smiled.

'Will you come and have a drink?' he asked.

'I don't mind if I do.'

They went into a tavern in one of the side streets of Piccadilly, where harlots congregated and men came to pick them up, and they drank a glass of beer. She chatted with the stranger and laughed with him. She told him a cock-and-bull story about herself. Presently, he asked if he could go home with her; no, she said, he couldn't do that, but they could go to an hotel. They got into a cab and drove to Bloomsbury, and there they took a room for the night. And next morning she took a bus to Trafalgar Square and walked through the park; when she got home her husband was just sitting down to breakfast. After breakfast they went back to the hospital to see about the child's funeral.

'Will you tell me something, Rosie?' I asked. 'What happened in the book after the child's death – did that happen too?'

She looked at me for a moment doubtfully; then her lips broke into her still beautiful smile.

'Well, it's all so many years ago, what odds does it make? I don't mind telling you. He didn't get it quite right. You see it was only guesswork on his part. I was surprised that he knew as much as he did; I never told him anything.'

Rosie took a cigarette and pensively tapped its end on the table, but she did not light it.

'We came back from the hospital just like he said. We walked back; I felt I couldn't sit still in a cab, and I felt all dead inside me. I'd cried so much I couldn't cry any more, and I was tired. Ted tried to comfort me, but I said: "For God's sake shut up." After that he didn't say any more. We had rooms in the Vauxhall Bridge Road then, on the second floor, just a sitting-room and a bedroom, that's why we'd had to take the poor little thing to the hospital; we couldn't nurse her in lodgings; besides, the landlady said she wouldn't have it, and Ted said she'd be looked after better at the hospital. She wasn't a bad sort, the landlady; she'd been a tart, and Ted used to talk to her by the hour together. She came up when she heard us come in.

' "How's the little girl tonight?" she said.

' "She's dead," said Ted.

'I couldn't say anything. Then she brought up the tea. I didn't want anything, but Ted made me eat some ham. Then I sat at the window. I didn't look round when the landlady came up to clear away. I didn't want anyone to speak to me. Ted was reading a book; at least he was pretending to, but he didn't turn the pages, and I saw the tears dropping on it. I kept on looking out of the window. It was the end of June, the twenty-eighth, and the days were long. It was just near the corner where we lived, and I looked at the people going in and out of the public-house and the trams going up and down. I thought the day would never come to an end; then all of a sudden I noticed that it was night. All the lamps were lit. There was an awful lot of people in the street. I felt so tired. My legs were like lead.

' "Why don't you light the gas?" I said to Ted.

' "Do you want it?" he said.

' "It's no good sitting in the dark," I said.

'He lit the gas. He began smoking his pipe. I knew that would do him good. But I just sat and looked at the street. I don't know what came over me. I felt that if I went on sitting in that room I'd go mad. I wanted to go somewhere where there were lights and people. I wanted to get away from Ted; no, not so much that, I wanted to get away from all that Ted was thinking and feeling. We only had two rooms. I went into the bedroom; the child's cot was still there, but I wouldn't look at it. I put on my hat and a veil and I changed my dress, and then I went back to Ted.

' "I'm going out," I said.

'Ted looked at me. I dare say he noticed I'd got my new dress on, and perhaps something in the way I spoke made him see I didn't want him.

' "All right," he said.

'In the book he made me walk through the park, but I didn't do that really. I went down to Victoria and I took a hansom to Charing Cross. It was only a shilling fare. Then I walked up the Strand. I'd made up my mind what I wanted to do before I came out. Do you remember Harry Retford? Well, he was acting at the Adelphi then, he had the second comedy part. Well, I went to the stage door and sent up my name. I always liked Harry Retford. I expect he was a bit unscrupulous and he was rather funny over money matters, but he could make you laugh, and with all his faults he was a rare good sort. You know he was killed in the Boer War, don't you?'

186

'I didn't. I only knew he'd disappeared and one never saw his name on playbills; I thought perhaps he'd gone into business or something.'

'No, he went out at once. He was killed at Ladysmith. After I'd been waiting a bit he came down and I said: "Harry, let's go on the razzle tonight. What about a bit of supper at Romano's?" "Not 'alf," he said. "You wait here, and the minute the show's over and I've got my make-up off I'll come down." It made me feel better just to see him; he was playing a racing tout, and it made me laugh just to look at him in his check suit and his billycock hat and his red nose. Well, I waited till the end of the show, and then he came down and we walked along to Romano's.

'"Are you hungry?" he said to me.

'"Starving," I said; and I was.

'"Let's have the best," he said, "and blow the expense. I told Bill Terris I was taking my best girl out to supper and I touched him for a couple of quid."

'"Let's have champagne," I said.

'"Three cheers for the widow!" he said.

'I don't know if you ever went to Romano's in the old days. It was fine. You used to see all the theatrical people and the racing men, and the girls from the Gaiety used to go there. It was *the* place. And the Roman. Harry knew him and he came up to our table; he used to talk in funny broken English; I believe he put it on because he knew it made people laugh. And if someone he knew was down and out he'd always lend him a fiver.

'"How's the kid?" said Harry.

'"Better," I said.

'I didn't want to tell him the truth. You know how funny men are; they don't understand some things. I knew Harry would think it dreadful of me to come out to supper when the poor child was lying dead in the hospital. He'd be awfully sorry and all that, but that's not what I wanted; I wanted to laugh.'

Rosie lit the cigarette that she had been playing with.

'You know how when a woman is having a baby, sometimes the husband can't stand it any more and he goes out and has another woman. And then when she finds out, and it's funny how often she does, she kicks up no end of a fuss; she says, that the man should go and do it just then, when she's going through hell, well, it's the limit. I always tell her not to be silly. It doesn't mean he doesn't love her, and isn't terribly upset, it doesn't mean anything, it's just nerves; if he wasn't so upset he wouldn't think of it. I know, because that's how I felt then.

'When we'd finished our supper Harry said: "Well, what about it?"

' "What about what?" I said.

'There wasn't any dancing in those days and there was nowhere to go.

' "What about coming round to my flat and having a look at my photograph album?" said Harry.

' "I don't mind if I do," I said.

'He had a little bit of a flat in the Charing Cross Road, just two rooms and a bath and a kitchenette, and we drove round there, and I stayed the night.

'When I got back next morning the breakfast was already on the table and Ted had just started. I'd made up my mind that if he said anything I was going to fly out at him. I didn't care what happened. I'd earned my living before, and I was ready to earn it again. For two pins I'd have packed my box and left him there and then. But he just looked up as I came in.

' "You've just come in time," he said. "I was going to eat your sausage."

'I sat down and poured him out his tea. And he went on reading the paper. After we'd finished breakfast we went to the hospital. He never asked me where I'd been. I didn't know what he thought. He was terribly kind to me all that time. I was miserable, you know. Somehow I felt that I just couldn't get over it, and there was nothing he didn't do to make it easier for me.'

'What did you think when you read the book?' I asked.

'Well, it did give me a turn to see that he did know pretty well what had happened that night. What beat me was his writing it at all. You'd have thought it was the last thing he'd put in a book. You're queer fish, you writers.'

At that moment the telephone bell rang. Rosie took up the receiver and listened.

'Why, Mr Vanuzzi, how very nice of you to call me up! Oh, I'm pretty well, thank you. Well, pretty and well, if you like. When you're my age you take all the compliments you can get.'

She embarked upon a conversation which, I gathered from her tone, was of a facetious and even flirtatious character. I did not pay much attention, and since it seemed to prolong itself I began to meditate upon the writer's life. It is full of tribulation. First he must endure poverty and the world's indifference; then, having achieved a measure of success, he must submit with a good grace to its hazards. He depends upon a fickle public. He is at the mercy of journalists who want to interview him, and photographers who want to take his picture, of editors who harry him for copy and tax-gatherers who harry him for income tax, of persons of quality who ask him to lunch and secretaries of institutes who ask him to lecture, of women who want to marry him and women who want to divorce him, of youths who want his autograph, actors who want parts and strangers who want a loan, of gushing ladies who want advice on their matrimonial affairs and earnest young men who want advice on their compositions, of agents, publishers, managers, bores, admirers, critics, and his own conscience. But he has one compensation. Whenever he has anything on his mind, whether it be a harassing reflection, grief at the death of a friend, unrequited love, wounded pride, anger at the treachery of someone to whom he has shown kindness, in short any emotion or any perplexing thought, he has only to put it down in black and white, using it as a theme of a story or the decoration of an essay, to forget all about it. He is the only free man.

Rosie put back the receiver and turned to me.

'That was one of my beaux. I'm going to play bridge to-night, and he rang up to say he'd call round for me in his car. Of course he's a Wop, but he's real nice. He used to run a big

189

grocery store down town, in New York, but he's retired now.'

'Have you never thought of marrying again, Rosie?'

'No.' She smiled. 'Not that I haven't had offers. I'm quite happy as I am. The way I look on it is this: I don't want to marry an old man, and it would be silly at my age to marry a young man. I've had my time and I'm ready to call it a day.'

'What made you run away with George Kemp?'

'Well, I'd always liked him. I knew him long before I knew Ted, you know. Of course I never thought there was any chance of marrying him. For one thing he was married already, and then he had his position to think of. And then when he came to me one day and said that everything had gone wrong and he was bust and there'd be a warrant out for his arrest in a few days and he was going to America and would I go with him, well, what could I do? I couldn't let him go all that way by himself, with no money perhaps, and him having been always so grand and living in his own house and driving his own trap. It wasn't as if I was afraid of work.'

'I sometimes think he was the only man you ever cared for,' I suggested.

' I dare say there's some truth in that.'

'I wonder what it was you saw in him.'

Rosie's eyes travelled to a picture on the wall that for some reason had escaped my notice. It was an enlarged photograph of Lord George in a carved gilt frame. It looked as if it might have been taken soon after his arrival in America; perhaps at the time of their marriage. It was a three-quarter length. It showed him in a long frock-coat, tightly buttoned, and a tall silk hat cocked rakishly on one side of his head; there was a large rose in his button-hole; under one arm he carried a silver-headed cane, and smoke curled from a big cigar that he held in his right hand. He had a heavy moustache, waxed at the ends, a saucy look in his eye, and in his bearing an arrogant swagger. In his tie was a horseshoe in diamonds. He looked like a publican dressed up in his best to go to the Derby.

'I'll tell you,' said Rosie. 'He was always such a perfect gentleman.'

Fiction

☐ **The Chains of Fate**	Pamela Belle	£2.95p
☐ **Options**	Freda Bright	£1.50p
☐ **The Thirty-nine Steps**	John Buchan	£1.50p
☐ **Secret of Blackoaks**	Ashley Carter	£1.50p
☐ **Lovers and Gamblers**	Jackie Collins	£2.50p
☐ **My Cousin Rachel**	Daphne du Maurier	£2.50p
☐ **Flashman and the Redskins**	George Macdonald Fraser	£1.95p
☐ **The Moneychangers**	Arthur Hailey	£2.95p
☐ **Secrets**	Unity Hall	£2.50p
☐ **The Eagle Has Landed**	Jack Higgins	£1.95p
☐ **Sins of the Fathers**	Susan Howatch	£3.50p
☐ **Smiley's People**	John le Carré	£2.50p
☐ **To Kill a Mockingbird**	Harper Lee	£1.95p
☐ **Ghosts**	Ed McBain	£1.75p
☐ **The Silent People**	Walter Macken	£2.50p
☐ **Gone with the Wind**	Margaret Mitchell	£3.95p
☐ **Wilt**	Tom Sharpe	£1.95p
☐ **Rage of Angels**	Sidney Sheldon	£2.50p
☐ **The Unborn**	David Shobin	£1.50p
☐ **A Town Like Alice**	Nevile Shute	£2.50p
☐ **Gorky Park**	Martin Cruz Smith	£2.50p
☐ **A Falcon Flies**	Wilbur Smith	£2.50p
☐ **The Grapes of Wrath**	John Steinbeck	£2.50p
☐ **The Deep Well at Noon**	Jessica Stirling	£2.95p
☐ **The Ironmaster**	Jean Stubbs	£1.75p
☐ **The Music Makers**	E. V. Thompson	£2.50p

Non-fiction

☐ **The First Christian**	Karen Armstrong	£2.50p
☐ **Pregnancy**	Gordon Bourne	£3.95p
☐ **The Law is an Ass**	Gyles Brandreth	£1.75p
☐ **The 35mm Photographer's Handbook**	Julian Calder and John Garrett	£6.50p
☐ **London at its Best**	Hunter Davies	£2.90p
☐ **Back from the Brink**	Michael Edwardes	£2.95p

☐	**Travellers' Britain**	Arthur Eperon	£2.95p
☐	**Travellers' Italy**		£2.95p
☐	**The Complete Calorie Counter**	Eileen Fowler	90p
☐	**The Diary of Anne Frank**	Anne Frank	£1.75p
☐	**And the Walls Came Tumbling Down**	Jack Fishman	£1.95p
☐	**Linda Goodman's Sun Signs**	Linda Goodman	£2.95p
☐	**The Last Place on Earth**	Roland Huntford	£3.95p
☐	**Victoria RI**	Elizabeth Longford	£4.95p
☐	**Book of Worries**	Robert Morley	£1.50p
☐	**Airport International**	Brian Moynahan	£1.95p
☐	**Pan Book of Card Games**	Hubert Phillips	£1.95p
☐	**Keep Taking the Tabloids**	Fritz Spiegl	£1.75p
☐	**An Unfinished History of the World**	Hugh Thomas	£3.95p
☐	**The Baby and Child Book**	Penny and Andrew Stanway	£4.95p
☐	**The Third Wave**	Alvin Toffler	£2.95p
☐	**Pauper's Paris**	Miles Turner	£2.50p
☐	**The Psychic Detectives**	Colin Wilson	£2.50p

All these books are available at your local bookshop or newsagent, or
can be ordered direct from the publisher. Indicate the number of copies
required and fill in the form below 12

....

Name..
(Block letters please)

Address..

Send to CS Department, Pan Books Ltd, PO Box 40, Basingstoke, Hants
Please enclose remittance to the value of the cover price plus:
35p for the first book plus 15p per copy for each additional book ordered
to a maximum charge of £1.25 to cover postage and packing
Applicable only in the UK

While every effort is made to keep prices low, it is sometimes
necessary to increase prices at short notice. Pan Books reserve
the right to show on covers and charge new retail prices which
may differ from those advertised in the text or elsewhere